Gabi Reigh

Gabi Reigh moved to the U.K. from Romania at the age of 12 and now teaches A-level English. In 2017, she won the Stephen Spender Prize which inspired her to translate more Romanian literature. As part of her Interbellum Series project, she has translated interwar novels, poetry and drama by Lucian Blaga, Liviu Rebreanu, Hortensia Papadat Bengescu, Max Blecher and Mihail Sebastian and her essay on the art of translation is featured in *The Women Writer's Handbook* (Aurora Metro Books).

Gabi's translations, articles and fiction have been published in *Modern Poetry in Translation, World Literature Today, Another Chicago Magazine, Open Democracy, Times Educational Supplement, The London Magazine, The Los Angeles Review of Books,* amongst others. She was shortlisted for the Society of Authors' Tom Gallon short story prize in 2018.

First published in the UK in 2023 by Aurora Metro Publications Ltd.

80 Hill Rise, Richmond, TW10 6UB UK

www.aurorametro.com   info@aurorametro.com

t: @aurorametro F: facebook.com/AuroraMetroBooks

Introduction copyright © 2023 Gabi Reigh

Compilation copyright © 2023 Gabi Reigh

Cover image: Frances Benjamin Johnston's *Self-Portrait (as "New Woman")*, 1896, Library of Congress collection

Cover design: copyright © 2023 Aurora Metro Publications Ltd.

Editor: Cheryl Robson

Aurora Metro Books would like to thank Bushra Mustafa-Dunne, Sze Hang Lo

Printed by 4edge, Essex, UK on sustainably resourced paper.

ISBNs:
978-1-912430-78-9 (print)
978-1-912430-79-6 (ebook)

Virginia's Sisters

Selected and introduced by
Gabi Reigh

AURORA METRO BOOKS

Contents

Introduction

Gabi Reigh

"I would venture to guess that Anon, who wrote so many poems without signing them, was often a woman." Virginia Woolf's much quoted line from *A Room of One's Own* seems an appropriate place to begin an introduction to this collection of women's writing from the first half of the twentieth century. Although some of the writers and artists included in this anthology such as Katherine Mansfield, Edith Wharton, Marina Tsvetaeva and Gabriela Mistral are well-known, the collection also brings to light the creativity of Virginia Woolf's "sisters" from thirteen different countries who have not received the global recognition they deserve and whose work has been translated into English for the first time, from eleven different languages.

The idea for this anthology began with my own obsession with a particular writer: Sorana Gurian (1913-1956), a Jewish-Romanian intellectual who was part of the underground opposition in fascist Romania during the Second World War. After fleeing persecution in Romania, she lived in Italy, Israel and eventually in Paris, where she died of cancer at the age of 43. Gurian wrote books in Romanian and in French, and while she achieved some level of recognition during her writing career in Paris, her earlier short story collections such as *The Days will Never Return* and *Episodes between Twilight and Darkness* disturbed the Romanian communist regime due to the "'decadent' amoralism, cosmopolitanism, defiant pessimism and eroticism"[1] with which they explored the inner

1   Burta-Cernat, Bianca. 2011. *Group Portrait of Forgotten Women*

lives of single women. This rebellion against the tastes of the establishment of her native country as well as Gurian's marginalised position as a (female) foreigner in France meant that Czeslow Milosz's prophecy, formulated in an article about his encounter with Gurian during her final days in Paris, was broadly fulfilled: "The name of Sorana Gurian will not be preserved in the chronicles of humanity."

When I first read Mislosz's account of this meeting – one of a tiny handful of articles written in English about Sorana Gurian – I was intrigued and saddened by the fate of this "lost" writer. I also took his words as a challenge to rescue her from the shadows of anonymity by giving her work a new life through translating it into English. But here I was faced with a seemingly insurmountable obstacle – how do you persuade publishers to print a translation of a writer whose work, although fresh, daring and beautiful, is largely unknown? I came to the conclusion that although Sorana Gurian might not attract a readership of her own, the very fact that she was an "obscure" female writer cheated of her place in the early twentieth century canon placed her in a sisterhood of many other female artists who shared her fate.

The idea then sprang to my mind that an anthology of their work, exploring the connections between their lives and themes, could be even more compelling. In their satirical art installation, the anonymous collective Guerrilla Girls wryly noted that one of "the Advantages of Being a Woman Artist" is "being included in revised versions of art history." Although this silver lining might strike us as bitter-sweet, I concluded that there is strength in numbers and that a collection of texts written by women from this period would amplify their voices.

In parallel with other texts included in this anthology, Sorana Gurian's 'Villa Myosotis' explores a woman's attempt to carve out an independent life in the shadow of personal struggles and dominant male influences. The story is a dreamlike reimagining of events in Gurian's own life; having been diagnosed with tuberculosis in her twenties, Gurian received treatment in the sanatorium town of Berck, in France, and whilst there, she discovered that she had occupied the same room as another Jewish-Romanian writer she admired, Max Blecher, who had died of the disease a year earlier. From this unsettling coincidence, Gurian developed a ghost story that allegorically reenacts her struggle to escape the spectre of death and the stifling influence of the male genius on her own creative development.

Like the rest of the stories in *Episodes between Twilight and Darkness*, 'Villa Myosotis' disturbed the wholesome, optimistic narrative that was taking shape in communist Romania, and consequently Gurian's art was not given the attention it deserved. This was a common motif for the writers included in this anthology. Yenta Serdatsky's story 'Unheard' acts as a symbol of their condition. Her heroine's attempts to express herself are constantly stymied by the voices of her male friends whose egotistical discourse renders her silent: "She wants to open up but the words get stuck in her throat... if only she could talk things out, have some relief from the weight on her heart." Serdatsky's protagonist might be voicing the author's own disappointments as her writing career faltered after misogynistic reviews of her short story collections and the fact that she was undercompensated, in comparison to her male colleagues, for her articles for the Yiddish newspaper *Forverts*.

Other writers found that, when the world did not listen to them, poetry gave them a voice. Despite her privileged upbringing as the child of aristocratic parents, the Italian poet Antonia Pozzi struggled to reconcile their expectations, her faith and her desire for romantic fulfilment and took her own life at the age of 26. Although her artistic voice was "unheard" during her lifetime, as all of her poems were published posthumously, Pozzi wrote in a letter to a friend that poetry gave her a psychological escape from the world. "The purpose of poetry", Pozzi writes, is "to take all the pain that agitates us and roars in our soul and mollify it, to transfigure it in the supreme calm of art, in the way the rivers flow into the vast blue sea. Poetry is a catharsis of pain, as the immensity of death is a catharsis of life."

The poetry of Anna Akhmatova, May Ziadeh and Magda Isanos also transforms pain into lyrical beauty. Persecuted and censored by the Stalinist authorities, Anna Akhmatova chose to remain in the Soviet Union even after her first husband was executed and her son was sent to a gulag, chronicling the "painful ulcer" of the social turmoil she witnessed in her poetry. The Palestinian-Lebanese poet May Ziadeh expresses the bereavement of the emigree in 'Goodbye, Lebanon', Myra Viola Wilds finds solace in her writing when her failing eyesight stops her from working as a dressmaker, while Magda Isanos, a Romanian poet whose brief life was tormented by polio, escapes her suffering through a 'Vegetal Reverie': "Unburdened of my soul/ I flee/ Towards the valleys, where the trees/Will share life with me/Muting all thoughts with flowers". Poetry becomes "the catharsis of pain", a space where, as Emily Dickinson put it, "the soul... stand[s] ajar, ready to welcome the ecstatic experience" and transcend the trials of the material world.

As well as physical suffering and political persecution, the texts in this anthology also highlight the challenges faced by women in patriarchal societies. From the very moment of their birth, as captured in Fani Popova-Mutafova's 'A Woman', where a baby girl is "greeted with disappointment, resignation and condescension" by everyone except her mother, the women in these short stories are forced to recognise their precarious foothold in the world.

In Katherine Mansfield's 'The Little Governess', the vulnerability of single women is startlingly exposed when the protagonist's trust is exploited by an older man. Maria Messina, described by the Sicilian writer Leonardo Sciascia as the

Introduction

"Italian Katherine Mansfield", explores the trials of marriage in the conservative society of early twentieth century Sicily in 'Coming Home', where an unhappily married young woman receives no encouragement from her family to break away from an unfulfilling relationship. Vanna, the heroine of the story, feels that marriage has transformed her into "a rag doll", "an ant", a "nothing" because her husband feels embarrassed by her as he tries to reinvent himself in Rome and obscure his Sicilian origins.

"To be rooted", wrote Simone Weil, "is perhaps the most important and least recognised need of the human soul." Like Vanna, Maria Messina understood the alienation caused by leaving one's home and arriving to the mainland as an outsider; although she escaped her rural roots by teaching herself to read and write before embarking on a literary career, she could never detach herself emotionally from the place of her birth even though, just like for her heroine, "there was no room for her [there]".

"There was no room", either, for divorced older women, even in the sophisticated, seemingly progressive circles of early twentieth century New York. In Edith Wharton's 'Autre Temps', Mrs. Lidcote returns home after a self-imposed exile in Europe following her divorce, to comfort her daughter after her own marriage breaks down. To her surprise, she discovers that her daughter's experience of divorce has been very different to her own, as the young woman has maintained her position in society. Yet ironically, Mrs. Lidcote is still regarded as a *persona non grata* in her native city because of her past. Considering this change in social mores and the injustice of being stigmatised by her divorce from many years ago, Mrs. Lidcote bitterly wonders: "If such a change was to come, why had it not come sooner?"

At the beginning of the twentieth century, the choices that women made in their personal lives could mean the difference between social integration and alienation. Simone de Beauvoir reflected that: "on the day when it will be possible for woman to love not in her weakness but in strength, not to escape herself but to find herself, not to abase herself but to assert herself – on that day love will become for her, as for man, a source of life and not of mortal danger."

While the commitment to a single life or the breakdown of marriage lowered women's social status, the pursuit of a same-sex relationship was an even greater gamble to take, an "assertion of the self" that was a vital "source of life" but also threatened the "mortal danger" of social exclusion. Fausta Cialente's debut novel, *Natalia,* was banned by Fascist authorities because it contained a "small lesbian episode" and a revised version was published in 1982. The same taboo topic was explored by two women writing at the same time in different continents – Ling Shuhua and Radclyffe Hall. The daughter of a concubine and a high-ranking official, Ling Shuhua's short stories became popular in her native China in the 1920s and 1930s. Interestingly, Shuhua became connected with the Bloomsbury circle through a twist of fate. While studying at Wuhan university, she began a romantic relationship with Vanessa Bell's son Julian and this led to a correspondence between Shuhua and Virginia Woolf, to whom she dedicated her memoirs. Later, Shuhua moved to England and met Woolf and her lover, Vita Sackville-West, in person. Shuhua's modern, liberal attitudes are reflected in 'Once upon a time', which portrays the forbidden relationship between two female students with warmth and compassion.

Like 'Once upon a Time', Radclyffe Hall's 'Miss Ogilvy Finds Herself' reflects the frustration felt by queer women who could not express their desires at the beginning of the twentieth century, but also offers an insight into how the First World War impacted their lives. Best known for her groundbreaking novel *The Well of Loneliness*, Radclyffe Hall is one of the early twentieth century's most prominent figures to write openly about lesbian relationships. In 'Miss Ogilvy Finds

Herself', she paints the portrait of a woman whose behaviour and desires place her on the edges of society and make her feel alienated from her family, so much so, that it takes the chaos of war to free her from their expectations and allow her to take an active role in shaping the world's events. In contrast, in the poem 'I Sit and Sew', the Harlem Renaissance writer Alice Dunbar-Nelson expresses her frustration with the fact that, as a woman, she cannot contribute to the war effort.

A very different perspective of war is offered in Natalya Kobrynska's short story 'Broken'. The translator Hanna Leliv was living in war-torn Ukraine when she submitted this story to the anthology, explaining that she found poignant parallels between its depiction of a family destroyed by the First World War and events that were affecting her home country in the present day. Kobrynska's story stands out from the rest of the texts included in the anthology because rather than being narrated solely from a female perspective, it uses both the husband and the wife as focalisers, as if to highlight the damage that war indiscriminately causes to everyone, male or female, as lives are destroyed for obscure political ends.

Many of the short stories and poems included in this anthology convey the trials experienced by women at different stages of their lives, in various social contexts. However, both the texts and the lives of the writers themselves bear testament to female strength and resilience. Carmen de Burgos's 'The Russian Princess' portrays a character in the winter of her life who refuses to "go gentle into that good night", challenging instead, the patriarchal world that judges women according to their youth and beauty. The self-proclaimed "Russian Princess", rising from the ashes of obscure old age, brings to mind Marina Tsvetaeva's evocation of female power – "I am the Phoenix; only in the fire I sing."

Like the characters they created, the writers also found the courage to challenge tradition and reshape their societies. Carmen de Burgos was the first woman in Spain to become a war correspondent and have her own column in a newspaper. May Ziadeh and Natalia Kobrynska campaigned for women's rights and Gabriela Mistral wrote articles arguing that education should be available to people of all social classes. Like Virginia Woolf, who famously claimed that a woman "must have money and a room of her own if she is to write fiction", Charlotte Perkins Gillman also encouraged women to become financially independent through lecture tours and her book *Women and Economics*.

Perkins Gillman is best known for her short story 'The Yellow Wallpaper', an analysis of suffocating domesticity and postpartum depression, as well as an indictment of the "rest cure" that was often enforced on women experiencing mental health problems. "The rest cure", developed by the 19th century physician Silas Weir Mitchell, was seen by Perkins Gillman as a tyrannical sanction aimed to silence women's voices when they disrupted the patriarchal establishment with their "hysterical" demands. In her 1915 feminist utopian novel *Herland*, Perkins Gillman imagines an exclusively female society devoid of such power dynamics, where women encourage each other to fulfil their potential:

"They developed their central theory of a Loving Power and assumed that its relation to them was motherly – that it desired their welfare and especially their development. Their relation to it, similarly, was filial, a loving appreciation and a glad fulfilment of its high purposes. Then, being nothing if not practical, they set their keen and active minds to discover the kind of conduct expected of them. This worked out in a most admirable system of ethics. The principle of Love was universally recognised – and used."

Other women took it upon themselves to build real life utopias. Dorka Talmon, an active participant in the Polish socialist movement, fled from antisemitic persecution in Europe and became one of the founding members of a

Kibbutz in Israel. Talmon recalls the "creationist" joy she felt as she anticipated belonging to a community where gender, nationality and class were unimportant and where everyone worked for the common good. Although she does not gloss over the "excruciating" and "acrimonious" debates between the commune's members about the technicalities of this utopia, Talmon nevertheless holds on to her faith that it is possible to build a better society: "We knew that without compromise and sensitivity, treating every member as a human being, we could not resolve continuous challenges and crises."

Talmon's account of her life would have never gained a readership beyond her immediate circle were it not for the fact that another woman, Mira Glover, who had grown up on the same Kibbutz and emigrated to England in the 1970s, found it in the commune's archives and submitted it to this anthology.

There are many other "Virginia's Sisters" out there whose voices are yet to reach us and I hope that, with time, the literary canon might expand and give them the pride of place they deserve. Even more importantly, perhaps, the resurrection of these forgotten literary ancestors might convince other women, who have never had the confidence to write, that their stories deserve to be heard. As Virginia Woolf's celebrated modernist short story tells us, even the minutiae of our ordinary lives, the smallest "mark on the wall", can be transformed into art.

As Hélène Cixous wrote: "I have been amazed more than once by a description a woman gave me of a world all of her own which she had been secretly haunting since childhood… I wished that woman would write and proclaim this unique empire so that other women, other unacknowledged sovereigns, might exclaim, 'I, too, overflow; my desires have invented new desires, my body knows unheard-of songs.'"[2]

---

2 *The Laugh of the Medusa,* by Hélène Cixous, translated by Paula and Keith Cohen

"Lock up your libraries if you like; but there is no gate, no lock, no bolt that you can set upon the freedom of my mind."

– Virginia Woolf

A Woman[1]

Fani Popova-Mutafova

translated by Petya Pavlova

A strange silence fell, full of quivering tension. Stranger still, as only a moment ago the room was brimming with all shades of human worry: the screams of the mother, the firm encouragement of the doctor, the pleading and weeping of her loved ones.

And now, silence.

And a weak, hot whisper:

"What is it?"

The doctor's gaze quickly brushes against the tiny red body, he smiles benevolently, his voice resounds with feigned enthusiasm:

"A girl."

This is how a woman comes into the world.

Greeted with disappointment, resignation and cond-escension. The mother is silent, listening to the child's cries, which pierce her heart with feelings she has never before experienced.

A girl. She sighs. And immediately realises that her disappointment does not come from within. Her arms open with the same warmth to take the newborn – regardless of whether it is a boy or a girl, her lips touch the delicate skin of

---

1 first published in 1936

the child's face with the same thirst; she presses the helpless body to her breast with the same immeasurable devotion. Perhaps, precisely because the newborn is a girl, a powerful feeling of care and protectiveness that will not leave her for the rest of her life, surges inside of her.

She gently strokes the delicate, dark-haired head with the tips of her fingers and smiles. Yet, from the first moment, she has started to defend her.

To defend her from the disappointment, from the coldness of the father, from the condescending smiles of relatives, from the insulting wishes for male offspring in the near future.

And the little girl falls asleep quietly, innocent as a small animal, her head resting trustingly on her mother's arm. Far away are the days when her heart would sicken at the difference between her female status and the proud brotherhood of men, the moment when the certainty of the inferiority of her sex will sink into her like a poison arrow. Mankind's lies have not yet touched the beauty of her spirit.

The man approaches excited. Different feelings fleet across his face – resignation, curiosity. But his eyes do not glow with the deep delight the mother has been imagining in the sleepless nights of the last few weeks. Not at all. There is no jubilation in his voice; his smile and his display of happiness are just a polite mask. With a guilty look, the mother turns her face to him, silently begging for forgiveness, for mercy; she watches his every look, every move, with a heavy heart.

A sharp pain eases inside her and a gentle glow spreads across her pale, grey, face as she notices the boundless amazement, awkwardness, love and fear with which the man takes the child, the man in whom the father is slowly born, the man who, with horror and joy, sees himself as a caricature in this tiny, wrinkled face.

During the night the mother suddenly wakes up, reaches for the crib with a worried face, and in the dim light tries to distinguish the features of the child, who is breathing deeply and quietly, with arms raised in little fists, one at each side of her head.

This is how it is going to be from now on. She will never have a moment of calm.

When snow blizzards cover the earth in a silent blanket of white, when the moon rises in the azure blue of the sky and fills the night with a mysterious radiance, when April winds shake the blossom from the branches and soft lights descend from the pink sky, when heavy mists press the sleeping earth and when cold rain lashes against the black windows – the mother's heart will tremble with worry: is her child happy? Is a hidden misfortune lurking? What does fate have in store for her? Will fame crown her precious forehead or will thorns draw blood from it? How many storms and how many precipices will hinder her footsteps? How many sunny moments will she enjoy and how much darkness will she endure?

And the mother is already alert, lying awake, untangling daydreams and worries.

A little girl was born. What would her path be like, bearing the cross of being a woman – to be a slave to nature, a cathode ray producing a spark of life?

She would live in the world of men, and in that world, she would seek to prove her worth, pointlessly chasing after male adoration or silently enduring the injustices of her female lot.

Her innate instinct to please others, to try to be fascinating, to be attracted to beautiful, glamourous objects, would be ridiculed and condemned. Her strong connection with nature would be undermined, her gift of fertility would be downplayed, the little joy that nature had bestowed upon her as a mother would be denied, but the hardship would remain.

At times, they would elevate her to the holy image of the Virgin Mother and at others bring her down into the mud, reduced to a level below that of an animal, which is at least pure and noble in its instincts. She would be surrounded by minders like a small child: the father, the brothers, the husband, the sons.

To free herself, she would choose between the wrong path and the joyless path, either by renouncing her female condition and seeking other opportunities for her spirit through hard work like a man, struggling to bring up children as a mother and working like a man to provide for her family. In this way she would go against God's will, taking on a double curse – to make a living with the sweat of her brow and to endure the pain of childbirth...

Or maybe she would look for new ways to gain power and influence to establish the parity of her kind, but then the women accustomed to the old yoke would be the first to assail her with insults...

A dark road to travel with no clear borders, with no clear goal...

***

The mother sighed and took the child in her arms. Its closeness made her melt with tenderness. She gently stroked the dark cheeks, the ears, the tiny nose, inhaled its warm scent, looked at the tiny nails and the tightly-shut eyelids with amazement. And she still couldn't believe that all of this was hers, just hers, and could not comprehend the miracle that had torn this part of her from her flesh, and turned it into something separate and independent.

For the hundredth time she explored the bland features; tried to find in them something of herself, of her husband. Several generations were hiding there, invisibly, wanting to live again in this fresh blood.

The eyebrows belonged to a grandfather, the forehead to an

uncle, the mouth to a grandmother.

This is how this first night passes, shrouded in the blue light of the night lamp, as if removed from all the days and nights on earth.

The morning light brings new joys, new surprises.

For the first time, the hungry, searching mouth of the child suckles her breast and then the mother suddenly feels at one with her deepest essence, and her vague sense of worry fades away – this is what it means to be a woman. Giving herself to the child to the last drop of blood.

Because her kingdom is called Love.

Thoughts

Myra Viola Wilds

What kind of thoughts now, do you carry
   In your travels day by day
Are they bright and lofty visions,
   Or neglected, gone astray?

Matters not how great in fancy,
   Or what deeds of skill you've wrought;
Man, though high may be his station,
   Is no better than his thoughts.

Catch your thoughts and hold them tightly,
   Let each one an honour be;
Purge them, scourge them, burnish brightly,
   Then in love set each one free.

"*The history of men's opposition to women's emancipation is more interesting perhaps than the story of that emancipation itself.*"

– Virginia Woolf

The Little Governess[1]

Katherine Mansfield

Oh, dear, how she wished that it wasn't night-time. She'd have
much rather travelled by day, much much rather. But the lady
at the Governess Bureau said: "You had better take an evening
boat and then if you get into a compartment for 'Ladies Only'
in the train you will be far safer than sleeping in a foreign hotel.
Don't go out of the carriage; don't walk about the corridors
and be sure to lock the lavatory door if you go there. The train
arrives at Munich at eight o'clock, and Frau Arnholdt says that
the Hotel Grunewald is only one minute away. A porter can
take you there. She will arrive at six the same evening, so you
will have a nice quiet day to rest after the journey and rub up
your German. And when you want anything to eat I would
advise you to pop into the nearest baker's and get a bun and
some coffee. You haven't been abroad before, have you?"

"No."

"Well, I always tell my girls that it's better to mistrust people
at first rather than trust them, and it's safer to suspect people
of evil intentions rather than good ones... It sounds rather
hard but we've got to be women of the world, haven't we?"

It had been nice in the Ladies' Cabin. The stewardess was
so kind and changed her money for her and tucked up her
feet. She lay on one of the hard pink-sprigged couches and
watched the other passengers, friendly and natural, pinning
their hats to the bolsters, taking off their boots and skirts,

---

1 short story published in 1915

opening dressing-cases and arranging mysterious rustling little packages, tying their heads up in veils before lying down. Thud, thud, thud, went the steady screw of the steamer. The stewardess pulled a green shade over the light and sat down by the stove, her skirt turned back over her knees, a long piece of knitting on her lap. On a shelf above her head there was a water-bottle with a tight bunch of flowers stuck in it. "I like travelling very much," thought the little governess. She smiled and yielded to the warm rocking.

But when the boat stopped and she went up on deck, her dress-basket in one hand, her rug and umbrella in the other, a cold, strange wind flew under her hat. She looked up at the masts and spars of the ship, black against a green glittering sky, and down to the dark landing-stage where strange, muffled figures lounged, waiting; she moved forward with the sleepy flock, all knowing where to go to and what to do except her, and she felt afraid. Just a little – just enough to wish – oh, to wish that it was daytime and that one of those women who had smiled at her in the glass, when they both did their hair in the Ladies' Cabin, was somewhere near now.

"Tickets, please. Show your tickets. Have your tickets ready."

She went down the gangway balancing herself carefully on her heels. Then a man in a black leather cap came forward and touched her on the arm. "Where for, Miss?" He spoke English – he must be a guard or a stationmaster with a cap like that. She had scarcely answered when he pounced on her dress-basket.

"This way," he shouted, in a rude, determined voice, and elbowing his way he strode past the people. "But I don't want a porter." What a horrible man! "I don't want a porter. I want to carry it myself." She had to run to keep up with him, and her anger, far stronger than she, ran before her and snatched the bag out of the wretch's hand. He paid no attention at all, but swung on down the long dark platform, and across a railway line.

"He is a robber." She was sure he was a robber as she stepped between the silvery rails and felt the cinders crunch under her shoes. On the other side – oh, thank goodness! – there was a train with Munich written on it. The man stopped by the huge lighted carriages. "Second class?" asked the insolent voice.

"Yes, a Ladies' compartment." She was quite out of breath. She opened her little purse to find something small enough to give this horrible man while he tossed her dress-basket into the rack of an empty carriage that had a ticket, *Dames Seules*, gummed on the window. She got into the train and handed him twenty centimes.

"What's this?" shouted the man, glaring at the money and then at her, holding it up to his nose, sniffing at it as though he had never in his life seen, much less held, such a sum.

"It's a franc. You know that, don't you? It's a franc. That's my fare!" A franc! Did he imagine that she was going to give him a franc for playing a trick like that just because she was a girl and travelling alone at night? Never, never! She squeezed her purse in her hand and simply did not see him – she looked at a view of St. Malo on the wall opposite and simply did not hear him.

"Ah, no. Ah, no. Four *sous*. You make a mistake. Here, take it. It's a franc I want." He leapt on to the step of the train and threw the money on to her lap. Trembling with terror she screwed herself tight, tight, and put out an icy hand and took the money – stowed it away in her hand.

"That's all you're going to get," she said. For a minute or two she felt his sharp eyes pricking her all over, while he nodded slowly, pulling down his mouth: "Ve-ry well. *Trrrès bien*." He shrugged his shoulders and disappeared into the dark. Oh, the relief! How simply terrible that had been! As she stood up to feel if the dress-basket was firm she caught sight of herself in the mirror, quite white, with big round eyes. She untied her "motor veil" and unbuttoned her green cape. "But it's all over now," she said to the mirror face, feeling in some way that it was more frightened than she.

People began to assemble on the platform. They stood together in little groups talking; a strange light from the station lamps painted their faces almost green. A little boy in red clattered up with a huge tea-wagon and leaned against it, whistling and flicking his boots with a serviette. A woman in a black alpaca apron pushed a barrow with pillows for hire. Dreamy and vacant she looked – like a woman wheeling a perambulator – up and down, up and down – with a sleeping baby inside it. Wreaths of white smoke floated up from somewhere and hung below the roof like misty vines.

"How strange it all is," thought the little governess, "and the middle of the night, too." She looked out from her safe corner, frightened no longer but proud that she had not given that franc. "I can look after myself – of course I can. The great thing is not to – "

Suddenly, from the corridor, there came a stamping of feet and men's voices, high and broken with snatches of loud laughter. They were coming her way. The little governess shrank into her corner as four young men in bowler hats passed, staring through the door and window. One of them, bursting with the joke, pointed to the notice *Dames Seules* and the four bent down the better to see the one little girl in the corner. Oh dear, they were in the carriage next door. She heard them tramping about, and then a sudden hush followed by a tall thin fellow with a tiny black moustache who flung her door open.

"If mademoiselle cares to come in with us," he said, in French. She saw the others crowding behind him, peeping under his arm and over his shoulder, and she sat very straight and still. "If mademoiselle will do us the honour," mocked the tall man. One of them could be quiet no longer; his laughter went off in a loud crack. "Mademoiselle is serious," persisted

the young man, bowing and grimacing. He took off his hat
with a flourish, and she was alone again.

"*En voiture. En voi-ture!*" Someone ran up and down beside
the train. "I wish it wasn't night-time. I wish there was another
woman in the carriage. I'm frightened of the men next door."
The little governess looked out to see her porter coming
back again – the same man making for her carriage with his
arms full of luggage. But – but what was he doing? He put
his thumbnail under the label *Dames Seules* and tore it right
off, and then stood aside squinting at her while an old man
wrapped in a plaid cape climbed up the high step.

"But this is a Ladies' compartment."

"Oh no, Mademoiselle, you make a mistake. No, no I assure
you. *Merci, Monsieur.*"

"*En voi-turre!*" A shrill whistle. The porter stepped off
triumphant and the train started. For a moment or two, big
tears brimmed her eyes and through them she saw the old man
unwinding a scarf from his neck and untying the flaps of his
Jaeger cap. He looked very old. Ninety at least. He had a white
moustache and big gold-rimmed spectacles with little blue
eyes behind them and pink wrinkled cheeks. A nice face – and
charming the way he bent forward and said in halting French:
"Do I disturb you, Mademoiselle? Would you rather I took
all these things out of the rack and found another carriage?"
What! that old man have to move all those heavy things just
because she…

"No, it's quite all right. You don't disturb me at all."

"Ah, a thousand thanks." He sat down opposite her and
unbuttoned the cape of his enormous coat and flung it off
his shoulders.

The train seemed glad to have left the station. With a
long leap it sprang into the dark. She rubbed a place in the
window with her glove but she could see nothing – just a tree
outspread like a black fan or a scatter of lights, or the line of

a hill, solemn and huge. In the carriage next door the young men started singing *"Un, deux, trois..."* They sang the same song over and over at the tops of their voices.

"I never could have dared to go to sleep if I had been alone," she decided. "I couldn't have put my feet up or even taken off my hat." The singing gave her a queer little tremble in her stomach and, hugging herself to stop it, with her arms crossed under her cape, she felt really glad to have the old man in the carriage with her. Careful to see that he was not looking she peeped at him through her long lashes. He sat extremely upright, the chest thrown out, the chin well in, knees pressed together, reading a German paper. That was why he spoke French so funnily. He was a German. Something in the army, she supposed – a Colonel or a General – once, of course, not now; he was too old for that now. How spick and span he looked for an old man. He wore a pearl pin stuck in his black tie and a ring with a dark red stone on his little finger; the tip of a white silk handkerchief showed in the pocket of his double-breasted jacket. Somehow, altogether, he was really nice to look at. Most old men were so horrid. She couldn't bear them doddery – or they had a disgusting cough or something. But not having a beard – that made all the difference – and then his cheeks were so pink and his moustache so very white.

Down went the German paper and the old man leaned forward with the same delightful courtesy: "Do you speak German, Mademoiselle?"

"Ja, ein wenig, mehr als Französisch," said the little governess, blushing a deep pink colour that spread slowly over her cheeks and made her blue eyes look almost black.

"Ach, so!" The old man bowed graciously. "Then perhaps you would care to look at some illustrated papers." He slipped a rubber band from a little roll of them and handed them across.

"Thank you very much." She was very fond of looking

at pictures, but first she would take off her hat and gloves. So she stood up, unpinned the brown straw and put it neatly in the rack beside the dress-basket, stripped off her brown kid gloves, paired them in a tight roll and put them in the crown of the hat for safety, and then sat down again, more comfortably this time, her feet crossed, the papers on her lap. How kindly the old man in the corner watched her bare little hand turning over the big white pages, watched her lips moving as she pronounced the long words to herself, rested upon her hair that fairly blazed under the light. Alas! how tragic for a little governess to possess hair that made one think of tangerines and marigolds, of apricots and tortoiseshell cats and champagne! Perhaps that was what the old man was thinking as he gazed and gazed, and that not even the dark ugly clothes could disguise her soft beauty. Perhaps the flush that licked his cheeks and lips was a flush of rage that anyone so young and tender should have to travel alone and unprotected through the night. Who knows he was not murmuring in his sentimental German fashion: *"Ja, es ist eine Tragoedie!* Would to God I were the child's grandpapa!"

"Thank you very much. They were very interesting." She smiled prettily handing back the papers.

"But you speak German extremely well," said the old man. "You have been in Germany before, of course?"

"Oh no, this is the first time" – a little pause, then – "this is the first time that I have ever been abroad at all."

"Really! I am surprised. You gave me the impression, if I may say so, that you were accustomed to travelling."

"Oh, well – I have been about a good deal in England, and to Scotland, once."

"So. I myself have been in England once, but I could not learn English."

He raised one hand and shook his head, laughing. "No, it

was too difficult for me… 'Ow-do-you-do. Please vich is ze vay to Leicestaire Squaare.'"

She laughed too. "Foreigners always say…" They had quite a little talk about it.

"But you will like Munich," said the old man. "Munich is a wonderful city. Museums, pictures, galleries, fine buildings and shops, concerts, theatres, restaurants – all are in Munich. I have travelled all over Europe many, many times in my life, but it is always to Munich that I return. You will enjoy yourself there."

"I am not going to stay in Munich," said the little governess, and she added shyly, "I am going to a post as governess to a doctor's family in Augsburg."

"Ah, that was it." Augsburg he knew; Augsburg – well – was not beautiful. A solid manufacturing town. But if Germany was new to her he hoped she would find something interesting there too.

"I am sure I shall."

"But what a pity not to see Munich before you go. You ought to take a little holiday on your way" – he smiled – "and store up some pleasant memories."

"I am afraid I could not do that," said the little governess, shaking her head, suddenly important and serious. "And also, if one is alone…"

He quite understood. He bowed, serious too. They were silent after that. The train shattered on, baring its dark, flaming breast to the hills and to the valleys. It was warm in the carriage. She seemed to lean against the dark rushing and to be carried away and away. Little sounds made themselves heard; steps in the corridor, doors opening and shutting – a murmur of voices – whistling… Then the window was pricked with long needles of rain… But it did not matter… it was outside… and she had her umbrella… she pouted, sighed, opened and shut her hands once and fell fast asleep.

The Little Governess

***

"Pardon! Pardon!" The sliding back of the carriage door woke her with a start. What had happened? Someone had come in and gone out again. The old man sat in his corner, more upright than ever, his hands in the pockets of his coat, frowning heavily.

"Ha! ha! ha!" came from the carriage next door. Still half asleep, she put her hands to her hair to make sure it wasn't a dream.

"Disgraceful!" muttered the old man more to himself than to her. "Common, vulgar fellows! I am afraid they disturbed you, gracious *Fräulein*, blundering in here like that."

No, not really. She was just going to wake up, and she took out her silver watch to look at the time. Half-past four. A cold blue light filled the windowpanes. Now when she rubbed a place she could see bright patches of fields, a clump of white houses like mushrooms, a road "like a picture" with poplar trees on either side, a thread of river. How pretty it was! How pretty and how different! Even those pink clouds in the sky looked foreign. It was cold, but she pretended that it was far colder and rubbed her hands together and shivered, pulling at the collar of her coat because she was so happy.

The train began to slow down. The engine gave a long shrill whistle. They were coming to a town. Taller houses, pink and yellow, glided by, fast asleep behind their green eyelids, and guarded by the poplar trees that quivered in the blue air as if on tiptoes, listening. In one house a woman opened the shutters, flung a red and white mattress across the window frame and stood staring at the train. A pale woman with black hair and a white woollen shawl over her shoulders. More women appeared at the doors and at the windows of the sleeping houses. There came a flock of sheep. The shepherd wore a blue blouse and pointed wooden shoes. Look! look what flowers – and by the railway station too! Standard roses like bridesmaids' bouquets, white geraniums, waxy pink ones that you would never see out of a greenhouse at home. Slower and slower. A man with a watering-can was spraying the platform. "A-a-a-ah!" Somebody came running and waving his arms. A huge fat woman waddled through the glass doors of the station with a tray of strawberries. Oh, she was thirsty! She was very thirsty! "A-a-a-ah!" The same somebody ran back again. The train stopped.

The old man pulled his coat round him and got up, smiling at her. He murmured something she didn't quite catch, but she smiled back at him as he left the carriage. While he was away the little governess looked at herself again in the glass, shook and patted herself with the precise practical care of a girl who is old enough to travel by herself and has nobody else to assure her that she is "quite all right behind." Thirsty and thirsty! The air tasted of water. She let down the window and the fat woman with the strawberries passed as if on purpose, holding up the tray to her.

"Nein, danke," said the little governess, looking at the big berries on their gleaming leaves. *"Wei viel?"* she asked as the fat woman moved away. "Two marks fifty, Fräulein."

"Good gracious!" She came in from the window and sat down in the corner, very sobered for a minute. Half a crown! "H-o-o-o-e-e-e!" shrieked the train, gathering itself together to be off again. She hoped the old man wouldn't be left behind. Oh, it was daylight – everything was lovely if only she hadn't been so thirsty. Where was the old man – oh, here he was – she dimpled at him as though he were an old accepted friend as he closed the door and, turning, took from under his cape a basket of the strawberries.

"If Fräulein would honour me by accepting these…"

"What, for me?" But she drew back and raised her hands as though he were about to put a wild little kitten on her lap.

"Certainly, for you," said the old man. "For myself it is twenty years since I was brave enough to eat strawberries."

"Oh, thank you so very much. *Danke bestens,*" she stammered, *"sie sind so sehr schön!"*

"Eat them and see," said the old man, looking pleased and friendly.

"You won't have even one?"

"No, no, no." Timidly and charmingly her hand hovered. They were so big and juicy she had to take two bites to them – the juice ran all down her fingers – and it was while she munched the berries that she first thought of the old man as her grandfather. What a perfect grandfather he would make! Just like one out of a book!

The sun came out, the pink clouds in the sky, the strawberry clouds were eaten by the blue. "Are they good?" asked the old man. "As good as they look?"

When she had eaten them she felt she had known him for years. She told him about Frau Arnholdt and how she had got the place. Did he know the Hotel Grunewald? Frau Arnholdt would not arrive until the evening. He listened, listened until he knew as much about the affair as she did, until he said – not looking at her – but smoothing the palms of his brown suède gloves together: "I wonder if you would let me show you a little of Munich today. Nothing much – but just perhaps a picture gallery and the Englischer Garten. It seems such a pity that you should have to spend the day at the hotel, and also a little uncomfortable... in a strange place."

"Nicht wahr?"

"You would be back there by the early afternoon or whenever you wish, of course, and you would give an old man a great deal of pleasure."

It was not until long after she had said "Yes" – because the moment she had said it and he had thanked her he began telling her about his travels in Turkey and attar of roses – that she wondered whether she had done wrong. After all, she really did not know him. But he was so old and he had been so very kind – not to mention the strawberries... And she couldn't have explained the reason why she said "No," and it was her last day in a way, her last day to really enjoy herself in.

"Was I wrong? Was I?" A drop of sunlight fell into her hands and lay there, warm and quivering.

"If I might accompany you as far as the hotel," he suggested, "and call for you again at about ten o'clock." He took out his pocket-book and handed her a card. "Herr Regierungsrat..."

He had a title! Well, it was bound to be all right! So after that the little governess gave herself up to the excitement of being really abroad, to looking out and reading the foreign advertisement signs, to being told about the places they came to – having her attention and enjoyment looked after by the charming old grandfather – until they reached Munich and the Hauptbahnhof.

"Porter! Porter!" He found her a porter, disposed of his own luggage in a few words, guided her through the bewildering crowd out of the station down the clean white steps into the white road to the hotel. He explained who she was to the manager as though all this had been bound to happen, and then for one moment her little hand lost itself in the big brown suede ones. "I will call for you at ten o'clock." He was gone.

"This way, Fräulein," said the waiter, who had been dodging behind the manager's back, all eyes and ears for the strange couple. She followed him up two flights of stairs into a dark bedroom. He dashed down her dress-basket and pulled up a clattering, dusty blind. Ugh! what an ugly, cold room – what enormous furniture! Fancy spending the day in here!

"Is this the room Frau Arnholdt ordered?" asked the little governess. The waiter had a curious way of staring as if there was something funny about her. He pursed up his lips about to whistle, and then changed his mind.

"Gewiss," he said. Well, why didn't he go? Why did he stare so?

"Gehen Sie," said the little governess, with frigid English simplicity. His little eyes, like currants, nearly popped out of his doughy cheeks. *"Gehen Sie sofort,"* she repeated icily. At the door he turned. "And the gentleman," said he, "shall I show the gentleman upstairs when he comes?"

Over the white streets big white clouds fringed with silver – and sunshine everywhere. Fat, fat coachmen driving fat cabs; funny women with little round hats cleaning the tramway lines; people laughing and pushing against one another; trees on both sides of the streets and everywhere you looked almost, immense fountains; a noise of laughing from the footpaths or the middle of the streets or the open windows. And beside her, more beautifully brushed than ever, with a rolled umbrella in one hand and yellow gloves instead of brown ones, her grandfather who had asked her to spend the day. She wanted to run, she wanted to hang on his arm, she wanted to cry every minute, "Oh, I am so frightfully happy!"

He guided her across the roads, stood still while she "looked," and his kind eyes beamed on her and he said "just whatever you wish." She ate two white sausages and two little rolls of fresh bread at eleven o'clock in the morning and she drank some beer, which he told her wasn't intoxicating, wasn't at all like English beer, out of a glass like a flower vase. And then they took a cab and really she must have seen thousands and thousands of wonderful classical pictures in about a quarter of an hour!

"I shall have to think them over when I am alone."... But when they came out of the picture gallery it was raining. The grandfather unfurled his umbrella and held it over the little governess. They started to walk to the restaurant for lunch. She, very close beside him so that he should have some of the umbrella too.

"It goes easier," he remarked in a detached way, "if you take my arm, Fräulein. And besides it is the custom in Germany." So she took his arm and walked beside him while he pointed out the famous statues, so interested that he quite forgot to put down the umbrella even when the rain was long over.

After lunch they went to a café to hear a gypsy band, but she did not like that at all. Ugh! such horrible men were there with heads like eggs and cuts on their faces, so she turned her chair and cupped her burning cheeks in her hands and watched her old friend instead… Then they went to the Englischer Garten.

"I wonder what the time is," asked the little governess. "My watch has stopped. I forgot to wind it in the train last night. We've seen such a lot of things that I feel it must be quite late."

"Late!" He stopped in front of her laughing and shaking his head in a way she had begun to know. "Then you have not really enjoyed yourself. Late! Why, we have not had any ice cream yet!"

"Oh, but I have enjoyed myself," she cried, distressed, "more than I can possibly say. It has been wonderful! Only Frau Arnholdt is to be at the hotel at six and I ought to be there by five."

"So you shall. After the ice cream I shall put you into a cab and you can go there comfortably." She was happy again. The chocolate ice cream melted – melted in little sips a long way down. The shadows of the trees danced on the tablecloths, and she sat with her back safely turned to the ornamental clock that pointed to twenty-five minutes to seven.

"Really and truly," said the little governess earnestly, "this has been the happiest day of my life. I've never even imagined such a day." In spite of the ice-cream her grateful baby heart glowed with love for the fairy grandfather.

So they walked out of the garden down a long alley. The day was nearly over. "You see those big buildings opposite," said the old man. "The third storey – that is where I live. I and the old housekeeper who looks after me." She was very interested. "Now just before I find a cab for you, will you come and see my little 'home' and let me give you a bottle of the attar of roses I told you about in the train? For remembrance?" She would love to.

"I've never seen a bachelor's flat in my life," laughed the little governess.

The passage was quite dark. "Ah, I suppose my old woman has gone out to buy me a chicken. One moment." He opened a door and stood aside for her to pass, a little shy but curious, into a strange room. She did not know quite what to say. It wasn't pretty. In a way it was very ugly – but neat, and, she supposed, comfortable for such an old man. "Well, what do you think of it?" He knelt down and took from a cupboard a round tray with two pink glasses and a tall pink bottle. "Two little bedrooms beyond," he said gaily, "and a kitchen. It's enough, eh?"

"Oh, quite enough." "And if ever you should be in Munich and care to spend a day or two – why, there is always a little nest – a wing of a chicken, and a salad, and an old man delighted to be your host once more and many many times, dear little Fräulein!" He took the stopper out of the bottle and poured some wine into the two pink glasses. His hand shook and the wine spilled over the tray. It was very quiet in the room. She said: "I think I ought to go now."

"But you will have a tiny glass of wine with me – just one before you go?" said the old man.

"No, really no. I never drink wine. I – I have promised never to touch wine or anything like that." And though he pleaded and though she felt dreadfully rude, especially when he seemed to take it to heart so, she was quite determined. "No, really, please."

"Well, will you just sit down on the sofa for five minutes and let me drink your health?" The little governess sat down on the edge of the red velvet couch and he sat down beside her and drank her health at a gulp.

"Have you really been happy today?" asked the old man, turning round, so close beside her that she felt his knee twitching against hers. Before she could answer he held her hands.

"And are you going to give me one little kiss before you go?" he asked, drawing her closer still.

It was a dream! It wasn't true! It wasn't the same old man at all. Ah, how horrible! The little governess stared at him in terror. "No, no, no!" she stammered, struggling out of his hands. "One little kiss. A kiss. What is it? Just a kiss, dear little Fräulein. A kiss."

He pushed his face forward, his lips smiling broadly; and how his little blue eyes gleamed behind the spectacles!

"Never – never. How can you!" She sprang up, but he was too quick and he held her against the wall, pressed against her his hard old body and his twitching knee, and though she shook her head from side to side, distracted, kissed her on the mouth. On the mouth! Where not a soul who wasn't a near relation had ever kissed her before…

She ran, ran down the street until she found a broad road with tram lines and a policeman standing in the middle like a clockwork doll.

"I want to get a tram to the Hauptbahnhof," sobbed the little governess. "Fräulein?" She wrung her hands at him. "The Hauptbahnhof. There – there's one now," and while he watched very much surprised, the little girl with her hat on one side, crying without a handkerchief, sprang on to the tram – not seeing the conductor's eyebrows, nor hearing the *hochwohlgebildete* Dame talking her over with a scandalised friend.

She rocked herself and cried out loud and said, "Ah, ah!" pressing her hands to her mouth. "She has been to the dentist," shrilled a fat old woman, too stupid to be uncharitable. *"Na, sagen Sie 'mal,* what toothache! The child hasn't one left in her mouth." While the tram swung and jangled through a world full of old men with twitching knees.

When the little governess reached the hall of the Hotel Grunewald the same waiter who had come into her room in the morning was standing by a table, polishing a tray of glasses. The sight of the little governess seemed to fill him out with some inexplicable important content. He was ready for her question; his answer came pat and suave. "Yes, Fräulein, the lady has been here. I told her that you had arrived and gone out again immediately with a gentleman. She asked me when you were coming back again – but of course I could not say. And then she went to the manager."

He took up a glass from the table, held it up to the light, looked at it with one eye closed, and started polishing it with a corner of his apron.

"… ?"

"Pardon, Fräulein? Ach, no, Fräulein. The manager could tell her nothing – nothing." He shook his head and smiled at the brilliant glass.

"Where is the lady now?" asked the little governess, shuddering so violently that she had to hold her handkerchief up to her mouth.

"How should I know?" cried the waiter, and as he swooped past her to pounce upon a new arrival his heart beat so hard against his ribs that he nearly chuckled aloud.

"That's it! that's it!" he thought. "That will show her." And as he swung the new arrival's box on to his shoulders – hoop! – as though he were a giant and the box a feather, he minced over again the little governess's words, *"Gehen Sie. Gehen Sie sofort. Shall I! Shall I!"* he shouted to himself.

"One is not born a woman,
one becomes one."

– Simone De Beauvoir

Villa Myosotis[1]

by Sorana Gurian

translated by Gabi Reigh

The house, modelled on a Swiss chalet – red brick, carved wooden balcony, pointed roof, iron fretwork and a weathervane – peered timidly over the dunes. An unremarkable house, only set apart from the others by its one crowning glory, the vines that choked its wind-sheltered southern wall like an emerald scarf. The luminous green of the vines brought into sharp relief the absence of any other greenery in this landscape painted in cold, leaden colours, its endless silver black dunes, ashen sand. Even the vegetation soaked up its sallow shades: rusty, thorny briars, rough, dull green, brittle grass, cursed to be rooted in sand. A dismal landscape, caving beneath the sadness of centuries, tormented by storms and wind, by its hopeless infertility. And beyond the dunes, the immense horizon, luminously bare, endlessly rolling towards the four cardinal points, like a gigantic, impotent dragon plummeting towards the grey tumult of the sea. Not a single tree, or flower, or shadow of a swaying branch, not even the familiar comfort of a hedge… Nothing was green… Far, far away, there were pine forests and heaths with blood-tipped thorns, swarming with wild rabbits… but so far away… Villa Myosotis was surrounded only by dunes, sand, thistles, and the heavy tread of that grand, imperious wind.

How had she ended up here, three kilometres away from

1   short story written in 1939, published in 1946

any other dwelling? No-one could answer that question, not even Li herself. She had stumbled across it one day, walking beside her horse, climbing and descending the dunes. She had stopped outside the villa. Its name was inscribed on a plaque, hanging on a single rusty nail. She read it and smiled.

"*Vergiss mein nicht... Ne m'oubliez pas...* Forget me not." Once, she too had wished so hard not to be forgotten. But now everything was imbued with the ashen colour of the landscape and Li was no longer tormented by dreams of immortality... She had come here, running away from noise, from anything that wasn't herself, from the town and its people... Her mare, Rêveuse, understood her and brought her to this house, offering its gift of desolation... She immersed herself in the dead landscape and drank its tranquility. The tranquility of sand drowsing beneath the sun, the calm light of the days pouring away without restless vibrations, the horizon, as blank as the gaze of the blind, the sea, turning its faint, glittering smile towards the thousand shades of grey land; even the wind seemed different here, as if it floated on a raft like an indolent king, accompanied by the dull symphony of the waves... Everything seemed familiar to her, as if it had been a realm she had often haunted in her dreams... The hot sand crunching beneath her bare feet, the rattle of hooves on the pebbles, the horizon dissected by the hunched spines of the dunes, but most of all the silence... The silence rustling with whispers, sighs, polished by the rhythmic breath of the sea; the silence of a day about to begin. She drew closer to the gate, holding the horse by the reins, its head nodding, its ears trembling. When she lifted her hand to ring the doorbell, a stone fell out of the wall, with a howl...

The summer seemed like it would never end. The days drained imperceptibly like sand, brief and insignificant, always the same and always different, fleeting, like the elongated shadow of the villa on the beach, short at noon, then long, like a Gothic castle, just before sunset, then suddenly large and heavy as it melted into the night's shadows, a phantom illuminated by moonlight, transforming into a medieval tower; and then at dawn the house regained its familiar shape, bathed in rosy light. And so, the days went on, pebbles tossed on a road going nowhere, soundless, colourless, pointless pebbles...

The summer passed; Li remained at Villa Myosotis. The rain lashed the windows, the wind howled its wrath; it slipped under the doors, shook the window frames, rattled the panes; it climbed up the house like a spiteful cat, spitting sand everywhere, on the terrace, on the balcony, under the doors. The mornings were foggy, drowned by avalanches of sand, as if the dunes were advancing towards the house, ready to stopper its exits with their hunchbacks of sand.

Li stared at the bruised horizon veiled in dust and stroked her dog Bobby, who came to her craving affection... She lay on the divan, lit a cigarette, closed her eyes. She smoked one cigarette after another, twisting the dial of the radio. Like a shell, the room echoed with nostalgic joy, the merriment of strangers, the melancholy of distant sunsets... Often, on such nights, her book, unread, would slip to the floor, startling the black cat asleep on the piano or the white fox terrier with a black patch on his eye that nestled at the girl's feet, or the black Alsatian with eyebrows like comma shaped flames and red paws. The animals watched over her with love and concern: the eyes of the cat were opal, minuscule headlights, Bobby's eyes were sapphires and Rikki, the Alsatian, had amber, phosphorescent eyes, an astonishing black gold, like a wolf's. And then, gradually, each of them fell asleep. Li would light another cigarette; violet beams flooded the room, the blast of a late ship would pierce the fog and the lighthouse relentlessly cast its plume of rays onto the window, at steady intervals.

Later, the weary violins on the radio would fall silent, and the night circled the house, turning the windows into black mirrors that reflected the room back to itself, and the vines

45

would suddenly transform into an immense bird pinned to the brickwork, feebly beating its thousands of wings, like an exaltation of larks. But Li paid no attention to them as she wandered through the coral islands of her dreams…

Once a week, her landlady, Florence Wainwright, invited her to afternoon tea; she was a tall, lanky American, with red hair pinned in a low bun and large gold earrings, like the ones worn by gypsy women in our country. She was a proud and humourless woman who wore long, low-cut dresses that revealed her saggy bosom and peculiar rings on her hands with black stones and the insignia of her aristocratic family, which no-one in Gotha had heard of. She had a mania for parrots and in her salon, which was decorated with reproductions of Gainsborough paintings and filled with faux antiques and moth-eaten furs, there were two gilded cages from which these birds constantly whistled and delivered their quick remarks. Li was struck by the uncanny parallels between these green parrots, with their inquisitive green eyes, curved beaks and quick retorts and their mistress's irregular features, prominent nose and gold teeth. The American woman had christened her Miss Sonia, because for her, Sonia was the ideal name for all Russian or Turkish girls, or indeed for girls from any countries that were so far away that it was improbable that they actually existed. The landlady served Miss Sonia green tea in minuscule cups and slices of white toast with marmalade. Sinking into the deep armchair, Li would silently smile, listening to her host's interminable stories. Florence was in love with an exiled Russian prince, who was now a painter, and also studied at a celebrated cookery school in Paris…

"Ah, this Eugen Ivanovici!", sighed the fifty-year-old woman, gazing at her lover's photograph which she kept in a locket that hung around her neck. "No, dear… it's not what you think… He suffers from a hernia so he can't have anything to do with women… he needs an operation… I offered to pay for it, of course, but he wouldn't hear of it… not until he's a qualified chef! He's simply delightful... You should taste his pork with bananas! You cannot imagine! He calls me – that's his little pet-name for me – King-Kong!"

Indeed, there was something about the woman's odd, large, slightly ridiculous body that brought to mind the enormous gorilla from that film... One day, bored of the tragedy of the debonair prince and his culinary adventures, Li asked Miss Wainwright if she had ever met another Romanian. The lady thoughtfully munched her last piece of cake, took another sip of tea and replied:

"Oh yes, my dear! He was a sweet boy, very nice, good looking, wonderful teeth! He went back... to Romania... he was suffering from Pott's disease... in fact, he used to live in your room!" She mentioned his name, but Li couldn't make it out on account of the pronunciation. They changed the subject.

Returning to her room, Li stopped for a moment in the doorway, stunned by the darkness, then turned on the light. It was as if she was seeing the sideboard, the Venetian mirror, the sofa, the piano, through different eyes; everything seemed strange, different, foreign. She no longer felt alone; something else had entered the room as soon as she began thinking about another life unfolding there.

As soon as she had started renting it, Li immediately started to make changes. She had put her books on the shelves, the flowers in a bowl, added brightly-coloured cushions, a painted fan, a model ship and her collection of crystal bottles immediately transformed the ambience of the space. The radio beside the sofa, the typewriter next to the window, a letter lying on the floor, a velvet belt, a stocking, a glove dropped down in haste, all of these created a warm, feminine atmosphere. Li had imbued the room with personality, bonhomie and a vaguely tropical scent. But now, something indistinct had wormed itself into the space framed by those yellow walls... Have you ever asked yourself who lived in your room before you? Haven't you ever suffered the torment of staying in a hotel room, haunted by the ghostly remnants of other lives? Haven't you ever stumbled across pages torn from unfamiliar books, or an empty envelope with an unknown address, a sewing needle pinned in the tablecloth, a hair on the dressing table, an empty perfume bottle? People pass through rooms, leaving their pain and disquiet behind. Pressing her forehead to the windowpane, Li wondered how many times her predecessor had stared desperately into the night... How many times had he cried in this silent room, how many times had he pressed the same electric light switch that she was pressing now? And because the touch of her fingers erased his touch, because they had slept in the same bed, because they had both walked through the same door, these things linked into an imperceptible, unrelenting chain that bound them together tighter and tighter, into a coil from which she could not escape...

Dissatisfied by Miss Wainwright's vague description, Li tried to gather more precise details about the man who had once lived in her room. She talked to the local people: the innkeeper, the postman, the hairdresser, the florist... But not many of the townsfolk remembered the sick Romanian; so, Li had to satisfy herself with the landlady's platitudes and her own imaginings until one evening when... The raindrops drummed on the roof like a thousand tiny hooves; the eye of the lighthouse slit the dark horizon diagonally with its gaze; the vines sighed like a giant, exhausted lung; after feeding the dogs, Li poured herself a cup of tea and started getting ready for bed; a small lamp covered with a floral shade filled the room with an opal glow; the piano keys glinted in the shadows; the chrysanthemums bled into the Chinese bowl; a book, whose pages she had absent-mindedly turned, slipped into the corner of the divan; the dogs, drowsy after their feed, had retreated to their usual places – Dick the Great, as photogenic as the wolfdogs in police films, was lying on his front, his tail on the ground, with his nose under the armchair, Bobby the fox terrier was resting his head on his mistress's feet, while Rikki, like a resplendent, steadfast coal sphinx, with his gold eyes and his ears pricked, followed her movements and listened out for noises coming from outside.

Someone rang the doorbell. At first, Li thought that she had imagined it, but Dick gave a short bark and rose to his feet. Another ring... The wolfdog growled and the fox terrier sprang to the floor. Li opened the door of her room and walked into the hall, followed by the dogs. As she unlocked the front door, the wind tore it from her hand and invaded the house, thrashing against the walls; Li's eyes could not penetrate the darkness outside. Dick started barking in an unfamiliar way.

"Who's there?" Li asked.

The eerie silence had unsettled her, and she was surprised by the shrillness of her voice.

"Is that you, Miss Florence?"

"No, Miss Florence has been away for a week now. May I help you?"

Struggling to adjust her eyes to the darkness, Li tried to make out the face of the man whose voice...

"Would you mind if I came in? You have a beautiful dog..."

Li reminded herself that she had a revolver in her room, that Dick the Great... might help her... But the stranger had already entered the hall. He was tall and thin; rivers of water were pouring down his black raincoat and his hat covered his eyes.

"I'm an old lodger, from a long time ago... It's been ages since I lived here..."

He pointed to Li's room.

"You? You have come back?"

"Are you surprised? So, Florence has told you about me! I'm delighted that she hasn't forgotten me!"

"Delighted" seemed a bit of an overstatement to Li. She wondered what his face looked like... She closed the door and replied: "You must be exhausted; did you walk all the way here?"

"Of course! As far as I know, this place isn't on the tramline!"

He was mocking her... Perhaps he was just tired?

"You can sleep here," Li said, feeling like the mistress of the house. "We have three empty rooms. Would you like a cup of tea? And we have bread, butter, everything... Are you hungry?"

"No, thank you, I'm not hungry", replied the stranger, "I'm never hungry, and I'm not tired either... You can't be tired when you don't exist." He took off his hat, hung it on a hook, then shook his raincoat. Li noticed that the man wore a grey jacket, had an oval face with irregular features, piercing dark eyes and chestnut hair.

"Please come in."

She opened the door to her room. The stranger stepped inside; the dogs simultaneously bared their teeth. Li told them to calm down but they kept growling. The stranger looked around.

"Everything looks so different... this room... the piano... my bed was over there, near the window... the curtains were red, but the mirror is still in the same place... and the wardrobe... the armchair used to be by the fireplace."

He walked to the piano, touched the keys, and then, hovering above them without pressing them, began to play. Li startled. Rachmaninov's Prelude in C sharp minor. The dogs, huddled together in a corner, still quietly growling, didn't dare approach; the cat was hiding under the wardrobe, a green glint shone in its eyes, like it did moments before its claws crushed a captured sparrow.

The prelude, vibrating with the tolling of funereal bells, with the irredeemable sadness of damp soil, with autumn, with the pain that tore apart the sombre chords, cleaved time apart like an open grave and filled the room with spectral shadows; the chimeric sounds rebounded from the walls.

The stranger played with his eyes closed, like a blind man. His fingers looked weary, long, jaundiced. Abruptly, the prelude collapsed into silence. Hoarsely, he asked: "You heard it? I often ask myself what it would take for the living to understand. It's something you wonder about when you die…"

Li didn't understand what he was talking about. The tick-tock of the clock waded through the waves of time. The stranger was sitting in the armchair in the shadows, while Li, lying on the sofa, was bathed in a halo of light. The dogs didn't dare move. Suddenly, Li sensed that something had changed but she couldn't fathom what exactly until she realised that she could no longer hear the clock… At that same moment, the voice from the shadows commanded: "Turn off the light." Li tried to protest, but her intense curiosity forced her to obey him. In the darkness, she felt her heart beating faster. Her mouth was dry, cold shivers ran up and down her spine.

"Now… I have everything just as it was before, can you hear the sound of the waves? So many times, I used to leave the door open so that I could better hear them… the waves… they were my friends… but you must get rid of the dogs, do you hear?"

"No," said Li, "the dogs sleep here."

"No, not in my room…" the stranger replied.

Li heard the door creak open, then the terrified scramble of the dogs running out. Silence.

"Don't worry, little girl… The dogs are in the kitchen… You see? It's better this way… I've dreamt so much of this moment… And you will, too… The return to the past you haven't managed to forget…"

His footsteps were so light that Li couldn't hear them, but she felt his presence, strangely, through her skin…

"This is where I waited for Solange, the night she wanted to die… She didn't die…" he laughed drily, "but brought me a dead crow as a gift … and the bitterness of love…"

Li felt the nerves vibrating in her temples and tried to turn on the light but a cold, dry hand gripped her arm.

"No, we don't need any light, I'm cold! Can't you see, Li… I'm cold… you took my room, and now you want to throw me out?"

"Tomorrow," she whispered, "you can have it back; I'll move back to town…"

"Tomorrow," the stranger gave a short laugh, "tomorrow – that word means nothing to me now; today, today, it's forever today, do you understand what today means?"

"Yes," answered the girl, suddenly alight with understanding, "today means you!"

The stranger sat down by her feet. Li could smell him; his coat bore the scent of damp earth, his hair smelled of rain, and her pity and compassion for that man who had endured such a long journey suddenly returned…

"I want to sleep beside you, Li! You are warm and you are alive, warm, alive, alive…"

The girl allowed herself to be carried by that fast, dark current into the realm of the cursed. The night was dense, hostile; the cat's green eyes sparkled in the darkness…

She awoke to the barking of the dogs; they were clawing at the door, whining pitifully and then barking sharply. The ashen light of the leaden sky filtered through the window; the clock had stopped at midnight… But at least it was morning. The rain had paused. Li got out of bed and opened the door; the dogs bounded inside the room, licking her face, almost toppling her with their rough affection. They followed her into the kitchen. Li warmed up the milk and shared her bread with them. A stray, pallid sunray bounced off the white drawers and made the red tiles sparkle. Li got down to business; after she swept up her room, she started calling on people from town, one after another: the milkman with the red nose and the green woollen jacket, the butcher who cycled to different houses bringing supplies, the stout, apple-shaped postman with the large moustache and tiny nose. The latter, doffing his gold-trimmed cap and handing her a pile of letters, said: "It looks like some good weather is coming our way… I think we should toast it with a glass of Dubonnet…"

Everything carried on as before; the dogs ran on the dunes, the cat had its head stuck in a bowl, licking it meticulously. Li scratched its ear. Minu turned its Siamese head towards her, and Li gazed at the triangular-shaped face with the squashed nose and narrow eyes. Droplets of milk quivered on the cat's long whiskers; she looked like a bendy, black velvet toy.

In the afternoon, the sky brightened to a pure azure blue; the colour poured down the dunes, bringing the sand to life, the sea was a pool of silver, the grass bent to the will of the wind.

Li wandered across the beach, followed by the dogs. Sometimes, one of them would loiter behind, rummaging through seashells, then race to catch them up, shake itself off, then run ahead. Li had the delicious feeling that she was on a walk with the best friends she had in the world. Towards the evening, the sky became rose-coloured, the sea rolled its golden waves, the beach, stripped bare by the retreating tide, was shrouded in violet mist. The rockpools seemed like the earth's resplendent wounds, mirroring the sunset. Gradually, the sky turned lilac. On the horizon, the last stray rays of sun looked green; a pale, haggard new moon clung precariously to the evening air. The wind turned cold. Fatigue weighed down Li's feet, like heavy water… She started climbing up the bank. But Bobby wanted to play, he pulled on her dress, hopped up and down the steps like a rabbit; Rikki stopped constantly for all sorts of different reasons – to sniff a stone, to investigate a dead crab, to dig a hole in the sand – and only Dick, heavy and dignified, walked beside his mistress and dutifully bared his teeth.

Alone, surrounded by the unutterable beauty of the dying day, Li starts to sing. Dick pricks his ears, then his rough, cautious tongue licks her bare arm. Cold grains of sand permeate through her cotton shoes. Wet shells sparkle. Li takes the key out of her pocket and tries to open the door. For the first time ever, the lock won't budge… As if it's warning her…

The dogs are asleep; Rikki and Bobby are huddled together, on the edge of the divan, both of them burying their noses in Li's knees. Dick the Great rises to get a drink and then falls asleep in the doorway. The cat is sharpening her claws on the green velvet armchair. The lamp pours its white light softly into the room.

Li is wearing a light dress of rose lace and she has put on some makeup because she has decided to go out into town. She is waiting, just like the open piano is waiting. The door, too, is waiting to be opened but there isn't a single noise, apart from the dogs' breathing, or the moaning of the wind outside that seems to be thrashing like a wounded creature. Occasionally she hears a wave crashing heavily against the sand. The whole house is waiting in silence; the vines are struggling like a bird caught in a trap.

Li keeps on waiting; she opens a book, looks at the black lines of text, deciphers a word, a phrase. Everything is outside of her; all of her senses are concentrated on the sounds around her, her whole body is an auditory nerve. She listens… She waits… The clock's hands are frozen at midnight, as if the whole of life had become one eternal midnight… Will no-one come?

One day, during afternoon tea, she asks Miss Florence: "I'd like you to change my curtains… do you still have the red ones?"

"Don't be silly, they've been devoured by moths, they're hideous!"

"It doesn't matter… and please, can I ask you something else? Could I put my typewriter in the hall?"

"Alright – why not? How funny you Romanians are!"

Bobby is white, small, like a porcelain figurine; he has long, triangular, black ears that make him look as if he is wearing a Dutch bonnet. His eyes are violet and he has a pink nose sprouting tiny hairs. When he is excited, he rises on his hind legs and starts jumping around in a circle – a graceful dance, like a boxer in the ring, as if readying himself for an attack from some hidden adversary. Once he wears himself out, he lies down next to Li, wagging his tail, his nose buried in her naked shoulder or her knees. His happiness is complete if he is then offered a sugar lump, or if she strokes his stomach, and on those occasions he throws himself on his back with a look of pure ecstasy on his face, like a spoiled dilettante.

Rikki is much more restrained and dignified, but also jealous and dictatorial, the quintessential canine Othello. Only an emergency of some kind could part him from his mistress. When she rebukes him, he hides under the bed and pretends to go to sleep. On those occasions, he will not answer to his name until he is reassured that he is a good dog. Then he comes out begrudgingly, but eventually cheers up and becomes his lively, obedient self once again. Li's laughter makes Rikki happy, he wags his tail and barks… He jumps on the bed, licks her, or fetches her slippers in his mouth…

Dick the Great is an enormous wolfdog, with olive eyes that turn green when he is furious. He has a huge, bushy tail that could knock over the coffee table that contains Li's cigarettes, her book, the basket of mandarins, the bowl filled with flowers and some bonbons. Dick always sleeps next to the door, but he often gets up in the middle of the night and sniffs Li, to check if she's awake… If he met her eye, then his ears would grow slack and he would push his nose under her hand, willing her to stroke him. Sometimes, he would get up on his front legs, resting his body on the edge of the mattress, and lie his head on her chest and close his eyes; it was as if he were listening to her heartbeat. Li called him 'boy' and sometimes 'Mr.'

"You can leave Dick tied up on the terrace, he won't be cold; look how thick his fur is... He mustn't sleep in the room... You will tie him up outside, won't you? And then maybe I'll come back..."

Dick spent the night on the terrace. In the morning, Li sees traces of blood outside; the wolfdog raises a wounded paw. The servant woman swears that she didn't throw any broken glass on the terrace but Li finds the fragments of a glass... She doesn't think it was her that broke it... She doesn't remember doing it... Li bandages Dick's leg and decides to keep the dogs in the kitchen from now on...

"I never had any animals in the room, I never had anyone there; I was always alone, even when I was in love, I always felt like I was part of a special tribe of people, the miserable few who possess a kind of second sight, like an additional lens attached to the retina... And because I was always alone, I turned bad... I'm not making any excuses, but loneliness, like certain illnesses, breeds tumours... When cancer gnaws at you, it... It's a form of revenge... reliving the days when... You keep on searching, searching, searching, until you find it..."

The days pass, ash tinted... the cat runs away and a hunter finds it in a rabbit trap. He brings it back to Villa Myosotis. Li looks at the bundle of black, damp fur. Touched, the man offers to bring her another kitten. Li shakes her head. No, she has no need for it now! She offers him some money and asks him if he knows of anyone who might be able to look after the dogs.

"I can pay," she says, "because I'm leaving tomorrow, and I can't take them with me."

The dogs leave. She stands on the front stairs and watches

them go, leaning on the railings. The vine leaves whisper as they caress her cheeks, their cold fingers as fragrant as chrysanthemums. The cat's bloody cadaver is like an unbearable reproach... Li tears off some rust-coloured leaves and covers the body... The days rush past her, in a flood. They seem not so much like days as the exhausting anticipation one feels waiting on a station platform for a train that is trudging its way slowly through the snow, somewhere far away.

The radio is covered with dust. A pile of unopened letters is slowly yellowing on a shelf – one day, it falls into the fire. One of these letters contained details about the former tenant of Villa Myosotis that Li would have found interesting... The man who had returned back to his own country paralysed, then died mid-June, around the time that Li first arrived here, amidst the desolate dunes... The writer of that letter would wait in vain for an answer, because it would never be held in the hands of the one for whom it was intended...

The vigil continues every evening. The doorbell rings. Li rushes to the door. She opens it. No-one. The ringing is so loud, but Li realises that it's actually the phone. Barefoot, in her pyjamas trimmed with black lace, the girl trembles as she approaches it. Suddenly, a light is switched on and the hall opens up like a crypt... Li can't tell anymore... Is this real or a dream? The phone rings again. Automatically, Li picks up the receiver, but it takes her a while to engage with that faraway voice, that living voice.

"What's the matter with you, dear? Are you sick? Your telephone is always engaged... Do you stay up all night talking? ...Have you been away? Why do I never see you in town these days?"

Li suddenly feels enraged. She doesn't understand anything anymore, has no idea who is on the other end of the line, or why they are calling her, or what they want. The stubborn, unmoving hands of the clock are mockingly still pointing to the same hour: 12 o'clock. Time drains away, gurgling its way down a funnel.

"Why weren't you answering?"

Li suddenly becomes aware of her silence and asks, as if waking from sleep: "Who is this?"

"It's me, Dr. Emile – what's the matter with you?"

Li now remembers the voice on the other end of the line, notices for the first time the cold floor beneath her bare feet, and begins to answer hesitantly, stumbling over her words, like an invalid learning to walk again after a long illness: "Yes, Emile, yes, I know, I have... been away, yes, away... No, I'm not drunk." But there he was, standing in the hall! Li could see his dark-circled eyes, his downturned mouth.

"Hang up!"

Li dropped the receiver and left it hanging like the body of a condemned man until the telephone started to purr again.

"You belong only to me, do you understand? You are all that I have left on this earth!"

Li listens to his voice, then lowers her eyelids so that she can better hear it, allowing herself to be enchanted by its spell. The fog closes in on her body, the lights go out, he takes her into his arms: "I hunger for you, Li..."

***

Doctor Emile is a tall, broad-shouldered man with long arms. There is something lithe about the way he moves, an adaptability that belies his heavy appearance, a lively, untamed, hidden energy. His facial features seem to have been painted in broad brushstrokes, without much detail; his lowered eyelids shield a steady, piercing gaze. But his lips seem too full, his skin too white to match the vitality exuding from that large body. Sometimes, when the doctor smiles, his face lights up with kindness and warmth. When he talks to women, he is masterful and contemptuous. By rights, they should hate him... but what's strange is that it is this very quality that endears him to them. His patients, in particular, come alive when he is near; they blush, stretch their necks like ponies roused by a familiar marching tune, their eyes sparkle, the blood rushes through their veins. The fact that Doctor Emile ignores them is enough to excite new erotic fantasies and they read his indifference as evidence of unquenchable lust. His self-assured air, his dismissive hand gestures that sweep away any concerns, even his relaxed, confident stride impresses his patients. Li had made his acquaintance by chance in the casino, and they became friends the day when, having just moved to Villa Myosotis, she had asked him: "Doctor, do you know the woman with the two parrots?"

And the doctor had answered: "I know what you mean – *pas deux sans trois,*" a reply that conveyed to her his utter disregard for the customary rules of politeness, but also his great sense of humour!

The abrupt ending of their telephone conversation concerned Emile and he called on her the next day, in the early evening. He found Li shivering on the bed, horribly thin, wearing makeup but practically naked. The room was blue with smoke, the ashtray full of cigarette butts. Orange peel was scattered on the carpet. The girl's eyes glowed with fever and darted about, nervously, suspicious. It was as if the room was filled with a different, strange atmosphere.

Li would not answer his questions, her eyes kept staring at the door. Emile touched her fingers and noticed that they were cold. Her arms and neck were covered with purple marks, but they didn't look like scratches... it was as if they had been created by suction... or bites... The doctor sat next to Li on the bed and started questioning her gently, calmly, full of kindness. And because he was patient, he managed to find out everything...

He didn't challenge her story, but held her close to him, stroking her shoulders. His fingers traced her hard, fragrant flesh, the sharp, red arrows of her breasts rising like flames. He embraced her, his mouth searching hers. Her head thrown back, Li looked towards the window and met the distressed eyes watching her from the other side of the glass... She saw the lips curling with hatred, the hat tilted down to reveal the cadaverous skull... A long howl, like a blast of wind...

"Let me go! Let me..." But Emile was clutching her in his arms, and he was alive...

The rain drummed on the roof all night long. The sea beat its gong, flares of sand crashed against the windows... A night tempest... The wind moaned like a man vanquished by pain, waiting on the doorstep...

***

In the morning, Li opened the door. The vines, torn from the wall like a vast, bloody, golden rag, were lying on the front steps of the villa...

The Mark on the Wall[1]

Virginia Woolf

Perhaps it was the middle of January in the present that I first looked up and saw the mark on the wall. In order to fix a date, it is necessary to remember what one saw. So now I think of the fire; the steady film of yellow light upon the page of my book; the three chrysanthemums in the round glass bowl on the mantelpiece. Yes, it must have been the wintertime, and we had just finished our tea, for I remember that I was smoking a cigarette when I looked up and saw the mark on the wall for the first time. I looked up through the smoke of my cigarette and my eye lodged for a moment upon the burning coals, and that old fancy of the crimson flag flapping from the castle tower came into my mind, and I thought of the cavalcade of red knights riding up the side of the black rock. Rather to my relief the sight of the mark interrupted the fancy, for it is an old fancy, an automatic fancy, made as a child perhaps. The mark was a small round mark, black upon the white wall, about six or seven inches above the mantelpiece.

How readily our thoughts swarm upon a new object, lifting it a little way, as ants carry a blade of straw so feverishly, and then leave it... If that mark was made by a nail, it can't have been for a picture, it must have been for a miniature – the miniature of a lady with white powdered curls, powder-dusted cheeks, and lips like red carnations. A fraud of course, for the people who had this house before us would have chosen pictures in that way – an old picture for an old room. That is

1   published in 1917

61

the sort of people they were – very interesting people, and I think of them so often, in such queer places, because one will never see them again, never know what happened next. They wanted to leave this house because they wanted to change their style of furniture, so he said, and he was in process of saying that in his opinion art should have ideas behind it when we were torn asunder, as one is torn from the old lady about to pour out tea and the young man about to hit the tennis ball in the back garden of the suburban villa as one rushes past in the train.

But as for that mark, I'm not sure about it; I don't believe it was made by a nail after all; it's too big, too round, for that. I might get up, but if I got up and looked at it, ten to one I shouldn't be able to say for certain; because once a thing's done, no-one ever knows how it happened. Oh! dear me, the mystery of life. The inaccuracy of thought! The ignorance of humanity! To show how very little control of our possessions we have – what an accidental affair this living is after all our civilization – let me just count over a few of the things lost in one lifetime, beginning, for that seems always the most mysterious of losses – what cat would gnaw, what rat would nibble – three pale blue canisters of book-binding tools? Then there were the bird cages, the iron hoops, the steel skates, the Queen Anne coal-scuttle, the bagatelle board, the hand organ – all gone, and jewels, too. Opals and emeralds, they lie about the roots of turnips. What a scraping paring affair it is to be sure! The wonder is that I've any clothes on my back, that I sit surrounded by solid furniture at this moment.

Why, if one wants to compare life to anything, one must liken it to being blown through the Tube at fifty miles an hour – landing at the other end without a single hairpin in one's hair! Shot out at the feet of God entirely naked! Tumbling head over heels in the asphodel meadows like brown paper parcels pitched down a shoot in the post office! With one's hair flying back like the tail of a racehorse. Yes, that seems to express the rapidity of life, the perpetual waste and repair; all so casual, all so haphazard...

But after life. The slow pulling down of thick green stalks so that the cup of the flower, as it turns over, deluges one with purple and red light. Why, after all, should one not be born there as one is born here, helpless, speechless, unable to focus one's eyesight, groping at the roots of the grass, at the toes of the Giants? As for saying which are trees, and which are men and women, or whether there are such things, that one won't be in a condition to do for fifty years or so. There will be nothing but spaces of light and dark, intersected by thick stalks, and rather higher up perhaps, rose-shaped blots of an indistinct colour – dim pinks and blues – which will, as time goes on, become more definite, become – I don't know what...

And yet that mark on the wall is not a hole at all. It may even be caused by some round black substance, such as a small rose leaf, left over from the summer, and I, not being a very vigilant housekeeper – look at the dust on the mantelpiece, for example, the dust which, so they say, buried Troy three times over, only fragments of pots utterly refusing annihilation, as one can believe.

The tree outside the window taps very gently on the pane... I want to think quietly, calmly, spaciously, never to be interrupted, never to have to rise from my chair, to slip easily from one thing to another, without any sense of hostility, or obstacle. I want to sink deeper and deeper, away from the surface, with its hard separate facts. To steady myself, let me catch hold of the first idea that passes... Shakespeare... Well, he will do as well as another. A man who sat himself solidly in an armchair, and looked into the fire, so – A shower of ideas fell perpetually from some very high Heaven down through his mind. He leant his forehead on his hand, and people, looking in through the open door – for this scene is supposed to take place on a summer's evening – But how dull this is, this historical fiction! It doesn't interest me at all. I wish I could hit upon a pleasant track of thought, a track indirectly reflecting credit upon myself, for those are the pleasantest thoughts, and very frequent even in the minds of modest, mouse-coloured people, who believe genuinely that they dislike to hear their own praises. They are not thoughts directly praising oneself; that is the beauty of them; they are thoughts like this:

"And then I came into the room. They were discussing botany. I said how I'd seen a flower growing on a dust heap on the site of an old house in Kingsway. The seed, I said, must have been sown in the reign of Charles the First. What flowers grew in the reign of Charles the First?" I asked – (but, I don't remember the answer). Tall flowers with purple tassels to them perhaps. And so it goes on. All the time I'm dressing up the figure of myself in my own mind, lovingly, stealthily, not openly adoring it, for if I did that, I should catch myself out, and stretch my hand at once for a book in self-protection. Indeed, it is curious how instinctively one protects the image of oneself from idolatry or any other handling that could make it ridiculous, or too unlike the original to be believed in any longer.

Or is it not so very curious after all? It is a matter of great importance. Suppose the looking glass smashes, the image disappears, and the romantic figure with the green of forest depths all about it is there no longer, but only that shell of a person which is seen by other people – what an airless, shallow, bald, prominent world it becomes! A world not to be lived in. As we face each other in omnibuses and underground railways we are looking into the mirror that accounts for the vagueness, the gleam of glassiness, in our eyes. And the novelists in future will realise more and more the importance of these reflections, for of course there is not one reflection but an almost infinite number; those are the depths they will explore, those the phantoms they will pursue, leaving the description of reality more and more out of their stories, taking a knowledge of it for granted, as the Greeks did and Shakespeare perhaps – but these generalizations are very worthless. The military sound of the word is enough. It recalls leading articles, cabinet ministers – a whole class of things indeed which as a child one thought the thing itself, the standard thing, the real thing, from which one could not depart, save at the risk of nameless damnation. Generalizations bring back somehow Sunday in London, Sunday afternoon walks, Sunday luncheons, and also ways of speaking of the dead, clothes, and habits – like the habit of sitting all together in one room until a certain hour, although nobody liked it. There was a rule for everything. The rule for tablecloths at that particular period was that they should be made of tapestry with little yellow compartments marked upon them, such as you may see in photographs of the carpets in the corridors of the royal palaces. Tablecloths of a different kind were not real tablecloths. How shocking, and yet how wonderful it was to discover that these real things, Sunday luncheons, Sunday walks, country houses, and tablecloths were not entirely real, were indeed half phantoms, and the damnation which visited the disbeliever in them was only a sense of illegitimate freedom. What now takes the place of those things I wonder, those real standard things? Men perhaps, should you be a woman; the masculine point of view which governs our lives, which sets the standard, which establishes Whitaker's Table of Precedency, which has become, I suppose, since the war, half a phantom to many men and women, which soon – one may hope, will be laughed into the dustbin where the phantoms go, the mahogany sideboards and the Landseer prints, Gods and Devils, Hell and so forth, leaving us all with an intoxicating sense of illegitimate freedom – if freedom exists...

In certain lights, that mark on the wall seems actually to project from the wall. Nor is it entirely circular. I cannot be sure, but it seems to cast a perceptible shadow, suggesting that if I ran my finger down that strip of the wall it would, at a certain point, mount and descend a small tumulus, a smooth tumulus like those barrows on the South Downs which are, they say, either tombs or camps. Of the two, I should prefer them to be tombs, desiring melancholy like most English people, and finding it natural at the end of a walk to think of the bones stretched beneath the turf... There must be some book about it. Some antiquary must have dug up those bones and given them a name... What sort of a man is an antiquary, I wonder? Retired Colonels for the most part, I daresay, leading parties of aged labourers to the top here, examining clods of earth and stone, and getting into correspondence with the neighbouring clergy, which, being opened at breakfast time, gives them a feeling of importance, and the comparison of arrowheads necessitates cross-country journeys to the county towns, an agreeable necessity both to them and to their elderly wives, who wish to make plum jam or to clean out the study, and have every reason for keeping that great question of the camp or the tomb in perpetual suspension, while the Colonel himself feels agreeably philosophic in accumulating evidence on both sides of the question. It is true that he does finally incline to believe in the camp; and, being opposed, indites a pamphlet which he is about to read at the quarterly meeting of the local society when a stroke lays him low, and his last conscious thoughts are not of wife or child, but of the camp and that arrowhead there, which is now in the case at the local museum, together with the foot of a Chinese murderess, a handful of Elizabethan nails, a great many Tudor clay pipes, a piece of Roman pottery, and the wine-glass that Nelson drank out of – proving I really don't know what.

No, no, nothing is proved, nothing is known. And if I were to get up at this very moment and ascertain that the mark on the wall is really – what shall we say? – the head of a gigantic old nail, driven in two hundred years ago, which has now, owing to the patient attrition of many generations of housemaids, revealed its head above the coat of paint, and is taking its first view of modern life in the sight of a white-walled fire-lit room, what should I gain? – Knowledge?

The Mark on the Wall

Matter for further speculation? I can think sitting still as well as standing up. And what is knowledge? What are our learned men save the descendants of witches and hermits who crouched in caves and in woods brewing herbs, interrogating shrew-mice and writing down the language of the stars? And the less we honour them as our superstitions dwindle and our respect for beauty and health of mind increases... Yes, one could imagine a very pleasant world. A quiet, spacious world, with the flowers so red and blue in the open fields. A world without professors or specialists or house-keepers with the profiles of policemen, a world which one could slice with one's thought as a fish slices the water with his fin, grazing the stems of the water-lilies, hanging suspended over nests of white sea eggs... How peaceful it is down here, rooted in the centre of the world and gazing up through the grey waters, with their sudden gleams of light, and their reflections – if it were not for *Whitaker's Almanack* – if it were not for the Table of Precedency!

I must jump up and see for myself what that mark on the wall really is – a nail, a rose-leaf, a crack in the wood? Here is nature once more at her old game of self-preservation. This train of thought, she perceives, is threatening mere waste of energy, even some collision with reality, for who will ever be able to lift a finger against Whitaker's Table of Precedency? The Archbishop of Canterbury is followed by the Lord High Chancellor; the Lord High Chancellor is followed by the Archbishop of York. Everybody follows somebody, such is the philosophy of Whitaker; and the great thing is to know who follows whom. Whitaker knows, and let that, so Nature counsels, comfort you, instead of enraging you; and if you can't be comforted, if you must shatter this hour of peace, think of the mark on the wall.

I understand Nature's game – her prompting to take action as a way of ending any thought that threatens to excite or to pain. Hence, I suppose, comes our slight contempt for men of action – men, we assume, who don't think. Still, there's no harm in putting a full stop to one's disagreeable thoughts by looking at a mark on the wall.

Indeed, now that I have fixed my eyes upon it, I feel that I have grasped a plank in the sea. I feel a satisfying sense of reality which at once turns the two Archbishops and the Lord High Chancellor to the shadows of shades. Here is something definite, something real. Thus, waking from a midnight dream of horror, one hastily turns on the light and lies quiescent, worshipping the chest of drawers, worshipping solidity, worshipping reality, worshipping the impersonal world which is a proof of some existence other than ours. That is what one wants to be sure of...

Wood is a pleasant thing to think about. It comes from a tree, and trees grow, and we don't know how they grow. For years and years they grow, without paying any attention to us, in meadows, in forests, and by the side of rivers – all things one likes to think about. The cows swish their tails beneath them on hot afternoons; they paint rivers so green that when a moorhen dives one expects to see its feathers all green when it comes up again. I like to think of the fish balanced against the stream like flags blown out; and of water-beetles slowly raiding domes of mud upon the bed of the river. I like to think of the tree itself: first the close dry sensation of being wood; then the grinding of the storm; then the slow, delicious ooze of sap. I like to think of it, too, on winter's nights standing in the empty field with all leaves close-furled, nothing tender exposed to the iron bullets of the moon, a naked mast upon an earth that goes tumbling, tumbling, all night long. The song of birds must sound very loud and strange in June; and how cold the feet of insects must feel upon it, as they make labourious progresses up the creases of the bark, or sun themselves upon the thin green awning of the leaves, and look straight in front of them with diamond-cut red eyes... One by one the fibres snap beneath the immense cold pressure of the earth, then the last storm comes and, falling, the highest branches drive deep into the ground again. Even so, life isn't done with; there are a million patient, watchful lives still for a tree, all over the world, in bedrooms, in ships, on the pavement, lining rooms, where men and women sit after tea, smoking cigarettes. It is full of peaceful thoughts, happy thoughts, this tree. I should like to take each one separately – but something is getting in the way... Where was I? What has it all been about? A tree? A river? The Downs? *Whitaker's Almanack?* The fields of asphodel? I can't remember a thing. Everything's moving, falling, slipping, vanishing... There is a vast upheaval of matter. Someone is standing over me and saying –

"I'm going out to buy a newspaper."

"Yes?"

"Though it's no good buying newspapers... Nothing ever happens. Curse this war; God damn this war! All the same, I don't see why we should have a snail on our wall."

Ah, the mark on the wall! It was a snail.

"A room is, after all, a place where you hide from the wolves. That's all any room is."

– Jean Rhys

Miss Ogilvy Finds Herself[1]

Radclyffe Hall

1.

Miss Ogilvy stood on the quay at Calais and surveyed the disbanding of her Unit, the Unit that together with the coming of war had completely altered the complexion of her life, at all events for three years.

Miss Ogilvy's thin, pale lips were set sternly and her forehead was puckered in an effort of attention, in an effort to memorise every small detail of every old war-weary, battered motor on whose side still appeared the merciful emblem that had set Miss Ogilvy free.

Miss Ogilvy's mind was jerking a little, trying to regain its accustomed balance, trying to readjust itself quickly to this sudden and paralysing change. Her tall, awkward body with its queer look of strength, its broad, flat bosom and thick legs and ankles, as though in response to her jerking mind, moved uneasily, rocking backwards and forwards. She had this trick of rocking on her feet in moments of controlled agitation. As usual, her hands were thrust deep into her pockets; they seldom seemed to come out of her pockets unless it were to light a cigarette, and as though she were still standing firm under fire while the wounded were placed in her ambulances, she suddenly straddled her legs very slightly and lifted her head and listened. She was standing firm under fire at that moment, the fire of a desperate regret.

---

1 extract from a short story written in 1926, published in 1934

Some girls came towards her, young, tired-looking creatures whose eyes were too bright from long strain and excitement. They had all been members of that glorious Unit, and they still wore the queer little forage-caps and the short, clumsy tunics of the French Militaire. They still slouched in walking and smoked Caporals in emulation of the Poilus. Like their founder and leader these girls were all English, but like her they had chosen to serve England's ally, fearlessly thrusting right up to the trenches in search of the wounded and dying. They had seen some fine things in the course of three years, not the least fine of which was the cold, hard-faced woman who commanding, domineering, even hectoring at times, had yet been possessed of so dauntless a courage and of so insistent a vitality that it vitalised the whole Unit.

"It's rotten!" Miss Ogilvy heard someone saying. "It's rotten, this breaking up of our Unit!" And the high, rather childish voice of the speaker sounded perilously near to tears.

Miss Ogilvy looked at the girl almost gently, and it seemed, for a moment, as though some deep feeling were about to find expression in words. But Miss Ogilvy's feelings had been held in abeyance so long that they seldom dared become vocal, so she merely said "Oh?" on a rising inflection – her method of checking emotion.

They were swinging the ambulance cars in midair, those of them that were destined to go back to England, swinging them up like sacks of potatoes, then lowering them with much clanging of chains to the deck of the waiting steamer. The porters were shoving and shouting and quarrelling, pausing now and again to make meaningless gestures, while a pompous official was becoming quite angry as he pointed at Miss Ogilvy's own special car – it annoyed him, it was bulky and difficult to move.

"Bon Dieu! Mais depechez-vous donc!" he bawled, as though he were bullying the motor.

Then Miss Ogilvy's heart gave a sudden, thick thud to see this undignified, pitiful ending, and she turned and patted the gallant old car as though she were patting a well-beloved horse, as though she would say: "Yes, I know how it feels – never mind, we'll go down together."

2.

Miss Ogilvy sat in the railway carriage on her way from Dover to London. The soft English landscape sped smoothly past: small homesteads, small churches, small pastures, small lanes with small hedges; all small like England itself, all small like Miss Ogilvy's future. And sitting there still arrayed in her tunic, with her forage-cap resting on her knees, she was conscious of a sense of complete frustration; thinking less of those glorious years at the Front and of all that had gone to the making of her, than of all that had gone to the marring of her from the days of her earliest childhood.

She saw herself as a queer little girl, aggressive and awkward because of her shyness; a queer little girl who loathed sisters and dolls, preferring the stable boys as companions, preferring to play with footballs and tops, and occasional catapults. She saw herself climbing the tallest beech trees, arrayed in old breeches illicitly come by. She remembered insisting with tears and some temper that her real name was William and not Wilhelmina. All these childish pretences and illusions she remembered, and the bitterness that came after. For Miss Ogilvy had found as her life went on that in this world it is better to be one with the herd, that the world has no wish to understand those who cannot conform to its stereotyped pattern. True enough in her youth she had gloried in her strength, lifting weights, swinging clubs and developing muscles, but presently this had grown irksome to her; it had seemed to lead nowhere, she being a woman, and then as her mother had often protested: muscles looked so appalling in evening dress – a young girl ought not to have muscles.

Miss Ogilvy's relation to the opposite sex was unusual and at that time added much to her worries, for no less than three men had wished to propose, to the genuine amazement of the world and her mother. Miss Ogilvy's instinct made her like and trust men for whom she had a pronounced fellow-feeling; she would always have chosen them as her friends and companions in preference to girls or women; she would dearly have loved to share in their sports, their business, their ideals and their wide-flung interests. But men had not wanted her, except the three who had found in her strangeness a definite attraction, and those would-be suitors she had actually feared, regarding them with aversion. Towards young girls and women, she was shy and respectful, apologetic, and sometimes admiring. But their fads and their foibles, none of which she could share, while amusing her very often in secret, set her outside the sphere of their intimate lives, so that in the end she must blaze a lone trail through the difficulties of her nature.

"I can't understand you," her mother had said, "you're a very odd creature – now when I was your age…"

And her daughter had nodded, feeling sympathetic. There were two younger girls who also gave trouble, though in their case the trouble was fighting for husbands who were scarce enough even in those days. It was finally decided, at Miss Ogilvy's request, to allow her to leave the field clear for her sisters. She would remain in the country with her father when the others went up for the Season.

Followed long, uneventful years spent in sport, while Sarah and Fanny toiled, sweated and gambled in the matrimonial market. Neither ever succeeded in netting a husband, and when the Squire died leaving very little money, Miss Ogilvy found to her great surprise that they looked upon her as a brother. They had so often jibed at her in the past, that at first she could scarcely believe her senses, but before very long it became all too real: she it was who must straighten out endless muddles, who must make the dreary arrangements for the move, who must find a cheap but genteel house in London and, once there, who must cope with the family accounts which she only, it seemed, could balance.

It would be: "You might see to that, Wilhelmina; you write, you've got such a good head for business." Or: "I wish you'd go down and explain to that man that we really can't pay his account till next quarter." Or: "This money for the grocer is five shillings short. Do run over my sum, Wilhelmina."

Her mother, grown feeble, discovered in this daughter a staff upon which she could lean with safety. Miss Ogilvy genuinely loved her mother, and was therefore quite prepared to be leaned on, but when Sarah and Fanny began to lean too with the full weight of endless neurotic symptoms incubated in resentful virginity, Miss Ogilvy found herself staggering a little. For Sarah and Fanny were grown hard to bear, with their mania for telling their symptoms to doctors, with their unstable nerves and their acrid tongues and the secret dislike they now felt for their mother. Indeed, when old Mrs. Ogilvy died, she was unmourned except by her eldest daughter who actually felt a void in her life – the unforeseen void that the ailing and weak will not infrequently leave behind them.

At about this time an aunt also died, bequeathing her fortune to her niece Wilhelmina who, however, was too weary to gird up her loins and set forth in search of exciting adventure – all she did was to move her protesting sisters to a little estate she had purchased in Surrey. This experiment was only a partial success, for Miss Ogilvy failed to make friends of her neighbours. Thus at fifty-five she had grown rather dour, as is often the way with shy, lonely people.

When the war came, she had just begun settling down – people do settle down in their fifty-sixth year – she was feeling quite glad that her hair was grey, that the garden took up so much of her time, that, in fact, the beat of her blood was slowing. But all this was changed when war was declared; on that day Miss Ogilvy's pulses throbbed wildly.

"My God! If only I were a man!" she burst out, as she glared at Sarah and Fanny, "if only I had been born a man!" Something in her was feeling deeply defrauded.

Sarah and Fanny were soon knitting socks and mittens and mufflers and Jaeger trench-helmets. Other ladies were busily working at depots, making swabs at the Squire's, or splints at the Parson's; but Miss Ogilvy scowled and did none of these things — she was not at all like other ladies.

For nearly twelve months she worried officials with a view to getting a job out in France — not in their way but in hers, and that was the trouble. She wished to go up to the front-line trenches, she wished to be actually under fire, she informed the harassed officials.

To all her enquiries she received the same answer: "We regret that we cannot accept your offer." But once thoroughly roused she was hard to subdue, for her shyness had left her as though by magic.

Sarah and Fanny shrugged angular shoulders: "There's plenty of work here at home," they remarked, "though of course it's not quite so melodramatic!"

"Oh... ?" queried their sister on a rising note of impatience — and she promptly cut off her hair: "That'll jar them!" she thought with satisfaction.

Then she went up to London, formed her admirable unit and finally got it accepted by the French, despite renewed opposition.

In London she had found herself quite at her ease, for many another of her kind was in London doing excellent work for the nation. It was really surprising how many cropped heads had suddenly appeared as it were out of space; how many Miss Ogilvies, losing their shyness, had come forward asserting their right to serve, asserting their claim to attention.

There followed those turbulent years at the front, full of courage and hardship and high endeavour; and during those years Miss Ogilvy forgot the bad joke that Nature seemed to have played her. She was given the rank of a French lieutenant and she lived in a kind of blissful illusion; appalling reality lay on all sides and yet she managed to live in illusion. She was competent, fearless, devoted and untiring. What then? Could any man hope to do better? She was nearly fifty-eight, yet she walked with a stride, and at times she even swaggered a little.

Poor Miss Ogilvy sitting so glumly in the train with her manly trench-boots and her forage-cap! Poor all the Miss Ogilvies back from the war with their tunics, their trench-boots, and their childish illusions! Wars come and wars go but the world does not change: it will always forget an indebtedness which it thinks it expedient not to remember.

I Sit and Sew

by Alice Dunbar-Nelson

I sit and sew – a useless task it seems,
My hands grown tired, my head weighed down with
dreams –
The panoply of war, the martial tred of men,
Grim-faced, stern-eyed, gazing beyond the ken
Of lesser souls, whose eyes have not seen Death,
Nor learned to hold their lives but as a breath –
But – I must sit and sew.

I sit and sew – my heart aches with desire –
That pageant terrible, that fiercely pouring fire
On wasted fields, and writhing grotesque things
Once men. My soul in pity flings
Appealing cries, yearning only to go
There in that holocaust of hell, those fields of woe –
But – I must sit and sew.

The little useless seam, the idle patch;
Why dream I here beneath my homely thatch,
When there they lie in sodden mud and rain,
Pitifully calling me, the quick ones and the slain?
You need me, Christ! It is no roseate dream
That beckons me – this pretty futile seam,
It stifles me – God, must I sit and sew?

First Steps[1]

by Dorka Talmon

translated by Mira Glover

The small boat, *Adria*, shook upon the waves of the stormy sea with 28 members on board. We were consumed with the weight of our mission and the anticipation of our new life. I remember vividly the arguments about the future awaiting us; the different proposals for the organisation of our new community and the overwhelming joy that we were all experiencing. Many of us suffered the effects of the stormy sea. But there were some "brave" ones who, despite the violent rocking of the boat, managed to fill their bellies with the 'luxurious' food we had stocked up: chocolate, salami, wine and cakes baked by mothers fearful for the fate of their children.

We arrived at the beaches of (the) Country on February 6th 1929, a dark and dreary day, yet we were full of faith and energy. To our great surprise, we were greeted by the top three, most senior, members of the kibbutz movement. They were dressed in winter clothes so characteristic of the proletarian style worn by the kibbutz members of that time. They represented to us the very ideal we yearned for.

At Hadera's train station, we were met by four men from the

---

1   The following is an article taken from a booklet, distributed to Kibbutz (commune) members to celebrate the Kibbutz's 30th anniversary (1961). It remains in the Kibbutz's archive. The Kibbutz was set up in 1931-2 in Palestine (since 1948, known as Israel).

local regiment and some veterans of Carkur[2] who led us to our designated training area. Our belongings were picked up and we went to join the other workers who received us (immigrants of the 5th Wave) with open arms and much joy. The longing for the new arrivals was so palpable in the Country, we sensed it in every step we took, a kind gaze and a warm smile. All was expressed in song and dance, so wonderful, so contagious – it was embedded in our memories for years to come.

We pegged our tents on a plot next to the women workers. The first, a large square military tent, was to provide us with a 'dining room'; an ancient ruin – a kitchen and the rest, our bedrooms. With a 'Creationist' joy, we began organising our lives. We were not discouraged by the distance of 300m separating the kitchen from the 'dining room', nor by the 3-time daily trips carrying heavy utensils in deep sand, nor carrying large, heavy baskets heaped with dried laundry. Our clothes had been stored in old stables next to which, washing and drying was done under open skies, vulnerable to nature's elements and horses kicking and turning the benches over, leaving our laundry to dry in the sand. We were clearly innocent settlers in those first days, unaware of our cunning neighbours who helped themselves to our clothes. And yet, despite the blistered hands and aching bones, the evenings were ignited with a storm of songs and dances that helped us forget the pain of transformation and proletarianization.

However, alongside the joyous creativity, contradicting thoughts concerning the Kibbutz's core principles emerged and were often very divisive. The thesis of monotheism was raised and differences in the approach to socialist Zionism became increasingly contentious: discussions turned into ongoing arguments.

Malaria and unemployment challenged us from within as we struggled with both. There were days when only one of

---

2   Arabic name of the place, later replaced by a Hebrew name

our members was fit for work. Myself and another member of our training camp nursed the sick, who were confined to bed, from morning to night. The surgery at Hadera became a hospital where members of other settlements, who suffered similar fate, met and debated similar struggles. On some occasions we managed to sneak out of the camp to join a meeting at a kibbutz nearby where we found a welcoming and warm bunch of people.

Lack of bread forced us to send members of our regiment further afield where they were working in a gravel mine: they too succumbed to malaria.

Meanwhile, in the camp, arguments became increasingly acrimonious and exasperating as a group of members insisted that only a monolithic kibbutz could survive in the face of external pressures. We decided that we could not share their views nor live in such an oppressive community. Our differences became too large to bridge and even debates chaired by the movement's leadership failed to resolve the issue. The only solution possible was to split the group.

We formed a regiment known as the "Hadera Regiment" and moved back to Hadera. Our main goal was to set up a kibbutz open to different ideas and opinions but founded on the major principles of the socialist National Kibbutz Movement. We rejected the narrow approach to the kibbutz's essence; we rejected the repressive atmosphere in which any thought or idea that was not in line with the accepted programme was silenced. We knew that without compromise and sensitivity, treating every member as a human being, we could not resolve continuous challenges and crises.

Thus, our fate was decided and 20 of us left the camp, united in our collective perception of the kibbutz, yet accepting the different political views amongst us. The total membership of our movement in the country was 240 and we were eagerly expecting further immigration. We had kept contact with the movement's members abroad and heard that they, too, were engaged in similar arguments to those that we had experienced.

In the meanwhile, we faced the riots of Av Tarpat[3] in August 1929. I was struck down by malaria and transported to a hospital away from the camp for the duration of the riots. After the first and bloodiest days of the riots, a message from the British High Commissioner defused the situation somewhat, tension subsided and public transport was restored.

On my return to Hadera, members of our regiment relayed to me their own role in trying to defend the Jewish community. We were all stunned and despondent due to the prevailing situation. The sky wept for the blood of the slaughtered in Hebron and Safed (and other locations). Little did we know then that we would witness much harsher and lengthier times of riots and wars.

It was during that time also that our regiment turned back to organise our lives. On New Year's Eve, a new group of immigrants joined us. Their representative was pleasantly surprised to find the place so clean and tidy, and the general atmosphere one of fresh energy. Our joy of welcoming the new arrivals knew no boundaries. In an effort to hide and reduce the tension we felt, we presented a relaxed, fresh and sparkling front, ready to meet the challenges of building a new home in a new kibbutz.

---

3   August 1929 Palestine riots (Meora'ot of Av Tarpat (5689 according to the Jewish calendar). From 23 to 29 August, 133 Jews and 116 Arabs killed of whom 67 Jews and 58 Arabs were killed in the Hebron Massacre, and in Safed 20 Jews were also killed.

Coming Home[1]

Maria Messina

translated by Juliette Neil

Upon disembarking, Vanna found her father and her two brothers, Antonio and Nené. Antonio busied himself with the luggage. Her father, folding her two hands in his just as he had when she was young, asked:

"Why are you here alone? Why did you leave so suddenly?"

"Later, Papa, I'll tell you later…" Vanna replied, blushing.

All four in the carriage, Antonio spoke:

"If you had told us earlier, someone would have found a way… what an idea, coming alone!"

It was her father who answered:

"She'll tell us later…"

At this, they all fell into an awkward silence.

"Are they well, at home?" asked Vanna, after a moment.

"Wonderful. Mama would like to have come, at least, but it wasn't possible. Her coming meant dragging the whole caravan along with her." This was Antonio.

"You'll find some new faces," added Nené.

"Right, Viola and Remigia. You wrote that you are all living together."

"Almost all together. We bought the little apartment next to our house. We wrote you about that, I think."

---

1 Published in 1921

85

"No. I don't know anything about it."

"No?! I thought we did. We bought it. It has eleven rooms, five for Luigi and six for Nené... the capitalists of the house. I'm with Papa. Every little family lives as they see fit, with complete freedom. But our meals we do together. Everyone pays a sum to Viola who manages it..."

"You're paying board, then?"

"Yes. But the difference is that it all stays in the family," explained Nené, raising his voice over the sound of the carriage wheel hitting fresh gravel. "It's convenient, you know. You spend half as much."

"Oh?" Vanna said, distracted. They fell quiet again.

Vanna was looking out at the road flanking the sea, the crescent port receding, the sleepy market with its sagging tents and battered benches; she recognised a few of the flowered terraces, the spot on the beach where, once, she used to swim. In her forlorn face, out of her soft and mournful eyes, a feverish light was shining. She was impatient to arrive, agitated and unsettled; she jumped with every bounce of the carriage.

Already the rosy wall and the green shutters were coming into view, and the terrace with its pergola of yellow roses. The driver flicked the air merrily with his whip; the horses slowed their trot.

Maria, her mother, and Ninetta were on the doorstep. The two sister in-laws – the new faces – showed themselves in the dining room. Vanna did not know them yet. They were both tall and sturdy; Viola very blonde and Remigia brunette; they were beautiful, in full bloom, with large breasts and the fairest skin, which immediately intimidated her, because Vanna was brown and skinny.

Her mother and Maria smothered Vanna in kisses. They watched her and spoke to her with visible anxiety. They worried to see her so dispirited and so changed, after three long years; they were almost too afraid to ask her anything because they could sense that she would speak of her distress.

Her mother quickly showed her to "the cat's room", an enormous room, once empty, which they called the cat's room because a tabby, now dead, used to come to sleep on the windowsill.

When Vanna was a little girl, every room had its own name. Any new tidbit the children overheard or which excited their imaginations led to a new and strange name. Thus there was the "prickly pear room," "the book room," the "pink room."

"We prepared this one because yesterday when you called, right then, we couldn't think of anywhere else," her mother explained.

"I'll be very happy here," said Vanna. Removing her scarf, she looked at her mother. She seemed to only be seeing her now that they were alone, and her breathing stilled. She found her mother smaller, humbler.

"And my room?" Vanna asked, laying her scarf on the bed.

"Which one?"

"The pink room. Where I was before."

"Oh! Ninetta sleeps there, now. What do you expect... now that there are so many of us! The rooms are all taken. And I told you, we didn't think you were coming this year."

"But even when you came with Guido, the first time," Antonio appeared, interrupting, "this was the room we made up for you."

"Oh, yes," replied Vanna. She was confused, she wanted to say that this time she meant to stay forever but she felt no-one would be happy about the idea. But her mother replied, in a soft and tired voice:

"I didn't think I would see you like this... after three years. Has something happened, Vannicchia?" Her lips were trembling as she said the words, which stuck in her throat like sobs. Vanna blushed deeply.

"Look." She spoke all at once: "I had a fight with him, a real fight."

Her brother furrowed his brow. Her mother placed the candle on the nightstand.

"And then what...?"

"I couldn't take it anymore. Why are you making that face, Antonio? Didn't you want me to come home?"

"What has that got to do with it? You're putting us all in the middle of it. Your husband will think that we..."

"No, no. He would never guess that I'd come back here."

"Don't be silly! What do you expect him to think, then? You're still the same, Vanna, living in a dreamworld!" Antonio was smiling, grimly. "What's Guido ever done to you? You'll see," he added, with a patronizing look, "I'll write to him and everything will be sorted out."

"No!" yelped Vanna, as if he'd slapped her. "Not that! I'd rather throw myself in the sea!"

Their mother signaled to Antonio to hush. Couldn't he see that Vanna, so stressed, so agitated, could not see sense? Why torture her?

"Tomorrow," she repeated, "after she's had a chance to rest..."

Alone, Vanna turned to face the window. She didn't feel like resting. Through the window she could make out the sea. She had always loved to watch the sea and its changing moods at night.

She felt the weight of the step she'd taken, but she did not regret it. Yes, she really had escaped. She'd argued with her husband, during the night. In the morning, in a frenzy, she filled her trunk with her few things, and left. She had sold her jewelry. In Naples, she telegraphed her father, letting him know that she was boarding the boat. She had done it all without a second thought, and with an efficiency that still shocked her – she, who had never even consulted a train schedule – as if someone had been guiding her at every step.

And so she had done something crazy. But now she was in her own home. She could stay here. Was this not her house, where she was born, where her youth had blossomed like a fine flower? She was stressed but slowly the events of the last few days were blurring together, ebbing away.

She watched the beam of the lighthouse glimmer across the sea. She was happy to see its light again, as if she had turned back the years, as if the lighthouse, in the quiet night, were greeting her.

Downstairs, confused and upset, they talked of Vanna, discussing what was to be done. Who was going to assume the responsibility of looking after a woman, so young, who had fled from her husband's house?

***

"Oh Vannicchia!" exclaimed Maria, stroking her sister-in-law's hand. "So what's wrong?" she said anxiously.

"Oh, you have no idea what Rome is like. Being alone there, not knowing a living soul, spending the day waiting around for the only person who is meant to love you…. He's out nearly the whole day. Always busy. His office is far away. Most of the time he gets a bite to eat in a trattoria. It wouldn't be possible, you see, to eat at home every day. The distances are too great. And in Rome, all their habits are different. Some evenings he comes home with two or three friends. Lawyers, like him. Or men who write for the papers. They talk for hours about things I don't understand: politics, theatre, philosophy. And I'm left to sit in the room next door. Ignored, I feel like nothing, nobody. Like one of those rag dolls I made when I was a girl.

I have no place in the life he lives. If we are together, he only notices me when he wants to complain about something. If we go out, he's almost ashamed; I probably look dowdy in my old dresses. I don't know anyone there and outside in the streets of Rome, I feel like an ant. But he knows everyone; it's strange that anyone could even find friends in that mass of people coming and going all the time. One day I sold my little gold watch; it was useless, and I bought myself a beautiful blue dress, store-made. He liked it, and he took me out to the theatre for once (he has free tickets for a box). It upset me, because I realised that he would be kinder if I weren't so poor, and I..."

"But you shouldn't have done that!" cried Maria.

"What?"

"Spent your own money."

Vanna smiled, wringing her hands.

"If only I had some money of my own! He's always saying that in a city like Rome you need to find a way to earn a little money, however you can. He's not very impressed with me, at all."

They were both talking in low voices, on the terrace facing the sea. Vanna spoke without bitterness.

She looked out at the sea, the fine sea of her youth, which seemed to wave at her from afar, its pearly foam breaking on the deserted beach. She was glad to be back. The sea air and relaxation was soothing her nerves. She fell suddenly quiet, thoughtful.

Maria's voice shook her. "Vanna!" she was saying. "Why didn't you tell us any of this when you came the first time? Why didn't you write to us, later?"

"Why?" repeated Vanna. "I don't know why I didn't. When I came home before, I'd been married less than a year. I didn't think it would always be that way. Write? A thousand times

Coming Home

I sat there, ready, ready to write! But all the reasons for my unhappiness seemed to vanish before me. I couldn't find the words to say what I meant. What did I have to complain about, really? What did I expect? That he would take pity on me? That he would love me a little? These aren't the kinds of things you can ask for. It's not his fault. It's not my fault. He made a mistake. He needed a different wife. A rich girl. More cultured. I'm nothing but a ball of lead at his feet. Why are you looking at me like that? It's the truth. Don't worry. I'm perfectly calm. I was stressed before, but I'm calm now. I didn't bring any money into the marriage. If he'd had more money, he could have funded the newspaper. That's the truth."

"The newspaper?"

"Didn't you know? That's one of his big dreams. But let me be, now, Maria. What does it matter? Just look at the sea. It's so wonderful! You don't know what it's like to long for the sea! I could smell the seaweed in your letters. It's hard to explain, Mariuccia."

Maria sighed.

"What about Viola? And Remigia?" she murmured in a whisper. "There are too many of us here!"

But Vanna wasn't listening. With her hands behind her head, she was staring at a sailboat crossing the open sea against the pink horizon. Down on the terrace, a fisherman was running along barefoot, balancing two baskets in his arms, the strong smell of fresh fish wafting through the air behind him.

Vanna felt herself relax, content to be home. She was glad to be close to Maria, her sweet sister-in-law who had come to her father's house many years before, and had been welcomed like another daughter, another sister.

She was small like her, brown like her. She reminded Vanna of the golden years of adolescence. The other two sister-in-laws Vanna did not like, no. She admired them, because they were shapely and strong, but she knew she would never love them.

While Vanna sat and talked on the terrace, she could hear their voices calling for Ninetta and ordering around the maid. They ran the house now. They held all the keys and dealt with all the communal family affairs. Remigia and Viola's in-laws had submitted to them. The two were always in agreement, opposing everyone else and especially Maria, who was so sweet-natured. Their dominating spirits needed always to be against something.

But when, humbly, Maria spoke to Remigia about Vanna, she cut her off from the outset, saying that Vanna had crossed a line, that the brothers had a duty to write to Rome to inform their brother-in-law. When she heard this, Vanna made Nené swear he would not write to her husband. It was useless, and cruel. Her husband didn't know, couldn't know where she was. Why tell him?

"I won't be a bother to you," she stammered, afraid. "I swear."

"Always with the melodrama!" Nené said, smiling. "But don't fret so. I won't tell him anything, but you did give us a surprise. Alright? We need to find out how things stand."

Reading the letter, Vanna felt somewhat reassured. But later, seeing the mailman pass below on the terrace, she became agitated again. It was the same postman, a little older, who had once brought her letters from her fiancé. She had waited for him many times, on the terrace, on beautiful, happy mornings which she had never experienced since then. Days when the sun shone brighter, the sea was bluer, when the sounds which came from the sky, from the sea, from the road, were vibrant and strong as the beating of her heart, and everything was lovely and rosy, like her lips as she called to him, "Sir! Make sure he writes to me!"

It was the same postman. But now as she watched him pass, she felt afraid, hoping he would not stop for her. She dreaded the reply from Rome. But she did not know how to explain, even to herself, exactly what she feared.

She spent the mornings lazing under the pergola of roses, while Maria worked beside her, reliving small, insignificant memories from a time not so long ago.

"Do you remember?" Maria would say, "that time when you wanted to try on my wedding dress! It fit you like a glove. I was convinced it would bring you good luck."

"Yes... I was eighteen and you were twenty-four. We had the same build. See? I stopped growing so that I would always look like you."

Maria was making a set of clothes for a baby. Vanna was helping: setting a ribbon to attach to a bit of lace. She was absorbed by sewing the tiny clothing on her lap. One morning, she said, speaking in a low voice:

"I was expecting one, too... do you remember?"

"Yes. Poor Vannicchia. We were all so heartbroken for you."

"I would have loved him... but he disappeared too, before he even had any features, a personality, any expression that I could have remembered him by. I'd made him such a nice set of clothes! It must be such a wonderful thing," she added, bowing her head slightly. "I think mothers must feel completely undone by tenderness when their baby's timid little hands brush against their face... Him? No. He doesn't care for children."

Maria began weeping. Vanna looked at her, surprised.

"Why are you crying? It's what happened. Maybe I just wasn't worthy to be a mother."

Vanna felt able to confide in Maria; the warm face which lit up her father's house. "You see, I'd never talk to my mother about these things," Vanna often said. "I don't know why. Either I have changed, or she has. I've tried to talk to her like before, when she would listen to all my trials and tribulations. But it's not the same. She doesn't understand what I mean, she doesn't see the truth, she doesn't want to know how I'm feeling, anymore, especially if it troubles her... I only make her scared, or else cry. I feel sorry for her."

"It's true," Maria would add, "she is pitiable. But you ought to explain your reasons to someone else. I know everything, but the others?"

"No, no," Vanna would exclaim. "I can speak to you because you understand me. The others wouldn't understand, they would say these are just my romantic whims. Don't tell the others, Maria. Believe me, our house has changed..."

Ninetta was changed too. She had become irritable. She cried like a child if they wouldn't go with her to the Piazza for a concert. She was nineteen and her greatest fear was that she would become an old maid, under the rule of her sister-in-laws, for she had no dowry and elderly parents.

One evening Vanna was called to the parlour. There were visitors. An old acquaintance was shocked that Vanna had come alone:

"From Rome?" she repeated, shaking her head.

"And your husband let you go?" cried Viola's neighbour.

They regarded her cooly, questioning and criticizing.

"What?! You don't know how long you'll be staying?"

"What an idea, sending your wife around like that, when she's so young! It's nothing to joke about! Travelling alone from the city..."

Vanna excused herself. Later she found Ninetta in tears.

"What's wrong?" she asked gently.

"What's wrong," Ninetta said, glaring at her, "is that people are vicious. That neighbour just kept at it, once she was alone with us, and we didn't know how to answer her..."

"It's a perfectly normal thing... to come and visit my

family…" Vanna replied quietly.

"Oh?!" Ninetta said with a sob. "Well, for some reason your behaviour seems to have upset everyone…"

Vanna looked sorrowfully at her little sister, speaking in this way, with such spite. She returned to the terrace without replying. She wasn't surprised after that, when, on visiting days, they left her alone. They mentioned her presence only to complain of it. The rest of the time, they almost forgot her.

At coffee, Viola would serve everyone and then say: "I forgot about Vanna…" and pour another cup. No-one rushed to call her down. Often Maria would go, in secret, to find her.

At the dinner table everyone was quiet, embarrassed. Ninetta fixed her eyes on her plate. Her father, confused, asked for the wine, quietly. Each of them felt ashamed in front of the others, each of them felt they were to blame for having allowed Vanna to run away. Viola's cold looks and Remigia's wrinkled brow were full of reproach. If Vanna had been more willing to put up with things, if Vanna had not known she would be welcomed home with open arms, Vanna would not have chosen, so swiftly, to pack up her things like a gypsy.

Her mother felt most at fault. She had not been able to teach Vanna the value of submission and sacrifice, the principal virtues of womanhood. The old woman had responsibilities to her younger daughter, to Ninetta, whose own prospects might suffer because of the sister's bad marriage.

Vanna gave up going out. She realised that Ninetta was ashamed of her, as though people in the neighbourhood knew of her escape.

"I'll stay home," she would say, "I don't like seeing people."

Maria would have walked with her along the beach, where in the evening they could go even without a hat. But Antonio, who walked that way twice a day to get to the office, preferred to take his wife out to the theatre or the café.

"Go," Vanna would tell her, smiling, when Maria, on her way out, gave her an apologetic hug. "I like being here on the terrace."

Viola and Remigia went out too, with their husbands. Her mother, too, was often dragged out to the café in the main street by Ninetta. But the poor woman was almost unrecognizable. The stress of trying to keep the peace between herself and her daughters-in-law – everyone knows that mother-in-laws have a horrible reputation – made her give up on herself. She would have preferred to live alone with her husband, but she stayed with her children because she loved them and because her husband's small pension would not have been enough to bring Ninetta out into society.

In the evenings, Vanna stayed on the terrace until late. She wasn't sorry to be alone. In the quiet of the night she sat listening to the vast and awesome murmur of the sea, of the waves crashing against the shore. The roses brushed against her hair. Her spirit was resting.

***

There was no answer from Rome. But when they had finally stopped waiting, a letter arrived: its wording was dry and flat. The lawyer wrote to his father-in-law that Vanna's departure had been improper for a lady, but that he would forgive all that "along with the inevitable anxieties that arise in conjugal life."

The letter made a good impression.

"The old devil," said Antonio, "isn't as bad as he's been made out to be."

And Viola added, reassured: "The truth is that you cannot know a man through the impressions of others."

From that day on they paid careful attention to Vanna. Viola and Remigia urged their mother-in-law to do her duty.

"If one has the right values!" reiterated Remigia. "I, for example, would never leave my home. And Nené is not always an angel, either!"

"Some things need to be understood!" said Viola. "When you don't bring a dime of dowry with you, you can't be so choosy!" Viola was very proud to have brought thirty thousand lire, in cash, to the household, which had allowed Luigi to start a business with Nené.

The old woman was mortified. Even Antonio, as much as Maria tried to move him to be understanding of Vanna, was persuaded that his sister was living a fantasy. He listened to his brothers, who all worked in the same office.

"My dear!" cried Viola, following her sister-in-law to the hidden corner under the pergola to whisper: "There aren't good or bad marriages, but there are prudent women and silly ones."

Vanna tried to dismiss their jibes, needling her from all sides. But soon she stopped trying to defend herself. Tired, barely paying attention, she listened to Luigi's reasoning, her mother's prayers, her sister-in-law's advice. They talked of nothing but a future full of risks and responsibility. When they forced her to answer, she always conceded: "Yes, yes…" she would say. "But leave me in peace," she'd beg.

She felt, in her heart, that her father's house had mutated, transformed, and was pushing her away, little by little.

"You can't go back!" whispered the soft fragrant roses blooming by her head.

"You can't go back!" warned the sea from afar, throwing its silver froth high onto the shore, as if it was trying to reach the terrace.

"You can't go back. Everything changes. Your brothers have new faces. Your mother has a new voice. Other women have taken your place while you were far away. And they take you in and treat you like a passing stranger."

Vanna heard the heavy words in the dark night.

"Oh, sea of mine!" she murmured, lacing her hands behind her head. "I crossed you twice with my heart full of hope. When I first left my home and when I returned to it. Oh my sea! You alone welcomed me when I returned... Can I cross you again, with faith in my heart?"

***

"Here," she said, showing the letter still damp with ink. "I wrote him."

Her face was paler than usual, and you could see that she had been crying. But her expression was gentle, as always.

She read it aloud to the family – everyone was there because it was nearly dinner-time – the few words with which she asked her husband for forgiveness and to come and retrieve her.

Folding the letter, she examined each face.

Everyone was silent. Maria, at the far end of the room, was crying quietly.

"Only," said Antonio, his voice cracking, "I would take out the last part. Why tell him you want to return? He can decide if he wants you to."

Viola looked at her brother-in-law with reproach. Vanna noticed and said, calmly:

"What use is it to only ask for forgiveness? Forgiveness for what? You all know that I did nothing to him. The point is this: I must go back."

"No!"

"You're in your own home!" they all said together. But their voices rang with an uncertainty that revealed their anxiety.

Vanna turned towards her room. On her way out she passed Maria, and wrapped her arms around her friend's waist which had grown thicker with the new life within.

"Silly goose!" she told Maria. "Why are you crying?" And she pulled her into her room, the "cat's room." There, where no-one else could see them, she cried too, her face on Maria's chest.

***

"It had to be done." Antonio said. "Vanna is twenty-two. She can't start her life with a scandal."

They wanted to convince themselves that they had done their duty. Yet they were unsettled by an odd apprehension.

Only Ninetta was happy. She rushed to tell the neighbours, her friends, that Vanna was leaving, called back to Rome by a husband who adored her and could not live without her.

No-one had the courage to be honest. No-one wanted to be the first, since no-one was the head of that house, to dare say what their hearts were telling them.

Vanna had begun to pack her trunk, and they acted indignant, saying that she was in a rush to leave, that no-one had wanted to get rid of her. They said these things to console themselves, as each felt they had been too hard on the poor creature who had come looking for a bit of love in her father's house. Vanna responded softly:

"It's better that he finds me ready. He won't stay long, you'll see. And anyway, what's the point in delaying, since we have to leave each other?"

She placed a handful of rose petals from the terrace in among her clothing. It was something to remind her of the old place she'd loved, and this too might soon change.

She tried to comfort Maria.

"You'll see," she told her, "I'll be better behaved than I was before, and things will be different for me."

She hoped so. Now that she had been pushed out from her father's house, she clung to the idea that her husband might be chastened. Waiting for him, she forced herself to remember him in his best moments, to find some hope in the future.

In the hours before his arrival, she begged her father and her brothers to put on a good front. On the evening of his arrival she insisted that Luigi, at least, should go and meet him.

Guido made an excellent impression on Remigia and Viola, who had never met him before. The close-cut, black-black moustache, the monocle worn on a thin gold chain, the light suit – all of it pleased the women who, without wanting to, compared him to Luigi and Nené, stuffed into their thick and comfortable, checkered shirts.

Immediately upon entering the room, he recounted, as if it were essential information, the time he had spent in Argentina to see a celebrated actress returned from America; the time he had written an article against a Milanese lawyer with whom he had a fierce rivalry...

He spoke with an accent that was emphatic and affected, as though he were speaking, not to relatives but to a group of friends, reunited for only a few moments. He seemed to have forgotten the point of his long journey and he made everyone else forget it too. Except that, when his eyes met those of his wife, he became hard, and cold. Vanna felt a painful shiver run from the nape of her neck to the bottom of her feet.

"Yes!" he was still saying as he started towards the cat's room to wash. "Being the head of a newspaper means having a weapon at the tips of your fingers!"

When Vanna closed the door and was alone with her husband, he became darker, cold. He said slowly, without looking at her:

"What the hell did you tell them?"

"Nothing. Didn't you see how they welcomed you?"

He calmed down a little then but his gaze remained hard. His eye, behind the glass of his monocle, looked dilated and red. Vanna's vision had gone blurry. Her husband seemed only to have that one eye, great and monstrous and round as that of a cyclops. They were quiet. They had nothing to say to each other.

He stripped down to his undershirt to wash. Drying himself off, he asked: "Who gave you the money?"

"What money?"

"To come here."

"I... had it."

"And now?"

"What do you mean, now?"

"How are you going to afford to leave again?"

"I... You..."

"I... You..." he repeated, sarcastically. "...You think I packed a bank in my suitcase?"

Vanna looked down. He came close and said in a whisper:

"I came here because you wanted me too. I didn't feel any need... to come. I didn't think I'd have to pay for your trip too."

Vanna was quiet.

"Understood?"

"Yes."

"So you'll see to it. It's already a lot that I came at all. Here you have three brothers, a father..."

"Yes," repeated Vanna.

It seemed to her that she was already back in Rome, in the apartment on the fourth floor. She grew very pale, almost gray. Her ears were whistling as though she'd taken a dose of quinine.

"Where are you going?" asked her husband suspiciously.

"To the terrace. I need some air."

"Watch it!" He warned in a voice that was calm but firm. "If you make me look bad…"

"Don't worry …"

Vanna went out, slowly, slowly. Crossing the dining room, Maria yelled to her, from the terrace:

"Look, Vanna. They told me to prepare the strawberries. Should I soak them in lemon or in Marsala wine?"

"Whatever you prefer, Maria," she replied, "…alright, do the Marsala…" she added, when her sister-in-law pressed her.

She went down the stairs. She went out onto the road, hugging the wall. A passing man looked at her curiously, he was saying something to her; it went unheard.

Vanna began to run towards the beach. She ran down to face the sea. The wind caught and tangled her hair.

A rush of water swelled to her feet…

Vegetal Reverie

Magda Isanos

translated by Gabi Reigh

Unburdened of my soul, I flee
Towards the valleys, where the trees
Will share life with me
Muting all thoughts with flowers
Scattering good and evil in the breeze.
In distant mountain forests I will dwell
Stirred from the night by kindest sunbeams
And as the gleeful swell
Of birdsong pierces the sky
I'll catch its tears
And hoard them on my cheek.
The wanton rain will wash away
The dusty ache of bygone years
And from those shadow fears, unroot me.
Adorned with starry gold
I'll trap the portly and astonished moon
In chains of branches
And curl up inside its nest
Cold rays and sap filling my mold
Until my body stretches, higher than the world
And, tearing off my sprigs of bloom
I'll play, on burnished strings,
my tenderest song
The fledgling happiness of being
Until the wood and all its speechless throng
Close tight around me, listening.

"*What a good thing there is no marriage or giving in marriage in the after-life; it will certainly help to smooth things out.*"

– Barbara Pym

The Iceberg[1]

Zelda Fitzgerald

Cornelia gazed out of the window and sighed, not because she was particularly unhappy, but because she had mortified her parents and disappointed her friends. Her two sisters, younger than she, were married and established for life long ago; yet here she remained at thirty years of age, like a belated apple or a faded bachelor's button, either forgotten or not deemed worth the picking. Her father did not scold. He kindly suggested that perhaps Neilie would do more for herself if the rest of the family would leave her alone. Her brother said, "Cornie's a fine girl and good looking enough, but she's got no magnetism. A fellow might as well try to tackle an iceberg."

For all that, the family cat found her responsive enough, and the little fox-terrier fairly adored her, to say nothing of a blue jay that insisted upon a friendly dispute every time she stole to her retreat in the old-fashioned Southern garden. Her mother said, "Cornelia is not sympathetic. She looks at a man with her thoughts a thousand miles away, and no man's vanity will stand for that. What good are beautiful clothes and musical genius if humanity is left out? No! No! Cornelia will never marry, Cornelia is my despair."

Now Cornelia sometimes grew weary of disapproval and resented it. "Mother," she would say, "is marriage the end and aim of life? Is there nothing else on which a woman might spend her energy? Sister Nettie is tied to a clerical man, and,

1 written in 1918, published in high school literary journal

between caring for the baby and making ends meet, looks older than I. Sister Blanche finds so little comfort in a worked-down husband that she has taken to foreign missions and suffrage for diversion. If I'm an economic proposition, I'll turn to business."

So, without more ado, she secretly took a course at business college, and taught the fingers that had rippled over Chopin and Chaminade to be equally dexterous on the typewriter. Her eyes seemed to grow larger and more luminous as she puzzled over the hieroglyphics of stenography.

"That Miss Holton is a wonder," said the manager of the college. "Yes, she's a social failure, but she bids fair to be a business success," agreed a young man who had once fallen into her indifferent keeping.

Just then the phone rang. "At once, you say! Wait a moment, I'll see." Proceeding softly to her desk, he said, "Miss Holton, I consider you quite efficient as a pupil. Do you care to answer an emergency call? The firm of Gimbel, Brown and Company wishes a stenographer at once. What do you say to the place?"

"What do I say? Why, it just hits the spot. Let me get my hat and I'm off."

"Well," said the manager, "I do like a girl who knows what she wants."

If her mother could only have heard that! Perhaps, after all, Cornelia had always known what she wanted – and failed to find it. Perhaps, after all, a social equation in trousers had not been just what Cornelia craved. Perhaps, after all, Cornelia was seeking self-expression. At any rate, she lost no time in finding Gimbel, Brown and company, and was not the least aghast that this was the mighty multi-millionaire Gimbel who needed her services.

"Miss Holton, you say? Cornelia Holton, the daughter of my old friend, Dan Holton? Why bless your heart, have a seat! This is so sudden! When did you enter the business arena, pray?"

Cornelia was not abashed. With her usual straight-forward earnestness, she said, "Yes, I'm Cornelia Holton, and I'm in business to stay. If the arena is full of Bulls and Bears, I'm here to wrestle. What can I do for you, Mr. Gimble?"

With a twinkle in his eye and a queer little smile, he pushed toward her the pile of snowy paper and began to dictate. North, South, East, and West the messages flew, and Cornelia's fingers flew with them. White, slender, and shapely, they graced the machine as they had the piano, and, when lunch hour came, her face had flushed, and the little brown curls clung to her forehead with a slight moisture of effort. Cornelia was beautiful over her first conquest of the typewriter!

As she rose to go, she blushed, and stammered, "Mr. Gimble, I'll thank you not to tell my parents of this. They have no knowledge of my business enterprise and would be quite horrified. You know, nothing succeeds like success. I have been a failure long enough." And she smiled as she left, the old grace of the distasteful ball-room clinging to her in spite of her steady resolve.

"Well, by Jove!" exclaimed Mr. Gimble. "By Jove!" he reiterated, "who'd-a thought a Holton woman would go into business! Why, that girl's mother was the greatest belle that this city ever produced. Well, she couldn't get married, maybe." So he too, went his way, thinking of the little wife that had died years ago and of the great emptiness that had taken her place, and that he had tried to fill with money.

Several months flew by. The Holtons had their shock when Cornelia announced her business success, and were again in the normal path of life. The cat said, "I told you so! I knew she had the element of success in her!" The little dog barked, "Doggone her! I always knew I didn't wag my tail for nothing." The blue jay noisily called, "Aw, come on now and let's finish our dispute. You can build a nest if I can, and you can hatch a family, too, if you try. Aw go awn!" But that was nothing to what the society world said when Cornelia Holton and James G. Gimble walked quietly to the study of the Reverend Devoted Divine and were made one. Even to the millions and the famous homestead was also a palace of art and aesthetic refinement.

Mrs. Holton fainted over her coffee-cup when she unfolded the morning paper and beheld the headlines, side-by-side with, and quite as large as the war news. Mr. Holton chuckled, as he emptied the water-bottle over her most expensive negligee. "I always said Cornelia had something up her sleeve."

"Well, the old girl must have warmed up at last," added her brother.

The front door opened and in walked the disheveled sisters, screaming, "Mamma, Mamma – Cornelia, the old maid – she has out-married us all!"

"Time spent with a cat is never wasted."

– Sidonie Gabrielle Colette

Jason Pau

The Russian Princess[1]

Carmen de Burgos

translated by Slava Faybysh

1.

The big-city noises were dying down little by little; everything was finally falling asleep that night. The din of voices, carriages, and streetcars had ceased, the din that carried all the way into Enrique's top-floor apartment on Fuencarral. He had been working with the window open, taking advantage of his delicious solitude, this feeling of living alone – he had sent his wife and daughters away for the summer.

Enrique loved them all very much, but he simply couldn't help letting out a sigh of relief when he saw them leaving with their hatboxes and suitcases and traveling trunks, where they kept all those fine clothes they'd be sporting out in the country, the fine clothes that dazzled everyone with their elegance, that they had worked and saved all winter for.

The truth was, though, everything Enrique did this year was out of sheer habit. It wasn't at all like in the past when he was held captive by some passion; or to be more precise, it was that in past years, the intoxication of feeling single had prompted him to start easy, crazy adventures.

His writer's curiosity, his creative imagination, idealised the women of the street, the neighbourhood girls, and clothed them with a certain grace. There was that night when he walked over to the Glorieta de Bilbao and helped that pretty servant fill her jug with water. He'd have had a hard time counting how many women had figured in his adventures those summers, if he ever bothered to remember. They were all one figure in his mind, and he thought of them with gratitude and a touch of pity. This was what women always inspired in him. He treated them all as if they were important señoras. He knew how to listen patiently to women, who enjoyed venting their pains and sorrows, as if they needed to come clean about something. Enrique tried not to add to their pain. But, except for a few big passions, his life was frivolous and gay, lived externally, like a sentimental novel.

He was always infatuated with two or three girls at a time. The French blonde who hitched herself to whatever man happened to be around attracted him because of her submissiveness and sophistication, her literary polish, and her long legs. He loved that other brunette artiste, the one with the beautiful soft silvery arms, how elusive she was.

He felt sorry in a loving way for the petite young girl with those big, anxious eyes, who was pushed by her mother's indiscretion into a life of relaxed morals. He would've liked to be able to be with all of them at once, bring them all together, keep a friendship with each and every one of them: Blanca, Gloria, María, Rosario...

His pained, loving, little wife was like a figure out of a silly Pérez Escrich melodrama. She put up with all of it and never stopped adoring her husband. She cried and cried over his infidelities, and the jealousy was so bad, the ailments, that she even neglected her two daughters at times; but deep down, she was happy to be the legitimate wife of a man so desired and spoiled as her Enrique. She admired him. He must have been superior to other men if he could maintain the household just from writing books. They lived off her husband's talent, so why should it be surprising that all the women who read his work and admired him would become infatuated.

"It's not his fault," she told her friends, "they're the ones who go chasing after men. The way girls are these days, a man's worth is not in his conquests, but how he fends them off."

Sometimes after the publication of a novel she'd come across fan letters in which the women made passionate declarations of love to her Enrique. They'd send portraits, describe all the beauty they'd offer him, and they praised and complimented him: "I can't stop looking at your picture. It feels like your eyes are looking back at me," one of them said. "Is it really possible that you have such beautiful eyes and gorgeous hair?"

Sometimes he received cryptic proposals from women who shrouded themselves in mystery, maybe society ladies, maybe married señoras: "I have lit a candle to Saint Rita," said one woman, "so that you will grant me an hour with you."

In all honesty, his wife was proud of this. She sometimes watched her husband with even more fascination, with even more respect. She felt envied, triumphant – the genius belonged to *her*. It's almost like being married to a tenor or a bullfighter, she proudly thought.

In any case, she had been more at peace for some time now. Enrique was spending more time at home, where he was a caring and attentive friend to his wife and daughters. It's true, though, he didn't like going out with them or taking them places because they compromised his image as a handsome heartthrob. Because of them he was seen as a husband and family man. He especially didn't like going out with them now that his daughters had begun wearing ankle-length dresses, attracting the attention of boys and other aficionados of budding adolescents. And as with all flirtatious men, it gave him a bad taste in his mouth to see his own ways reflected towards his daughters. It bothered him to see the desirous looks directed at the only flesh he had ever truly respected, the only flesh he had ever treated as consubstantial and godly. But at home, in private, he spoiled his daughters, he lavished them with gifts, and brought them candies and cakes every night. He ruled in the way only a young, handsome father can, with real affection that earned his children's admiration.

But underneath it all he was exhausted. *All those novels I wrote just so my publisher could get rich!* he thought. He didn't want to admit it, but this was the beginning of a decline. Old age was starting to set in, and it was getting to him. He made efforts to stay young, watch his weight, take care of his teeth, and laugh in moderation to avoid showing his receding gums. He walked with his legs close together, with good posture, and he thought the salt-and-pepper curls overhanging his temples looked more blond than gray. He attributed all this to the flirting, not his years. "It's the side effect of all the chastity," he joked.

But what bothered him most of all was that his novels were becoming less popular, and his fame as a writer was diminishing, precisely now that he was becoming more aware of his responsibilities. His novels were becoming more formulaic now. They seemed to veer further from what the public wanted, though they all used to love the vague novels he wrote in his youth – maybe they were a bit morbid at times, but the hearts of very human women beat in their pages.

Sometimes he attributed this to the fads that sometimes influence literature, like trends in tailcoats, but other times he blamed himself for giving in to idleness and having fewer dealings with women. Women had always been his inspiration… but now he was just tired.

That summer he was determined to overcome his difficulties with his work – without giving in to his addiction to women. So he stayed home alone, buried in the book that was to be his masterwork, teasing out and polishing the plot with such care.

He scarcely saw anyone. He'd wake up late, and for his bath he'd throw a bucket of cold water over his head, since there was no bathtub anyways. He'd rub himself with eau de cologne, brush his teeth, clean his nails, dress himself, and make his own lunch: fried eggs, steak and a cup of coffee. He made it on the gas in the clumsy way of men not used to cooking. Sometimes the monotony was so great, he lost his appetite, but he forced himself to continue his regimen. *Who knows*, he thought, *maybe there's a great idea under this steak!*

Enrique wasn't the disgruntled type. He remembered the happy times of his youth, when he had nothing. That was when he had produced the most, the best work! A novelette every week, and he barely had to think about it! Those novelettes had made a fortune for his publisher, and he sold them for a plate of lentils!

The housekeeper took advantage of his short afternoon walks to clean his room and make his dinner. Enrique always breathed a sigh of relief when he came home and saw everything was in order. *The old witch is taking good care of me*, he'd say to himself, smiling, thinking how puzzled the poor woman must have been not to see any hairpins or any other traces of women that year.

He worked near the balcony, peaceful and happy in pajamas and slippers, with his coffee pot on the table and his cigarette case well stocked. His only concern was the novel, and he worked on it until the windows filled with the cobalt-blue of early morning. Then he got ready for bed, slurped his two eggs – although he never much had an appetite for them – but that was what Victor Hugo did, always worried about feeding his brain.

And he didn't think about women. He was a new man now and dreaded getting involved in the kind of dramas that had hounded him in the past. He no longer had anyone to cry over him or threaten him, like that grief-stricken widow who'd spew vitriol at him whenever she had the chance. He started to think women were more trouble than they were worth.

But soon more letters started coming, and this stirred him and piqued his curiosity. Although these weren't the usual perfumed coquettish letters written on exquisite paper. They were on lined commercial paper and had a pointed, aristocratic script, indicating that the writer was not young. This handwriting was of an older generation of women and was unlike that of today's twenty or thirty-year-olds, who all seemed to write like Ursuline nuns. This handwriting was more compact, less robust in its strokes, but stronger overall and more uniform. This was a woman who was getting on in years, fairly well-educated, and with a pleasant, though somewhat forced style.

When he saw the first letter, and how long it was, he hesitated to read it, but it had that irresistible charm of a woman's letter. It was a strange letter. It didn't promise the usual romantic rendezvous, or even just a harmless bit of flirtation. This was a mature lady who expressed herself in a bilingual style, in bad Spanish and bad French. She apologised for being educated in England and for her continuous travels that made her speak different languages. This lady was the guardian and protector of a young princess. A little fairy-tale princess. No less than an *authentic* Russian princess who had been orphaned and ruined during the war, but had managed to escape. She was in hiding as she was being pursued by a secret lover, an old politician. The princess wanted to earn her living as an actress, and her great, perfect, sculptural beauty, and her slanting eyes with their unique, tragic stamp, would assure her success.

They knew Enrique would be going to the New World, where he would be busy with conferences and the theatre, and they wanted to put themselves under his protection and offer him the opportunity to be Princess Natasha's manager.

The bait was well placed. At the bottom of it, Enrique pictured a beautiful woman, princess or not. Unveiling her mystery would be quite delicious. And he also glimpsed a chance to stand out, to shine a powerful spotlight on himself. The extraordinary figure of D'Annunzio, who had driven so many crazy, was his example. *What would he have been without Duse or Rubenstein?* he thought, *Would he have ever reached those heights of fame?*

So a correspondence began between the novelist and Madame Marques, who didn't keep her home address from him, a simple house in the district of Chamberí.

He became fascinated by the enigma of these letters that were so full of contradictions. He lost himself in them, but never really managed to figure them out. *I should just let this go,* he thought. But the picture in his mind of the two beautiful women was irresistible.

Madame Marques, who wanted to publish a memoir titled *The Blue Book*, didn't entice him very much. He wouldn't have recommended she become a writer, but she assured him that while she wasn't twenty-three like Natasha, she was still young and seductive.

Natasha on the other hand must have been adorable. Madame Marques had described her several times. She assured him all she had to do was make a few movements of her divine white arms as she descended the stairs, and the crowd would erupt in cheers of "Ave, Natasha," like the journalists had done at the Paris Opera. "They received her in a private session," she wrote. Then on a whim, her godmother, an eminent lady, had suggested she play the role of Sappho, with stupendous jewels, her own, and the director had gladly agreed to it. The press unanimously agreed she was "the revelation of the year."

Another time she wrote, "If your eye isn't accustomed to the *cutlassfish face* of modern Spanish painters, you will love Natasha's little round face, her short little nose, and her graceful, childlike features. Overall, she is quite precious with her small little head, long neck, and harmonious nymph lines like in the Vatican Museum. She also has a certain *je ne sais quoi*, some extremely beautiful natural movements, *chic* as you would not believe."

Not for the world would he miss the chance to see this marvel. With all the sensuality oozing from the description, he didn't think about how unusual the young princess's situation was, how she was protected by a poor, lonely lady, even though sometimes there was a powerful godmother or a rich aunt who figured into the stories. She was simply a princess who was hiding from a powerful man who was after her, and she wanted to act in the theatre.

Madame Marques wrote to him, "She has an incredible wealth of Tatar, Mongol, and Persian suits for the stage. And among other marvels, she possesses the last suit that the unfortunate Tsarina wore at court and the authentic tunic that was Rasputin's enchantment, with the large cross and the five-metre rosary." Despite the Russian princess's influence on him, Enrique had sense enough to react against this height of absurdity.

And she always added something in the letters to gently push him away. "Natasha knows nothing of the flirtation innate in Spanish women, although this excites you Spanish men. I know how much it pleases you. Natasha has her own special ideas, which I share, about 'love,' which in our view, is simply a small step from possession. She very gracefully rejects 'animalism.' She struggles with these negative ideas, and only favours *chastity*, which she has proven is *scientific*. Courting her passionately would simply be nonsense in this country, to be expected of a Patagonian."

Was being difficult just another well-thought-out way to attract him even more?

But she did seem sincere when she wrote things like, "Don't you believe, dear maestro, that our virtue is based on religion or the excuse of established conventions. It is pure logic, for saintly Beauty and saintly Poetry. That is what we are fervently devoted to, our *raison d'être*. We are too idealistic to fall into the horrid trap of love. We fear it would be anti-aesthetic. In summary, it is a terrible appetite of the masses. We impose abstention. You must understand, extraordinary man that you are, we adhere to ideas of Beauty and Poetry, and Art with its sacred fire."

It seemed to him they were somewhat abusing this sacred fire, and Art, and grand ideas, but ultimately he was receptive to them. Madame Marques opened her letters with "Most gentle maestro." She told him he was charming, *the most extraordinary rare bird of Spain*, and she flattered his ego.

"The princess and I both know you are young, handsome, and *talenteux*, you must have so many women fighting over you, standing in line at your door. It scares us because women are so jealous here and their stridency is frightful."

He wondered about her more and more. He really believed Madame Marques to be distinguished, but she was always disparaging Spain and other women.

"No Spanish woman could hold a candle to Natasha," she said. "Especially the middle class, whom I consider riffraff like the rest of them. The Spanish woman is educated (and here I'll use a phrase from Montmartre Boulevard) *ne comme je te pousse*, in a slapdash way, and she becomes the epitome of imperfection. For us aristocrats on the other hand, who have received an exquisite education, the first thing we are taught is self-control, self-mastery, which is strength, security, independence. Natasha is thus an extraordinary personality, and her serene philosophy is shocking to others, and that is why I have accepted this noble undertaking, which any Spanish woman would have rejected."

It seemed she was able to guess the bad state this would put Enrique in because she added, "I assume you are amenable to hearing the truth without injury to your patriotism, as would be the case, of course, with so many of the *eminent one-eyed men* (my expression, but they say it is true) who form what they call *L'elite*, a word I do not know how to translate."

To finally lay his doubts to rest, Enrique insisted on seeing the princess. His writer's imagination and his great talent urged him forward. He didn't see Natasha the woman, but Beauty incarnate, Art made flesh. He adored this superior woman, her creamy arms, her rhythmic movements, her slanting eyes, the Tatar suit and Rasputin's rosary. But he had to see her... to see her at all costs.

But Madame Marques resisted. For a young woman from Siberia, the summer in Madrid was simply horrid. She had left for cooler climes. She went to Toledo, then to El Escorial to see some antique dealers so she could sell some El Grecos her aunt kept in Nice. There was really no way out of this scheduling mess they were in.

Then Enrique tried his hand at subterfuge. He wrote to Madame Marques that he had a contract ready, and he needed to see Natasha so she could sign it. There was no time to waste, or they would lose this opportunity.

That night when he came home, he found a long letter from Madame Marques. Natasha had consented to see him. Enrique felt his heart beating like in his first flush of youth. Natasha was real! (He had even doubted that) And he was going to see her!

But slowly, after that first burst of enthusiasm, he noticed something strange about the letter:

"As a courtesy to you, I have taken it *upon myself* for you to see Natasha in a modest temporary room. The landlady is a young widow (don't tell anyone but I think she sees men), but that is how this country is. A façade of virtue. All lies. I would send Natasha to your home, which I'm sure is *chorming*, just as you are *chorming* and original, but then I would have to go with *toilette de Ville* and with *tenue* that is absolutely not the same as her stage costumes, and you must judge her in these.

"Therefore, it would be best if you came next Friday at *nine o'clock at night. She will be waiting for you*, and since I will have some errands to do at that hour, I will leave you two alone, something I am glad to do so you will be able to talk freely without anyone watching.

"It was not easy for her to consent to be seen, but she felt it was necessary so she could sign the contract."

The windows were now filled with blue and looked like canvases ready to paint. Enrique continued turning the letter over in his hand, and he couldn't make sense of the misgivings that were obsessing him.

How is it that this princess who is so modest consents to see me alone? Why is her stern guardian leaving? How can it be that she paints herself as being so distinguished and aristocratic, with her polyglot speech, and suddenly she gossips and says vulgar things like the landlady of the house sees men, and other such things?

He decided to put these preoccupations out of his mind, saying to himself that if anything, it was just another pretty girl to help him pass the time. But a fantasy had taken root during these weeks of correspondence. Natasha lived in his heart now, and he was afraid her image would fade away, her rhythms, her pale arms, her sculptural body, her little face with its slanting eyes, her treasure chest of Tatar costumes, and the Tsarina's dresses... even the five-metre rosary and Rasputin's tunic.

2.

It gave him a thrill, the tremble in his heart, the excitement that he had tried in vain to feel when he came close to a woman. He didn't want to admit he was going downhill, and he laid the blame on them. *The conquest wasn't always a sure thing before,* he thought, *there used to be doubt. There was time to feel desire. Now they're so easy, I'm not interested.* That was why this exceptional, admirable woman, full of difficulties, was such a strong tonic, why she made his heart skip a beat.

He climbed the steep, dirty staircase and stopped in front of a square wood door. It was grease-polished and worm-eaten.

He discreetly pulled the chain to ring the bell, and the door opened instantaneously as if by a wind.

A tall, dark-haired woman with big, black eyes was walking away down the hallway after opening for him. He took off his hat, somewhat disconcerted, unsure if he should ask for Madame Marques or the princess. The lady stopped; she was beautiful, and she probably would have attracted his attention if it weren't for his obsession with the princess.

An unpleasant nasal voice with a forced foreign accent issued from the adjacent room: "Come in, caballero."

He opened the little door and found himself in a room where the walls and ceiling were covered with coloured cloth, giving it the look of a used-clothing store. In the back, taking up most of the little room, was the bed, also heaped with cloths and cushions, and lit from behind by the soft light of an incandescent bulb under a red shade.

Standing next to the bed was a woman wearing black, with a large hat and a thick veil that made it hard to see her face. "Oh, friend and admired maestro!" she exclaimed, "I am happy to see you here *à mon côté*." It was Madame Marques. He bowed and gave her a gentlemanly kiss on the hand as his eyes searched keenly for Natasha.

She noticed his impatience. "She will come. She is getting dressed. Will you be so kind as to wait here in the meantime?" She raised a piece of fabric that was hiding a little door, and Enrique found himself in the kitchen, a small kitchen that was obviously not used very often.

"You must excuse us," Madame Marques continued. "You can see what conditions we are living in, and how painful this is for people of our lineage."

He looked at her closely. She was thin, but still shapely. She was wearing gloves. It was hard to see her features and hard to tell if she was young or old. He didn't know what to say. For the first time in his life, he had lost his nerve.

"I must go," continued Madame Marques. "In a moment, you will hear the bell, and then you may return to our cabinet, where you will see Natasha. You'll see, she will make an impression... but you're a man of the world... isn't that right?"

"Señora..."

"Not another word. Soon we'll have a chance to speak at length." She waved goodbye with perfect distinction, with the good form of a woman of high society, in a way that cannot be faked. Then she disappeared.

Ten minutes later, the longed-for bell rang. Enrique darted into the picturesque little room. On the bed, almost on her back, with her elbow on a cushion and her head in her hand, there was a woman. He looked at her avidly. She was wearing an eastern costume, something like an odalisque, with loose-fitting trousers tied at the ankle. "Natasha Your Highness!"

The princess lifted her long left arm, which had been resting along the length of her body, and stretched it out to him as if to hold him back. The divine white arm raised in that triumphant gesture was an old, squalid arm. His expertise with women had helped him see through the artifice – she raised it covering the outer part of her arm, only letting him see the milkier, shinier, more youthful inner part, soft as bird feathers.

Her hands were old, perfumed hands, although the pointed metal fingernails that lengthened each of her ten fingers made them look somewhat strange.

"Thank you for having come," she said, in the proper and foreign way Madame Marques had described in her letters. "It is much audacity on my part to have an eminence like yourself come see me here."

The novelist, with his good manners, resisted the urge to run out of there and replied courteously, "Wherever you are, princess, it is a palace."

She sighed and raised her eyes in ecstasy. "Oh, my palaces in Saint Petersburg and Moscow. Where are my gardens and my lovely sitting rooms?"

Enrique, without paying much attention to her words, took advantage of her daydreaming to take a good look at her. *How old is this hag?* he thought.

She pushed her bosom out towards him, showing a multitude of rare jewels, fringes, and gold, and shook her head, atop of which sat something like a shining warrior's helmet. "We were too considerate to the riffraff. The Tsar's government was too weak, the Russian nobility was too benevolent, the Tsar was a father to all... They should have given them all fifty lashes!"

He kept quiet.

"And the writers there, what horror! What doctrines they spread among the masses! You don't write that way, do you?"

"No."

"They unleashed the beast! You writers are the true assassins! It's because of you that I, who had servants kneeling before me, find myself in need of a contract."

"But..."

"Don't say anything. Yes, I know... Art is redemption!"

"And..."

"Wait. You're no common man... I know you won't speak to me of love."

"I..."

"I forbid it."

"It's that..."

"I need you to take a good look at me, admire me. Would you be so kind as to go into the next room? I would like you to see me the way we noble Russians dressed."

"You look lovely just like that. You don't have to bother."

"I want to wear the disgraced Tsarina's dress in your honour, an exquisite gown, only befitting a star, something very grand."

"Another day maybe."

"I want you to see me now, this ugly thing on my head *n'est pas charmant*. Please go into the room once more."

Enrique did as she asked. He stooped down and went through the little door she pointed to. Once again, he found himself in the kitchen. As in the bedroom, there were no chairs. He felt like pacing, but there wasn't enough room for that. He needed to clear his mind of this nightmare, that woman with her strange, skeletal voice that felt like a hailstorm.

He began to wonder what this preposterous adventure was leading to. *It must be a case of insanity,* he thought. There was no princess. The woman who had received him a moment ago and the one on the bed dressed as an odalisque were one and the same. Madame Marques and the princess were the same person. There was no doubt she was playing the dual role, but to what end? Was she crazy? Did she want an affair? Did she really think she could obtain a role in the theatre this way?

He was lost in his conjectures when he heard the falsetto voice attempting to sound different from Madame Marques: "Enter, caballero."

He found the princess dressed in a fantastical court dress, standing by the headboard of her bed under the incandescent light. He froze when he saw how ridiculous it was. Her arms and bosom were covered with a mesh of crocheted gold thread and coloured beads, some that looked like pearls and others precious stones. She was wearing buttons on her fingers as if they were jewels, and the same sort of tiara on her head.

Her cloak was supposed to be made of ermine skins, but it must have been white rabbit fur with spots of black velvet sewn in. The gilded mesh had a shine like tobacco. Everything was tragically grotesque, and there was something about it that was like a magician's act or a fairground show.

He felt sorry for her and furious at the same time. The woman had created another woman, brought her Natasha to life. The princess did live in his imagination, but he felt as if she had been killed and replaced by this other woman. But at the same time he thought there was something about her that did match his imagination. This frightful vision had slanting eyes, the result of makeup and something pulling her temples back. A round, dry little face with purple lipstick, and everything enveloped in shadow. His princess in a death shroud.

Natasha seemed to be enjoying the silence, which she took for admiration and respect. She lifted her arm again with that movement she thought was irresistible and asked, "Tell me, how do you find me?"

"Señora…"

"I see you are choked with emotion. But now I want you to see me wearing another dress of fantasy."

"I beg you, don't tire yourself out, Your Highness."

"It is necessary."

He realised he would have to resign himself to seeing the entire wardrobe on this rather shabby mannequin. This was his penance for the illusions he had cultivated in his mind. It was better to face the situation, remain patient, though not without some irony. He bowed respectfully and went back through the little door, sighing as he murmured, "The Thin Door!"

When he returned, the princess had put on a Spanish outfit, the finishing touch being the *sombrero calañés*. "This dress belonged to Lola Montez. I wanted to pay homage to the typical Spanish woman."

Now he was playing his part: "Magnificent!"

"Don't you know we Russians can conquer the Spanish soul. There must be some hidden connection between our two peoples. The type, the character, even the accent is similar."

"That's true."

"But we differ in education. Spain is more backwards. Don't be offended."

"Me?"

"Be so kind as to leave. You'll see me in another dress."

This time it was dazzling. She was wrapped in a sort of lamé made from candy wrappers. She seemed to be completely covered with necklaces of coloured and transparent beads, and on her head she wore something like a Byzantine crown, multicoloured and shining.

"This dress is from the Caucasus region. A mountain bride. They dress this way, the most beautiful women on Earth who are born in this region where I am from."

"Everyone knows that!"

"In the Caucasus, the physical culture of the woman is the most important thing. From the time she is born, the girl is made to be beautiful. She is rubbed with ointments, she is perfumed, she is educated so she can be sold at a high price. They are the mothers of all the sultans and princes of the East.

"Marvelous!"

"But I still have one more *tenue* I'd like you to see."

"My God, don't bother yourself anymore, princess."

"Are you tired?"

"No, not at all. Why would you think that?"

"Good, then wait another moment… this will be the last one for tonight… you won't regret it."

Enrique went back into the kitchen and leaned against the wall. *Let's see what she does now! If I go in and she's nude, I'll make a run for it. But still, I'd like to make it out of here without offending her.* In a certain way, he respected the grandeur of her obsession, the duplicity of the double personality, her effort to create another younger, beautiful, triumphant woman inside herself.

This daydream merged with the novelist's previous fantasy.

He understood the desire of Madame Marques to relive her past, the memory of her youth, the beautiful woman who was adulated in her day. And the grandest, most surprising thing about it was that it wasn't a small idea. It had such deep roots, such certainty, that she wanted to impose it on others and even take it to the stage. He knew this wasn't about flirtation. He respected her for the lofty sentiments that were at the bottom of her desire and her monomania.

At certain moments, he found himself fascinated by her grand imagination. He felt as if he were backstage seeing a performance of one of those ancient plays in which the protagonist, without the other characters knowing it, plays a dual role.

As he stood there waiting in the squalid kitchen, he thought a miracle would happen and he would find both Natasha and Madame Marques when he went back into the room. He lost himself so thoroughly in his thoughts that Natasha had to call him twice.

He saw her covered with a shining, black, hooded cloak. It was sort of a full-body costume, and though it was made of goatskin, it looked more like a monkey's fur.

"You will now see me in a historic outfit, one that is destined for the museum. An authentic suit belonging to Rasputin." She let the cloak fall to the floor with an elegant gesture, revealing a silk tunic full of beaded embroidery that resembled Egyptian hieroglyphs. On her chest, dropping down past her knees, a large silver and blue cross. Around her waist was the famous five-metre rosary, with beads the size of walnuts, each a different size and strangely multicoloured.

Enrique sincerely admired the woman's performance.

"Oh, if you could only understand the thrill it gives me to put on these garments! Rasputin was truly an exceptional man. He was a disaster for Russia, but I can't erase him from my imagination, that figure with his mysterious eyes surrounded by all his followers. He was a Christ-like figure, but a Christ followed by the aristocrats instead of by the poor and a gang of fishermen."

She stopped, but since Enrique kept quiet, she continued. "And he was a martyr too. Since he was immune to poison, they had to kill him with gunfire, kicking, punching, they destroyed him like a rabid wolf… and they gouged his eyes out. What horror!"

"But did you love him or hate him?" Enrique asked.

"My mind hates him, and my heart loves him. He was a great and extraordinary man. Whether an angel or a demon, there was something magnificent in him. It's no lie that on the day he died, bloody stigmata appeared at the altars of churches."

"Did you ever deal with him personally?"

"Very much, all the women of the court did… But let's sit down. We don't have any sofas or divans here. We're not in one of my sitting rooms in Saint Petersburg, after all. Come sit next to me *sur le lit*."

"I'm fine right here."

"You are respectful and *chorming*," she said in English, "Not many Spanish men know how to treat a lady. Care for a cigarette?"

Enrique realised he was going to have to play along. Sitting down on the bed, he took the box of cigarettes, and prepared himself to follow this adventure to its end, since now there was no fear of any romantic advances.

"Rasputin," continued the princess, "had a real fondness for me. He often singled me out among all the ladies who adored him. I had trouble more than once with him. The Tsarina was furious… jealous."

"Weren't you scared?"

"No. He would never dream of going too far with me. He knew the Tsar was my most fervent admirer."

"I see."

"He called me 'Divine Natasha.'"

"Like I do."

"Don't, or you'll upset me... no flattery! Do you see this famous rosary? It's authentic. He put it on me once so I would dance with him at court. It was like a consecration of my art."

"You were an artist back then, Your Highness?"

"There's no need for titles here, my friend. It sounds bad in these walls. I perceive your deference in the tone of your voice. There's no need to say the words. Yes, in Russia we noble maidens learned to dance, do gymnastics, play music, recite poetry. The Russian Imperial College of Dance was something unique in the world. You'll allow me to cry when I see how we are losing our art, our monuments, our museums, our grandeur."

Enrique didn't feel like participating in this sentimental second act. "If you will allow me to retire," he said as he stood up, "I would be honoured to return when you next invite me."

The expression on the mask between the folds of Rasputin's tunic changed, and she asked angrily, "But aren't we going to sign the contract?"

"I brought a few notes with me, but I must confess, Princess, I'm in no mood for these things now. Art, Beauty, Royalty... I'm enchained by my respect."

"I understand, but we mustn't squander this opportunity."

"Well, do you have your identity card and your working papers?"

"No... you see, an old minister of the Tsar, who later became one of the traitors who killed him, is in the top leadership now. He wanted to take advantage, he imprisoned me, but I escaped... Dear Lord, what haven't I suffered!"

"I don't know if I should be sorry about it, since that's the reason we have you here in Spain now."

"Yes, my aunt knew Madame Marques, a wonderful spirit. Such a worthy woman, still young and beautiful."

"Lovely!"

"You will be able to sign the contract with her."

"Could the three of us meet?"

"Oh that won't be necessary. I was thinking of going to see my aunt. I need her to see reason, to understand that my pride will not allow me to live at her expense. I want to prove it's a lie that we noble Russian exiles are good for nothing but to be waiters and servants, that we are worth as much as the French, who knew how to make themselves respected, to ply their arts and trades in every country."

She changed the subject and continued, "But let's not talk about that. I feel that the white-hot rage of my people is coming over me. To think that a princess of Romanov blood, may be called one day to fulfill the highest of destinies, would need papers to sign a simple contract!"

"It's the barbarity of the law, señora."

"Fine. Then tomorrow you may return to see Madame Marques. She will await you at this hour." She solemnly put her hand out to him, and he kissed it whispering words of admiration and respect. On the way out, he bowed so deeply it was as if he really were standing before the Empress of All Russia.

His head was swimming after that strange adventure, so instead of opening the door out to the street, he accidentally pushed open the other door at the back, the one from which the beautiful dark-haired woman had come to let him in earlier. He found himself disconcerted in front of her. The woman stood up, surprised in her private chambers, with her hair and clothes mussed. Enrique noticed her beautiful dark arms were uncovered. This ruddy, full-blooded Spanish woman looked even better in contrast with the mummy princess.

"Excuse me, señora, I made a mistake. I was trying to leave."

"It's this way." She walked towards him amiably to show him the door, and as she came close, he was enveloped in the pleasant smell of lilac perfume emanating from her body like a natural scent.

He didn't move. Suddenly, he was no longer in a rush. The woman must have noticed the impression she had caused because her smile was somewhere between satisfied and mocking.

Enrique came even closer to her with his conquistador's audacity, and taking her hand, he said, almost in her ear, "I'd rather stay now."

"You want to see the princess again?" she asked without rejecting him.

"You're the only princess here. I'd like to adore you."

"Just like that? So suddenly?"

Here he switched to the informal *tú*: "I don't need any more time to see your beauty. Allow me to stay." He took her into his arms, with an audacity picked up from a life of womanizing.

She smiled and didn't consent or reject him.

"Should I stay then?" he asked.

"I'm not alone."

"So what do we do?"

Now she too began to address him with the informal *tú*: "Wait for me on Santa Engracia. I'll come out in a moment."

"Can we have dinner together?"

"Oh no, not dinner."

"Why not?"

"I wonder what you would think of me if we did that?" she said, recovering her sense of propriety.

"That aside from being divine, you're generous and friendly... Will you come?"

Then he began almost begging her. Encarnación, for that was her name, could make up for his earlier disappointment. If she consented, his efforts to spruce himself up for that adventure – at the bottom of which was just the simple desire for a fling with a beautiful woman – wouldn't have been in vain.

He kept on pleading using both his voice and his eyes, hugging her tightly, with all the force of impassioned desire, which must have had an effect on her. "Say you'll come, you'll let me adore you."

She lowered her eyes gracefully and mumbled, "Yes... I'll come."

3.

A morning breeze brought in a bit of mild air through the open window, like a fan blowing from the top of Guadarrama over the suffocating city. Enrique felt an infinite melancholy seep into his bones, but the gentle, peaceful weather relaxed his body.

After the act of love-making – which is often followed by a bout of depression – it was the time for sharing confidences. He called her Encarna, and like most simple souls, she felt the need to pour out her intimate secrets.

He had observed this in almost all the women, regardless of social class, who had passed through his arms. Saints and sinners had this in common: they awakened early for confession. Enrique knew to listen with interest, to ask questions, to get all the little details from these poor souls. Maybe the reason women loved him so much was because of his compassion, because of the tenderness with which he listened to their boring lives, which they never tried to hide.

And so it was often the case that while he'd forget these women entirely, they always kept the memory of him close to their hearts. Their time with him stood out among all the others.

That first night, he didn't have to wait long for Encarnación to appear. She came dressed in a black suit and a lace mantilla that made her look even more sexy and beautiful. She wasn't very elegant, but she was an eyeful, her skirt clinging to her voluptuous curves. It was just the right length to show off her legs, with their thin ankles, thick calves and small, graceful, arched feet.

Her outfit with its low neckline and short sleeves had the look of an everyday housedress, and the way it revealed the smooth, polished, pink-marble hue of her arms and bosom, conveyed a sense of ripeness to her body. She offered herself up like chilled fruit to a thirsty customer. One could see that she had taken care to wear what all novices in the art of flirtation consider to be supreme *chic*. Silk stockings and high heels, along with a very bright nail polish and lipstick.

It was clear that this widow, who had been married to some deep-pocketed businessman, was only now beginning her life of freedom. If Enrique wasn't the first to be with her, he was one of the first.

He had had to make quite an effort to get her to have dinner with him at La Bombilla. But once there, with the help of the music and some cheap wine, she was a lovely companion. She ate and laughed wholeheartedly, whetting both his appetite and his enthusiasm. They even danced a few waltzes and polkas. When he asked her where she wanted to go, she answered without hesitating: "Home."

"But isn't Madame Marques there?"

"No, she only comes when there's an appointment to see the princess."

"So you knew?"

Encarna burst out laughing. "I know everything. I read a lot of the letters she writes, and the replies, too. If I didn't think it would go to your head, I would tell you something."

"What?"

"No."

"Tell me."

"You think I came out by chance to open the door for you?"

"What do you mean?"

"I knew who you were… I've read a lot of your novels. I'm an admirer of yours. When I found out you were coming, I wanted to meet you."

Enrique rewarded her confession with a hug and a big kiss on the lips. It reaffirmed his conquest and his usual prestige. "Did you see her after I left?" he asked.

"Yes, I asked her what happened, and she said, 'He's charming, but he was so impressed, he was dumbstruck, speechless. Hypnotised. It happens to all of them who see Natasha.'"

Encarna told him her whole story as they lay there in bed. Enrique listened distractedly, but pretended to pay close attention. Those beautiful arms of hers only had the power to keep him interested for that one night. He probably would never see them again, or remember what they talked about.

It was the same story with every widow. A husband who had no idea what love-making is all about. The tyranny, the brutalization, the mediocrity of a life with no prospect other than to be his obedient servant, without any outlet for the spirit, a lifeless existence… And then being able to breathe finally as a widow. The shock of newfound freedom, and not knowing what to do with it.

"But you did have some fun, don't deny it," said Enrique, reminding her of the little game she played with his letters.

"No, don't think that. Don't get me wrong, I won't pretend to be a saint, but I'm not like other women. If I've come here tonight with you, it's because you are... because I like you."

"I like you too."

"Don't get the wrong idea. I'm a very respectable woman. I would never go out with a man just for personal gain. I've always had to pay for my whims."

Enrique couldn't help but smile at Encarnación's strange idea of honour. But obviously she was sincere about it.

"It's true. I've paid for my whims. I've never taken a céntimo from anyone. And if I were to ever have the misfortune of becoming pregnant, I'd give birth and go to the Royal Palace with my child in my arms."

She was proud to be independent. She had enough money to be able to live modestly. The only reason she rented the room to Madame Marques was because it didn't get in her way. The lady actually lived somewhere else under a different name. But deep down, Encarnación hated Madame Marques because of the way she looked down on her and thought she was superior.

"I'm not sure why I haven't kicked her out yet," she said. "The truth is I feel sorry for her. She was very high class, but a little crazy, and the story of her ancestors has really gone to her head. Would you believe she doesn't even say hello or goodbye to me? She says blue bloods don't have to have these courtesies towards us commoners."

"But was she really a great lady?"

"Yes, extremely rich. She had her own carriages."

"A widow?"

"Yes, and I don't think she was too bad looking either."

"I know."

This comment awakened Encarna's jealousy. "I don't see

how you would know that. She always has a scarf tied under her chin so you can only see the front of her face, and she wears a piece of metal on her head to pull back her temples."

"Where does she get the money to live?"

"She has a few old friends that take care of her, but she's always dreaming about being independent, setting something up for herself. She has it in her head that she's some kind of amazing artist, and she's going to make a big splash the second she steps on the stage."

"Poor woman."

"She had her big debut in a small theatre. She played an Indian princess with a mask."

"Was it successful?"

"You need to ask? How could it possibly have been successful? The police had to intervene to stop the public from assaulting her. They sent insulting notes to her dressing room!"

"And what does she say about it?"

"She says they're only jealous."

Although he resented the fact that Madame Marques had tricked him, he felt a great compassion for her. Maybe it was a mistake sometimes, but he always saw women – the weaker, more delicate sex – as vulnerable to men's lust and the vulgarity and mockery of the public.

Encarnación told him about how the poor woman spent her life searching for some artist or writer who would be dazzled by her beauty, who would open the doors to fame and glory. She was obsessed by these delusions of grandeur, and she spent her days writing to every young politician and writer offering up Natasha for the theatre.

Encarna listed off the names of the most well-known artists, some of whom were his friends, some of whom were famous celebrities, so although he was worried, he couldn't help but laugh.

"I've seen the letters," said Encarna. "There's a poet with a thick beard who's very excited to take her to South America. He wrote to Madame Marques that the divine Natasha will never have to worry about anything. He'll take care of everything for the trip."

"But has he seen the princess?"

"No, only Madame Marques. It's not easy for her to dress up as the princess."

"How can she possibly think she can fool people?"

"It's her madness. She tells me she's an artist, says being an artist takes off thirty years. She says she looks so *precious* with her ridiculous dresses, that I wouldn't even recognise her myself. Actually, her real talent is writing. Everyone bites."

Yes, he thought. *Everyone bites.*

But he knew it wasn't her writing talent that seduced the men, and now that he was disenchanted, the whole thing seemed tacky and foolish. What all these men were hoping for was fresh meat and adventure – the prestige of having been with an extraordinary young woman.

Encarna continued naming names. A parade of novelists, poets, journalists, and politicians. It was a procession of deluded men lusting after a helpless little woman who needed work. But he wouldn't be the one to open their eyes! And it wasn't only his sense of self-preservation that forced him to be quiet. He saw them as fools, the kind that allow themselves to be conned by a pigeon drop or fake remedies. They get swindled thinking they're the ones doing the swindling.

The poor woman would have no trouble continuing her little performance and there would be no shortage of men to take the bait. Men's vanity provided an ample playing field and was the best guarantee of secrecy. Obviously, everyone would keep quiet.

And he had to admit, the bait wasn't bad. It wasn't some

commonplace dish, but a delicious plate of caviar with a Russian princess whose eyes had seen the horrors of death and destruction. In Spain, despite boasting of all its democrats, deep down there is still an attraction to aristocrats. Everyone goes wild for a great lady or some other great celebrity.

Novels featuring aristocrats, which allowed commoners to feel they were sitting in great drawing rooms, sold out quickly. Clubs prospered if they were headed by some shriveled up viscount or *marquesa* of dubious fame – the members could boast they knew aristocrats of such and such lineage.

A princess, especially an exotic one, would always have admirers in Spain, willing slaves. No matter what she wanted, everyone would say yes. She could be as audacious as she wanted, without consequence. The tragic thing in this case was that the woman could not maintain the illusion.

"And the outfits?"

Encarna let out a laugh. "Didn't you get a good look? Wait a second, you'll see." She jumped off the bed and walked out, returning a short while later with an armful of clothes. She obviously enjoyed ridiculing Madame Marques. It was as if they were rivals.

A psychologist like Enrique couldn't be fooled. Encarna was jealous of "Natasha." He caressed the dresses with the delight of those great lovers of women who believe they can perceive a heartbeat or the heat of a woman's body in her clothes.

"This must be Rasputin's tunic," he said to break the silence.

"Yes, and the Tsarina's dress. Look at them." She showed some outfits patched together from pieces of different fabric, with paper appliqué and coloured beads that were simply dyed macaroni.

"Look," continued Encarna, taking a cruel pleasure in ridiculing her rival. "This lamé fabric is just a wool shawl of mine. It was so old I was going to throw it out, and she asked me if she could have it. Look how patiently she wrapped each strand in tinfoil. And these long fringes that are starting to chip off are just dyed noodles."

It was more absurd than he could have imagined.

Little by little, caught up in the excitement of the exhibition, Encarna forgot her resentment and almost began admiring her. What an extraordinary woman, making a pretense of wealth with these scant items at her disposal. "She fixes everything. She makes jewels and tiaras with buttons she finds. She makes earrings and bracelets and necklaces with coloured beads or a little pasta. She knows how to make an old rag look like a suit of diamonds if you don't look too close."

Through these dresses, he understood Madame Marques's spirit better than when he had seen her in real life. He realised what a frivolous and vain woman she was. She hadn't known how to enjoy her youth and came to old age poor, ruined, full of unsatisfied, tormenting desires. Enrique needed to get that nightmarish figure out of his mind, and his eyes passed from the clothes to the beautiful arms holding out a linen cloak smeared with metallic paint.

He brushed away the poor, elegant outfits so industriously put together, and they fell to the floor with the sound of precious jewels and silk. He drew the delicate milky-skinned woman towards him. He wanted to get the bad taste out of his mouth. And the thought of all the men who would be disillusioned after him was even more depressing.

But he could still salvage his image of himself as an eternal Don Juan. Encarna was exactly the kind of lithe, attractive woman that appealed to men.

Nevertheless, he felt a deep dissatisfaction, the kind people feel when they are counting on certain business profits that never come, or if they mistakenly think they've won the lottery. Then when they're disappointed, they feel devastated. Things don't go back to the way they were, it feels as if everything has been lost.

However, Encarna's beauty could not compensate for what he felt that he had lost. She fell short of the storybook fantasy he yearned for, though at another time she would have suited him just fine.

This strange obsession of Madame Marques's, her tragic performance – well, it seemed that she had made such a desperate attempt to create this other personality that she really had come to create "Natasha" in his mind. Enrique felt it.

Despite everything, the image of the Russian princess had left such a vivid impression that it continued to live on in his heart and mind, and this gave rise to a general malaise, as though the hope for all his unrealised longings had been fatally extinguished.

Bring to Me All

Marina Tsvetaeva

translated by Nina Kossman

Bring to me all that's of no use to others:
My fire must burn it all!
I lure life, and I lure death
As weightless gifts for my fire.

Fire loves light-weighted things:
Last year's brushwood, wreathes, words.
Fire blazes from this kind of food.
You will rise from it purer than ash!

I am the Phoenix; only in the fire I sing.
Provide for my miraculous life!
I burn high – and I burn to the ground.
From now on let your nights be light-filled.

The icy fire – the fiery fount.
I hold high my tall form,
I hold high my high rank
Of Confidante and Heiress!

"*Women have served all these centuries as looking glasses possessing the magic and delicious power of reflecting the figure of man at twice its natural size.*"

– **Virginia Woolf**

Autres Temps[1]

Edith Wharton

1.

Mrs. Lidcote, as the huge menacing mass of New York defined itself far off across the waters, shrank back into her corner of the deck and sat listening with a kind of unreasoning terror to the steady onward drive of the screws.

She had set out on the voyage quietly enough – in what she called her "reasonable" mood – but the week at sea had given her too much time to think of things and had left her too long alone with the past.

When she was alone, it was always the past that occupied her. She couldn't get away from it, and she didn't any longer care to. During her long years of exile she had made her terms with it, had learned to accept the fact that it would always be there, huge, obstructing, encumbering, bigger and more dominant than anything the future could ever conjure up. And, at any rate, she was sure of it, she understood it, knew how to reckon with it; she had learned to screen and manage and protect it as one does an afflicted member of one's family.

There had never been any danger of her being allowed to forget the past. It looked out at her from the face of every acquaintance, it appeared suddenly in the eyes of strangers when a word enlightened them: "Yes, the Mrs. Lidcote, don't you know?" It had sprung at her the first day out, when, across the dining-room, from the captain's table, she had seen

1 first published in 1911

Mrs. Lorin Boulger's revolving eye-glass pause and the eye behind it grow as blank as a dropped blind. The next day, of course, the captain had asked: "You know your ambassadress, Mrs. Boulger?" and she had replied that, no, she seldom left Florence, and hadn't been to Rome for more than a day since the Boulgers had been sent to Italy. She was so used to these phrases that it cost her no effort to repeat them. And the captain had promptly changed the subject.

No, she didn't, as a rule, mind the past, because she was used to it and understood it. It was a great concrete fact in her path that she had to walk around every time she moved in any direction. But now, in the light of the unhappy event that had summoned her from Italy – the sudden unanticipated news of her daughter's divorce from Horace Pursh and remarriage with Wilbour Barkley – the past, her own poor miserable past, stared up at her with eyes of accusation, became, to her disordered fancy, like the afflicted relative suddenly breaking away from nurses and keepers and publicly parading the horror and misery she had, all the long years, so patiently screened and secluded.

Yes, there it had stood before her through the agitated weeks since the news had come – during her interminable journey from India, where Leila's letter had overtaken her, and the feverish halt in her apartment in Florence, where she had had to stop and gather up her possessions for a fresh start – there it had stood grinning at her with a new balefulness which seemed to say: "Oh, but you've got to look at me now, because I'm not only your own past but Leila's present."

Certainly it was a master-stroke of those arch-ironists of the shears and spindle to duplicate her own story in her daughter's. Mrs. Lidcote had always somewhat grimly fancied that, having so signally failed to be of use to Leila in other ways, she would at least serve her as a warning. She had even abstained from defending herself, from making the best of her case, had stoically refused to plead extenuating circumstances, lest Leila's impulsive sympathy should lead to deductions that might react disastrously on her own life. And now that very thing had happened, and Mrs. Lidcote could hear the whole of New York saying with one voice: "Yes, Leila's done just what her mother did. With such an example what could you expect?"

Yet, if she had been an example, poor woman, she had been an awful one; she had been, she would have supposed, of more use as a deterrent than a hundred blameless mothers as incentives. For how could anyone who had seen anything of her life in the last eighteen years have had the courage to repeat so disastrous an experiment?

Well, logic in such cases didn't count, example didn't count, nothing probably counted but having the same impulses in the blood; and that was the dark inheritance she had bestowed upon her daughter. Leila hadn't consciously copied her; she had simply "taken after" her, had been a projection of her own long-past rebellion.

Mrs. Lidcote had deplored, when she started, that the *Utopia* was a slow steamer, and would take eight full days to bring her to her unhappy daughter; but now, as the moment of reunion approached, she would willingly have turned the boat about and fled back to the high seas. It was not only because she felt still so unprepared to face what New York had in store for her, but because she needed more time to dispose of what the *Utopia* had already given her. The past was bad enough, but the present and future were worse, because they were less comprehensible, and because, as she grew older, surprises and inconsequences troubled her more than the worst certainties.

There was Mrs. Boulger, for instance. In the light, or rather the darkness, of new developments, it might really be that Mrs. Boulger had not meant to cut her, but had simply failed to recognise her. Mrs. Lidcote had arrived at this hypothesis simply by listening to the conversation of the persons sitting next to her on deck – two lively young women with the latest Paris hats on their heads and the latest New York ideas in them. These ladies, as to whom it would have been impossible for a person with Mrs. Lidcote's old-fashioned categories to determine whether they were married or unmarried, "nice" or "horrid," or any one or other of the definite things which young women, in her youth and her society, were conveniently assumed to be, had revealed a familiarity with the world of New York that, again according to Mrs. Lidcote's traditions, should have implied a recognised place in it. But in the present fluid state of manners what did anything imply except what their hats implied – that no-one could tell what was coming next?

They seemed, at any rate, to frequent a group of idle and opulent people who executed the same gestures and revolved on the same pivots as Mrs. Lidcote's daughter and her friends: their Coras, Matties and Mabels seemed at any moment likely to reveal familiar patronymics, and once one of the speakers, summing up a discussion of which Mrs. Lidcote had missed the beginning, had affirmed with headlong confidence: "Leila? Oh, Leila's all right."

Could it be her Leila, the mother had wondered, with a sharp thrill of apprehension? If only they would mention surnames! But their talk leaped elliptically from allusion to allusion, their unfinished sentences dangled over bottomless pits of conjecture, and they gave their bewildered hearer the impression not so much of talking only of their intimates, as of being intimate with everyone alive.

Her old friend Franklin Ide could have told her, perhaps; but here was the last day of the voyage, and she hadn't yet found courage to ask him. Great as had been the joy of discovering his name on the passenger-list and seeing his friendly bearded face in the throng against the taffrail at Cherbourg, she had as yet said nothing to him except, when they had met: "Of course, I'm going out to Leila."

She had said nothing to Franklin Ide because she had always instinctively shrunk from taking him into her confidence. She was sure he felt sorry for her, sorrier perhaps than anyone had ever felt; but he had always paid her the supreme tribute of not showing it. His attitude allowed her to imagine that compassion was not the basis of his feeling for her, and it was part of her joy in his friendship that it was the one relation seemingly unconditioned by her state, the only one in which she could think and feel and behave like any other woman.

Now, however, as the problem of New York loomed nearer, she began to regret that she had not spoken, had not at least questioned him about the hints she had gathered on the way. He did not know the two ladies next to her, he did not even, as it chanced, know Mrs. Lorin Boulger; but he knew New York, and New York was the sphinx whose riddle she must read or perish.

Almost as the thought passed through her mind his stooping shoulders and grizzled head detached themselves against the blaze of light in the west, and he sauntered down the empty deck and dropped into the chair at her side.

"You're expecting the Barkleys to meet you, I suppose?" he asked.

It was the first time she had heard anyone pronounce her daughter's new name, and it occurred to her that her friend, who was shy and inarticulate, had been trying to say it all the way over and had, at last, shot it out at her only because he felt it must be now or never.

"I don't know. I cabled, of course. But I believe she's at – they're at – his place somewhere."

"Oh, Barkley's; yes, near Lenox, isn't it? But she's sure to come to town to meet you."

He said it so easily and naturally that her own constraint was relieved, and suddenly, before she knew what she meant to do, she had burst out: "She may dislike the idea of seeing people."

Ide, whose absent short-sighted gaze had been fixed on the slowly gliding water, turned in his seat to stare at his companion.

"Who? Leila?" he said with an incredulous laugh.

Mrs. Lidcote flushed to her faded hair and grew pale again. "It took me a long time – to get used to it," she said.

His look grew gently commiserating. "I think you'll find – " he paused for a word "– that things are different now – altogether easier."

"That's what I've been wondering – ever since we started." She was determined now to speak. She moved nearer, so that their arms touched, and she could drop her voice to a murmur. "You see, it all came on me in a flash. My going off to India and Siam on that long trip kept me away from letters for weeks at a time; and she didn't want to tell me beforehand – oh, I understand that, poor child! You know how good she's always been to me; how she's tried to spare me. And she knew, of course, what a state of horror I'd be in. She knew I'd rush off to her at once and try to stop it. So she never gave me a hint of anything, and she even managed to muzzle Susy Suffern – you know Susy is the one of the family who keeps me informed about things at home. I don't yet see how she prevented Susy's telling me; but she did. And her first letter, the one I got up at Bangkok, simply said the thing was over – the divorce, I mean – and that the very next day she'd – well, I suppose there was no use waiting; and he seems to have behaved as well as possible, to have wanted to marry her as much as – "

"Who? Barkley?" he helped her out. "I should say so! Why what do you suppose – ?" He interrupted himself. "He'll be devoted to her, I assure you."

"Oh, of course; I'm sure he will. He's written me – really beautifully. But it's a terrible strain on a man's devotion. I'm not sure that Leila realises – "

Ide sounded again his little reassuring laugh. "I'm not sure that you realise. They're all right."

It was the very phrase that the young lady in the next seat had applied to the unknown "Leila," and its recurrence on Ide's lips flushed Mrs. Lidcote with fresh courage.

"I wish I knew just what you mean. The two young women next to me – the ones with the wonderful hats – have been talking in the same way."

"What? About Leila?"

"About a Leila; I fancied it might be mine. And about society in general. All their friends seem to be divorced. Some of them seem to announce their engagements before they get their decree. One of them – her name was Mabel – as far as I could make out, her husband found out that she meant to divorce him by noticing that she wore a new engagement-ring."

"Well, you see, Leila did everything 'regularly,' as the French say," Ide rejoined.

"Yes, but are these people in society? The people my neighbours talk about?"

He shrugged his shoulders. "It would take an arbitration commission a good many sittings to define the boundaries of society nowadays. But at any rate they're in New York; and I assure you you're not; you're farther and farther from it."

"But I've been back there several times to see Leila." She hesitated and looked away from him. Then she brought out slowly: "And I've never noticed – the least change – in – in my own case – "

"Oh," he sounded deprecatingly, and she trembled with the fear of having gone too far. But the hour was past when such scruples could restrain her. She must know where she was and where Leila was. "Mrs. Boulger still cuts me," she brought out with an embarrassed laugh.

"Are you sure? You've probably cut her; if not now, at least in the past. And in a cut if you're not first you're nowhere. That's what keeps up so many quarrels."

The word roused Mrs. Lidcote to a renewed sense of realities. "But the Purshes," she said, "– the Purshes are so strong! There are so many of them, and they all back each other up, just as my husband's family did. I know what it means to have a clan against one. They're stronger than any number of separate friends. The Purshes will never forgive Leila for leaving Horace. Why, his mother opposed his marrying her because of – of me. She tried to get Leila to promise that she wouldn't see me when they went to Europe on their honeymoon. And now she'll say it was my example."

Her companion, vaguely stroking his beard, mused a moment upon this; then he asked, with seeming irrelevance, "What did Leila say when you wrote that you were coming?"

"She said it wasn't the least necessary, but that I'd better come, because it was the only way to convince me that it wasn't."

"Well, then, that proves she's not afraid of the Purshes."

She breathed a long sigh of remembrance. "Oh, just at first, you know – one never is."

He laid his hand on hers with a gesture of intelligence and pity. "You'll see, you'll see," he said.

A shadow lengthened down the deck before them, and a steward stood there, proffering a Marconigram.

"Oh, now I shall know!" she exclaimed.

She tore the message open, and then let it fall on her knees, dropping her hands on it in silence.

Ide's enquiry roused her: "It's all right?"

"Oh, quite right. Perfectly. She can't come, but she's sending Susy Suffern. She says Susy will explain." After another silence she added, with a sudden gush of bitterness: "As if I needed any explanation!"

She felt Ide's hesitating glance upon her. "She's in the country?"

"Yes. 'Prevented last moment. Longing for you, expecting you. Love from both.' Don't you see, the poor darling, that she couldn't face it?"

"No, I don't." He waited. "Do you mean to go to her immediately?"

"It will be too late to catch a train this evening; but I shall take the first tomorrow morning." She considered a moment. "Perhaps it's better. I need a talk with Susy first. She's to meet me at the dock, and I'll take her straight back to the hotel with me."

As she developed this plan, she had the sense that Ide was still thoughtfully, even gravely, considering her. When she ceased, he remained silent a moment; then he said almost ceremoniously: "If your talk with Miss Suffern doesn't last too late, may I come and see you when it's over? I shall be dining at my club, and I'll call you up at about ten, if I may. I'm off to Chicago on business tomorrow morning, and it would be a satisfaction to know, before I start, that your cousin's been able to reassure you, as I know she will."

He spoke with a shy deliberateness that, even to Mrs. Lidcote's troubled perceptions, sounded a long-silenced note of feeling. Perhaps the breaking down of the barrier of reticence between them had released unsuspected emotions in both. The tone of his appeal moved her curiously and loosened the tight strain of her fears.

"Oh, yes, come – do come," she said, rising. The huge threat of New York was imminent now, dwarfing, under long reaches of embattled masonry, the great deck she stood on and all the little specks of life it carried. One of them, drifting nearer, took the shape of her maid, followed by luggage-laden stewards, and signing to her that it was time to go below. As they descended to the main deck, the throng swept her against

Mrs. Lorin Boulger's shoulder, and she heard the ambassadress call out to someone, over the vexed sea of hats: "So sorry! I should have been delighted, but I've promised to spend Sunday with some friends at Lenox."

2.

Susy Suffern's explanation did not end till after ten o'clock, and she had just gone when Franklin Ide, who, complying with an old New York tradition, had caused himself to be preceded by a long white box of roses, was shown into Mrs. Lidcote's sitting-room.

He came forward with his shy half-humourous smile and, taking her hand, looked at her for a moment without speaking.

"It's all right," he then pronounced.

Mrs. Lidcote returned his smile. "It's extraordinary. Everything's changed. Even Susy has changed, and you know the extent to which Susy used to represent the old New York. There's no old New York left, it seems. She talked in the most amazing way. She snaps her fingers at the Purshes. She told me – me, that every woman had a right to happiness and that self-expression was the highest duty. She accused me of misunderstanding Leila; she said my point of view was conventional! She was bursting with pride at having been in the secret, and wearing a brooch that Wilbour Barkley'd given her!" Franklin Ide had seated himself in the armchair she had pushed forward for him under the electric chandelier. He threw back his head and laughed. "What did I tell you?"

"Yes, but I can't believe that Susy's not mistaken. Poor dear, she has the habit of lost causes, and she may feel that, having stuck to me, she can do no less than stick to Leila."

"But she didn't – did she? – openly defy the world for you? She didn't snap her fingers at the Lidcotes?"

Mrs. Lidcote shook her head, still smiling. "No. It was enough to defy my family. It was doubtful at one time if they would tolerate her seeing me, and she almost had to disinfect herself after each visit. I believe that, at first, my sister-in-law wouldn't let the girls come down when Susy dined with her."

"Well, isn't your cousin's present attitude the best possible proof that times have changed?"

"Yes, yes; I know." She leaned forward from her sofa-corner, fixing her eyes on his thin, kindly face, which gleamed on her indistinctly through her tears. "If it's true, it's – it's dazzling. She says Leila's perfectly happy. It's as if an angel had gone about lifting gravestones, and the buried people walked again, and the living didn't shrink from them."

"That's about it," he assented.

She drew a deep breath, and sat looking away from him down the long perspective of lamp-fringed streets over which her windows hung.

"I can understand how happy you must be," he began at length.

She turned to him impetuously. "Yes, yes; I'm happy. But I'm lonely, too – lonelier than ever. I didn't take up much room in the world before; but now – where is there a corner for me? Oh. since I've begun to confess myself, why shouldn't I go on? Telling you this lifts a gravestone from me! You see, before this, Leila needed me. She was unhappy, and I knew it, and though we hardly ever talked of it, I felt that, in a way, the thought that I'd been through the same thing, and down to the dregs of it, helped her. And her needing me helped me. And when the news of her marriage came my first thought was that now she'd need me more than ever, that she'd have no-one but me to turn to. Yes, under all my distress there was a fierce joy in that. It was so new and wonderful to feel again that there was one person who wouldn't be able to get on without me! And now what you and Susy tell me seems to have taken my child from me; and just at first that's all I can feel."

"Of course it's all you feel." He looked at her musingly. "Why didn't Leila come to meet you?"

"That was really my fault. You see, I'd cabled that I was not sure of being able to get off on the *Utopia,* and apparently my second cable was delayed, and when she received it she'd already asked some people over Sunday – one or two of her old friends, Susy says. I'm so glad they should have wanted to go to her at once; but naturally I'd rather have been alone with her."

"You still mean to go, then?"

"Oh, I must. Susy wanted to drag me off to Ridgefield with her over Sunday, and Leila sent me word that of course I might go if I wanted to, and that I was not to think of her, but I know how disappointed she would be. Susy said she was afraid I might be upset at her having people to stay, and that, if I minded, she wouldn't urge me to come. But if they don't mind, why should I? And of course, if they're willing to go to Leila it must mean – "

"Of course. I'm glad you recognise that," Franklin Ide exclaimed abruptly. He stood up and went over to her, taking her hand with one of his quick gestures. "There's something I want to say to you," he began –

***

The next morning, in the train, through all the other contending thoughts in Mrs. Lidcote's mind there ran the warm undercurrent of what Franklin Ide had wanted to say to her.

He had wanted, she knew, to say it once before, when, nearly eight years earlier, the hazard of meeting at the end of a rainy autumn in a deserted Swiss hotel had thrown them for a fortnight into unwonted propinquity. They had walked and talked together, borrowed each other's books and newspapers, spent the long chill evenings over the fire in the dim lamplight of her little pitch-pine sitting-room; and she had been wonderfully comforted by his presence, and hard frozen places in her had melted, and she had known that she would be desperately sorry when he went. And then, just at the end, in his odd indirect way, he had let her see that it rested with her to have him stay.

She could still relive the sleepless night she had given to that discovery. It was preposterous, of course, to think of repaying his devotion by accepting such a sacrifice, but how to find reasons to convince him? She could not bear to let him think her less touched, less inclined to him than she was: the generosity of his love deserved that she should repay it with the truth. Yet, how let him see what she felt, and yet refuse what he offered? How confess to him what had been on her lips when he made the offer: "I've seen what it did to one man; and there must never, never be another"? The tacit ignoring of her past had been the element in which their friendship lived, and she could not suddenly, to him of all men, begin to talk of herself like a guilty woman in a play.

Somehow, in the end, she had managed it, had averted a direct explanation, had made him understand that her life was over, that she existed only for her daughter, and that a more definite word from him would have been almost a breach of delicacy. She was so used to behaving as if her life were over! And, at any rate, he had taken her hint, and she had been able to spare her sensitiveness and his. The next year, when he came to Florence to see her, they met again in the old friendly way; and that till now had continued to be the tenor of their intimacy.

And now, suddenly and unexpectedly, he had brought up the question again, directly this time, and in such a form that she could not evade it: putting the renewal of his plea, after so long an interval, on the ground that, on her own showing, her chief argument against it no longer existed.

"You tell me Leila's happy. If she's happy, she doesn't need you – need you, that is, in the same way as before. You wanted, I know, to be always in reach, always free and available if she should suddenly call you to her or take refuge with you. I understood that – I respected it. I didn't urge my case because I saw it was useless. You couldn't, I understood well enough, have felt free to take such happiness as life with me might give you while she was unhappy, and, as you imagined, with no hope of release. Even then I didn't feel as you did about it; I understood better the trend of things here. But ten years ago the change hadn't really come; and I had no way of convincing you that it was coming. Still, I always fancied that Leila might not think her case was closed, and so I chose to think that ours wasn't either. Let me go on thinking so, at any rate, till you've seen her, and confirmed with your own eyes what Susy Suffern tells you."

3.

All through what Susy Suffern told and retold her during their four-hours' flight to the hills this plea of Ide's kept coming back to Mrs. Lidcote. She did not yet know what she felt as to its bearing on her own fate, but it was something on which her confused thoughts could stay themselves amid the welter of new impressions, and she was inexpressibly glad that he had said what he had, and said it at that particular moment. It helped her to hold fast to her identity in the rush of strange names and new categories that her cousin's talk poured out on her.

With the progress of the journey Miss Suffern's communications grew more and more amazing. She was like a cicerone preparing the mind of an inexperienced traveller for the marvels about to burst on it.

"You won't know Leila. She's had her pearls reset. Sargent's to paint her. Oh, and I was to tell you that she hopes you won't mind being the least bit squeezed over Sunday. The house was built by Wilbour's father, you know, and it's rather old-fashioned – only ten spare bedrooms. Of course that's small for what they mean to do, and she'll show you the new plans they've had made. Their idea is to keep the present house as a wing. She told me to explain – she's so dreadfully sorry not to be able to give you a sitting-room just at first. They're thinking of Egypt for next winter, unless, of course, Wilbour gets his appointment. Oh, didn't she write you about that? Why, he wants Borne, you know – the second secretaryship. Or, rather, he wanted England; but Leila insisted that if they went abroad she must be near you. And of course what she says is law. Oh, they quite hope they'll get it. You see Horace's uncle is in the Cabinet – one of the assistant secretaries – and I believe he has a good deal of pull – "

"Horace's uncle? You mean Wilbour's, I suppose," Mrs. Lidcote interjected, with a gasp of which a fraction was given to Miss Suffern's flippant use of the language.

"Wilbour's? No, I don't. I mean Horace's. There's no bad feeling between them, I assure you. Since Horace's engagement was announced – you didn't know Horace was engaged? Why, he's marrying one of Bishop Thorbury's girls: the red-haired one who wrote the novel that everyone's talking about: *This Flesh of Mine*. They're to be married in the cathedral. Of course Horace can, because it was Leila who – but, as I say, there's not the least feeling, and Horace wrote himself to his uncle about Wilbour."

Mrs. Lidcote's thoughts fled back to what she had said to Ide the day before on the deck of the *Utopia*. "I didn't take up much room before, but now where is there a corner for me?" Where indeed in this crowded, topsy-turvy world, with its headlong changes and helter-skelter readjustments, its new tolerances and indifferences and accommodations, was there room for a character fashioned by slower, sterner processes and a life broken under their inexorable pressure? And then, in a flash, she viewed the chaos from a new angle, and order seemed to move upon the void.

If the old processes were changed, her case was changed with them; she, too, was a part of the general readjustment, a tiny fragment of the new pattern worked out in bolder, freer harmonies. Since her daughter had no penalty to pay, was not she herself released by the same stroke? The rich arrears of youth and joy were gone; but was there not time enough left to accumulate new stores of happiness? That, of course, was what Franklin Ide had felt and had meant her to feel. He had seen at once what the change in her daughter's situation would make in her view of her own. It was almost – wondrously enough! – as if Leila's folly had been the means of vindicating hers.

***

Everything else for the moment faded for Mrs. Lidcote in the glow of her daughter's embrace. It was unnatural, it was almost terrifying, to find herself standing on a strange threshold, under an unknown roof, in a big hall full of pictures, flowers, firelight, and hurrying servants, and in this spacious unfamiliar confusion to discover Leila, bareheaded, laughing, authoritative, with a strange, young man jovially echoing her welcome and transmitting her orders; but once Mrs. Lidcote had her child on her breast, and her child's "It's all right, you old darling!" in her ears, every other feeling was lost in the deep sense of well-being that only Leila's hug could give.

The sense was still with her, warming her veins and pleasantly fluttering her heart, as she went up to her room after luncheon. A little constrained by the presence of visitors, and not altogether sorry to defer for a few hours the "long talk" with her daughter for which she somehow felt herself tremulously unready, she had withdrawn, on the plea of fatigue, to the bright luxurious bedroom into which Leila had again and again apologised for having been obliged to squeeze her.

The room was bigger and finer than any in her small apartment in Florence, but it was not the standard of affluence implied in her daughter's tone about it that chiefly struck her, nor yet the finish and complexity of its appointments. It was the look it shared with the rest of the house, and with the perspective of the gardens beneath its windows, of being part of an "establishment" – of something solid, avowed, founded on sacraments and precedents and principles. There was nothing about the place, or about Leila and Wilbour, that suggested either passion or peril: their relation seemed as comfortable as their furniture and as respectable as their balance at the bank.

This was, in the whole confusing experience, the thing that confused Mrs. Lidcote most, that gave her at once the deepest feeling of security for Leila and the strongest sense of apprehension for herself. Yes, there was something oppressive in the completeness and compactness of Leila's well-being. Ide had been right: her daughter did not need her. Leila, with her first embrace, had unconsciously attested the fact in the same phrase as Ide himself, and as the two young women with the hats. "It's all right, you old darling!" she had said; and her mother sat alone, trying to fit herself into the new scheme of things which such a certainty betokened.

Her first distinct feeling was one of irrational resentment. If such a change was to come, why had it not come sooner? Here was she, a woman not yet old, who had paid with the best years of her life for the theft of the happiness that her daughter's contemporaries were taking as their due. There was no sense, no sequence, in it. She had had what she wanted, but she had had to pay too much for it. She had had to pay the last, bitterest price of learning that love has a price: that it is worth so much and no more. She had known the anguish of watching the man she loved discover this first, and of reading the discovery in his eyes. It was a part of her history that she had not trusted herself to think of for a long time past: she always took a big turn about that haunted corner. But now, at the sight of the young man downstairs, so openly and jovially Leila's, she was overwhelmed at the senseless waste of her own adventure, and wrung with the irony of perceiving that the success or failure of the deepest human experiences may hang on a matter of chronology.

Then gradually, the thought of Ide returned to her. "I chose to think that our case wasn't closed," he had said. She had been deeply touched by that. To everyone else, her case had been closed so long! *Finis* was scrawled all over her. But here was one man who had believed and waited, and what if what he believed in and waited for were coming true? If Leila's "all right" should really foreshadow hers?

As yet, of course, it was impossible to tell. She had fancied, indeed, when she entered the drawing-room before luncheon, that a too-sudden hush had fallen on the assembled group of Leila's friends, on the slender, vociferous, young women and the lounging golf-stockinged young men. They had all received her politely, with the kind of petrified politeness that may be either a tribute to age or a protest at laxity; but to them, of course, she must be an old woman because she was Leila's mother, and in a society so dominated by youth the mere presence of maturity was a constraint.

One of the young girls, however, had presently emerged from the group, and, attaching herself to Mrs. Lidcote, had listened to her with a blue gaze of admiration which gave the older woman a sudden happy consciousness of her long-forgotten social graces. It was agreeable to find herself attracting this young Charlotte Wynn, whose mother had been among her closest friends, and in whom something of the soberness and softness of the earlier manners had survived. But the little colloquy, broken up by the announcement of luncheon, could of course result in nothing more definite than this reminiscent emotion.

No, she could not yet tell how her own case was to be fitted into the new order of things; but there were more people – "older people" Leila had put it – arriving by the afternoon train, and that evening at dinner she would doubtless be able to judge. She began to wonder nervously who the new-comers might be. Probably she would be spared the embarrassment of finding old acquaintances among them; but it was odd that her daughter had mentioned no names.

Leila had proposed that, later in the afternoon, Wilbour should take her mother for a drive: she said she wanted them to have a "nice, quiet talk." But Mrs. Lidcote wished her talk with Leila to come first, and had, moreover, at luncheon, caught stray allusions to an impending tennis match in which her son-in-law was engaged. Her fatigue had been a sufficient pretext for declining the drive, and she had begged Leila to think of her as peacefully resting in her room till such time as they could snatch their quiet moment.

"Before tea, then, you duck!" Leila with a last kiss had decided; and presently Mrs. Lidcote, through her open window, had heard the fresh, loud voices of her daughter's visitors chiming across the gardens from the tennis court.

4.

Leila had come and gone, and they had had their talk. It had not lasted as long as Mrs. Lidcote wished, for in the middle of it Leila had been summoned to the telephone to receive an important message from town, and had sent word to her mother that she couldn't come back just then, as one of the young ladies had been called away unexpectedly and arrangements had to be made for her departure. But the mother and daughter had had almost an hour together, and Mrs. Lidcote was happy. She had never seen Leila so tender, so solicitous. The only thing that troubled her was the very excess of this solicitude, the exaggerated expression of her daughter's annoyance that their first moments together should have been marred by the presence of strangers.

"Not strangers to me, darling, since they're friends of yours," her mother had assured her.

"Yes, but I know your feeling, you queer wild mother. I know how you've always hated people." (Hated people! Had Leila forgotten why?) "And that's why I told Susy that if you preferred to go with her to Ridgefield on Sunday I should perfectly understand, and patiently wait for our good hug. But you didn't really mind them at luncheon, did you, dearest?"

Mrs. Lidcote, at that, had suddenly thrown a startled look at her daughter. "I don't mind things of that kind any longer," she had simply answered.

"But that doesn't console me for having exposed you to the bother of it, for having let you come here when I ought to have ordered you off to Ridgefield with Susy. If Susy hadn't been stupid she'd have made you go there with her. I hate to think of you up here all alone."

Again Mrs. Lidcote tried to read something more than a rather obtuse devotion in her daughter's radiant gaze. "I'm glad to have had a rest this afternoon, dear; and later – "

"Oh, yes, later, when all this fuss is over, we'll more than make up for it, shan't we, you precious darling?" And at this point Leila had been summoned to the telephone, leaving Mrs. Lidcote to her conjectures.

These were still floating before her in cloudy uncertainty when Miss Suffern tapped at the door.

"You've come to take me down to tea? I'd forgotten how late it was," Mrs. Lidcote exclaimed.

Miss Suffern, a plump, peering, little woman, with prim hair and a conciliatory smile, nervously adjusted the pendent bugles of her elaborate black dress. Miss Suffern was always in mourning, and always commemorating the demise of distant relatives by wearing the discarded wardrobe of their next of kin. "It isn't exactly mourning," she would say; "but it's the only stitch of black poor Julia had – and of course, George was only my mother's step-cousin."

As she came forward, Mrs. Lidcote found herself humorously wondering whether she were mourning Horace Pursh's divorce in one of his mother's old black satins.

"Oh, did you mean to go down for tea?" Susy Suffern peered at her, a little fluttered. "Leila sent me up to keep you company. She thought it would be cozier for you to stay here. She was afraid you were feeling rather tired."

"I was, but I've had the whole afternoon to rest in. And this wonderful sofa to help me."

"Leila told me to tell you that she'd rush up for a minute before dinner, after everybody had arrived, but the train is always dreadfully late. She's in despair at not giving you a sitting-room; she wanted to know if I thought you really minded."

"Of course I don't mind. It's not like Leila to think I should." Mrs. Lidcote drew aside to make way for the housemaid, who appeared in the doorway bearing a table spread with a bewildering variety of tea-cakes.

"Leila saw to it herself," Miss Suffern murmured as the door closed. "Her one idea is that you should feel happy here."

It struck Mrs. Lidcote as one more mark of the subverted state of things that her daughter's solicitude should find expression in the multiplicity of sandwiches and the piping-hotness of muffins; but then everything that had happened since her arrival seemed to increase her confusion.

The note of a motor-horn down the drive gave another turn to her thoughts. "Are those the new arrivals already?" she asked.

"Oh, dear, no; they won't be here till after seven." Miss Suffern craned her head from the window to catch a glimpse of the motor. "It must be Charlotte leaving."

"Was it the little Wynn girl who was called away in a hurry? I hope it's not on account of illness."

"Oh, no; I believe there was some mistake about dates. Her mother telephoned her that she was expected at the Stepleys, at Fishkill, and she had to be rushed over to Albany to catch a train."

Mrs. Lidcote meditated. "I'm sorry. She's a charming young thing. I hoped I should have another talk with her this evening after dinner."

"Yes, it's too bad." Miss Suffern's gaze grew vague.

"You do look tired, you know," she continued, seating herself at the tea-table and preparing to dispense its delicacies. "You must go straight back to your sofa and let me wait on you. The excitement has told on you more than you think, and you mustn't fight against it any longer. Just stay quietly up here and let yourself go. You'll have Leila to yourself on Monday."

Mrs. Lidcote received the tea-cup which her cousin proffered, but showed no other disposition to obey her injunctions. For a moment she stirred her tea in silence; then she asked: "Is it your idea that I should stay quietly up here till Monday?"

Miss Suffern set down her cup with a gesture so sudden that it endangered an adjacent plate of scones. When she had assured herself of the safety of the scones she looked up with a fluttered laugh. "Perhaps, dear, by tomorrow you'll be feeling differently. The air here, you know – "

"Yes, I know." Mrs. Lidcote bent forward to help herself to a scone. "Who's arriving this evening?" she asked.

Miss Suffern frowned and peered. "You know my wretched head for names. Leila told me – but there are so many – "

"So many? She didn't tell me she expected a big party."

"Oh, not big: but rather outside of her little group. And of course, as it's the first time, she's a little excited at having the older set."

"The older set? Our contemporaries, you mean?"

"Why – yes." Miss Suffern paused as if to gather herself up for a leap. "The Ashton Gileses," she brought out.

"The Ashton Gileses? Really? I shall be glad to see Mary Giles again. It must be eighteen years," said Mrs. Lidcote steadily.

"Yes," Miss Suffern gasped, precipitately refilling her cup.

"The Ashton Gileses; and who else?"

"Well, the Sam Fresbies. But the most important person, of course, is Mrs. Lorin Boulger."

"Mrs. Boulger? Leila didn't tell me she was coming."

"Didn't she? I suppose she forgot everything when she saw you. But the party was got up for Mrs. Boulger. You see, it's very important that she should – well, take a fancy to Leila and Wilbour – his being appointed to Rome virtually depends on it. And you know Leila insists on Rome in order to be near you. So she asked Mary Giles, who's intimate with the Boulgers, if the visit couldn't possibly be arranged; and Mary's cable caught Mrs. Boulger at Cherbourg. She's to be only a fortnight in America; and getting her to come directly here was rather a triumph."

"Yes, I see it was," said Mrs. Lidcote.

"You know, she's rather – rather fussy; and Mary was a little doubtful if – "

"If she would, on account of Leila?" Mrs. Lidcote murmured.

"Well, yes. In her official position. But luckily, she's a friend of the Barkleys. And finding the Gileses and Fresbies here will make it all right. The times have changed!" Susy Suffern indulgently summed up.

Mrs. Lidcote smiled. "Yes; a few years ago it would have seemed improbable that I should ever again be dining with Mary Giles and Harriet Fresbie and Mrs. Lorin Boulger."

Miss Suffern did not at the moment seem disposed to enlarge upon this theme; and after an interval of silence Mrs. Lidcote suddenly resumed: "Do they know I'm here, by the way?"

The effect of her question was to produce in Miss Suffern an exaggerated excess of peering and frowning. She twitched the tea-things about, fingered her bugles, and, looking at the clock, exclaimed amazedly: "Mercy! Is it seven already?"

"Not that it can make any difference, I suppose," Mrs. Lidcote continued. "But did Leila tell them I was coming?"

Miss Suffern looked at her with pain. "Why, you don't suppose, dearest, that Leila would do anything – ? "

Mrs. Lidcote went on: "For, of course, it's of the first importance, as you say, that Mrs. Lorin Boulger should be favourably impressed, in order that Wilbour may have the best possible chance of getting Borne."

"I told Leila you'd feel that, dear. You see, it's actually on your account – so that they may get a post near you – that Leila invited Mrs. Boulger."

"Yes, I see that." Mrs. Lidcote, abruptly rising from her seat, turned her eyes to the clock. "But, as you say, it's getting late. Oughtn't we to dress for dinner?"

Miss Suffern, at the suggestion, stood up also, an agitated hand among her bugles. "I do wish I could persuade you to stay up here this evening. I'm sure Leila'd be happier if you would. Really, you're much too tired to come down."

"What nonsense, Susy!" Mrs. Lidcote spoke with a sudden sharpness, her hand stretched to the bell. "When do we dine? At half-past eight? Then I must really send you packing. At my age it takes time to dress."

Miss Suffern, thus projected toward the threshold, lingered there to repeat: "Leila'll never forgive herself if you make an effort you're not up to." But Mrs. Lidcote smiled on her without answering, and the icy lightwave propelled her through the door.

5.

Mrs. Lidcote, though she had made the gesture of ringing for her maid, had not done so.

When the door closed, she continued to stand motionless in the middle of her soft, spacious room. The fire which had been kindled at twilight danced on the brightness of silver and mirrors and sober gilding; and the sofa toward which she had been urged by Miss Suffern heaped up its cushions in inviting proximity to a table laden with new books and papers. She could not recall having ever been more luxuriously housed, or having ever had so strange a sense of being out alone, under the night, in a windbeaten plain. She sat down by the fire and thought.

A knock on the door made her lift her head, and she saw her daughter on the threshold. The intricate ordering of Leila's fair hair and the flying folds of her dressing-gown showed that she had interrupted her dressing to hasten to her mother; but once in the room she paused a moment, smiling uncertainly, as though she had forgotten the object of her haste.

Mrs. Lidcote rose to her feet. "Time to dress, dearest? Don't scold! I shan't be late."

"To dress?" Leila stood before her with a puzzled look. "Why, I thought, dear – I mean, I hoped you'd decided just to stay here quietly and rest."

Her mother smiled. "But I've been resting all the afternoon!"

"Yes, but – you know, you do look tired. And when Susy told me just now that you meant to make the effort – "

"You came to stop me?"

"I came to tell you that you needn't feel in the least obliged – "

"Of course. I understand that."

There was a pause during which Leila, vaguely averting herself from her mother's scrutiny, drifted toward the dressing-table and began to disturb the symmetry of the brushes and bottles laid out on it.

"Do your visitors know that I'm here?" Mrs. Lidcote suddenly went on.

"Do they? – Of course – why, naturally," Leila rejoined, absorbed in trying to turn the stopper of a salts-bottle.

"Then won't they think it odd if I don't appear?"

"Oh, not in the least, dearest. I assure you they'll all understand." Leila laid down the bottle and turned back to her mother, her face alight with reassurance.

Mrs. Lidcote stood motionless, her head erect, her smiling eyes on her daughter's. "Will they think it odd if I do?"

Leila stopped short, her lips half-parted to reply. As she paused, the colour stole over her bare neck, swept up to her throat, and burst into flame in her cheeks. Thence, it sent its devastating crimson up to her very temples, to the lobes of her ears, to the edges of her eyelids, beating all over her in fiery waves, as if fanned by some imperceptible wind.

Mrs. Lidcote silently watched the conflagration, then she turned away her eyes with a slight laugh. "I only meant that I was afraid it might upset the arrangement of your dinner-table if I didn't come down. If you can assure me that it won't, I believe I'll take you at your word and go back to this irresistible sofa." She paused, as if waiting for her daughter to speak; then she held out her arms. "Run off and dress, dearest; and don't have me on your mind." She clasped Leila close, pressing a long kiss on the last afterglow of her subsiding blush. "I do feel the least bit overdone, and if it won't inconvenience you to have me drop out of things, I believe I'll basely take to my bed and stay there till your party scatters. And now run off, or you'll be late; and make my excuses to them all."

6.

The Barkleys' visitors had dispersed, and Mrs. Lidcote, completely restored by her two days' rest, found herself, on the following Monday alone with her children and Miss Suffern.

There was a note of jubilation in the air, for the party had "gone off" so extraordinarily well, and so completely, as it appeared, to the satisfaction of Mrs. Lorin Boulger, that Wilbour's early appointment to Rome was almost to be counted on. So certain did this seem that the prospect of a prompt reunion mitigated the distress with which Leila learned of her mother's decision to return almost immediately to Italy. No-one understood this decision; it seemed to Leila absolutely unintelligible that Mrs. Lidcote should not stay on with them till their own fate was fixed, and Wilbour echoed her astonishment.

"Why shouldn't you, as Leila says, wait here till we can all pack up and go together?"

Mrs. Lidcote smiled her gratitude with her refusal. "After all, it's not yet sure that you'll be packing up."

"Oh, you ought to have seen Wilbour with Mrs. Boulger," Leila triumphed.

"No, you ought to have seen Leila with her," Leila's husband exulted.

Miss Suffern enthusiastically appended: "I do think inviting Harriet Fresbie was a stroke of genius!"

"Oh, we'll be with you soon," Leila laughed. "So soon that it's really foolish to separate."

But Mrs. Lidcote held out with the quiet firmness which her daughter knew it was useless to oppose. After her long months in India, it was really imperative, she declared, that she should get back to Florence and see what was happening to her little place there; and she had been so comfortable on the *Utopia* that she had a fancy to return by the same ship. There was nothing for it, therefore, but to acquiesce in her decision and keep her with them till the afternoon before the day of the *Utopia's* sailing. This arrangement fitted in with certain projects which, during her two days' seclusion, Mrs. Lidcote had silently matured. It had become to her of the first importance to get away as soon as she could, and the little place in Florence, which held her past in every fold of its curtains and between every page of its books, seemed now to her, the one spot where that past would be endurable to look upon.

She was not unhappy during the intervening days. The sight of Leila's well-being, the sense of Leila's tenderness, were, after all, what she had come for; and of these she had had full measure. Leila had never been happier or more tender; and the contemplation of her bliss, and the enjoyment of her affection, were an absorbing occupation for her mother. But they were also a sharp strain on certain overtightened chords, and Mrs. Lidcote, when at last she found herself alone in the New York hotel to which she had returned the night before embarking, had the feeling that she had just escaped with her life from the clutch of a giant hand.

She had refused to let her daughter come to town with her; she had even rejected Susy Suffern's company. She wanted no viaticum but that of her own thoughts; and she let these come to her without shrinking from them as she sat in the same high-hung sitting-room in which, just a week before, she and Franklin Ide had had their memorable talk.

She had promised her friend to let him hear from her, but she had not kept her promise. She knew that he had probably come back from Chicago, and that if he learned of her sudden decision to return to Italy it would be impossible for her not to see him before sailing; and as she wished above all things not to see him she had kept silent, intending to send him a letter from the steamer.

There was no reason why she should wait till then to write it. The actual moment was more favourable, and the task, though not agreeable, would at least bridge over an hour of her lonely evening. She went up to the writing-table, drew out a sheet of paper and began to write his name. And as she did so, the door opened and he came in.

The words she met him with were the last she could have imagined herself saying when they had parted. "How in the world did you know that I was here?"

He caught her meaning in a flash. "You didn't want me to, then?" He stood looking at her. "I suppose I ought to have taken your silence as meaning that. But I happened to meet Mrs. Wynn, who is stopping here, and she asked me to dine with her and Charlotte, and Charlotte's young man. They told me they'd seen you arriving this afternoon, and I couldn't help coming up."

There was a pause between them, which Mrs. Lidcote at last, surprisingly broke with the exclamation: "Ah, she did recognise me, then!"

"Recognise you?" He stared. "Why – ?"

"Oh, I saw she did, though she never moved an eyelid. I saw it by Charlotte's blush. The child has the prettiest blush. I saw that her mother wouldn't let her speak to me."

Ide put down his hat with an impatient laugh. "Hasn't Leila cured you of your delusions?"

She looked at him intently. "Then you don't think Margaret Wynn meant to cut me?"

"I think your ideas are absurd."

She paused for a perceptible moment without taking this up then she said, at a tangent: "I'm sailing tomorrow, early. I meant to write to you – there's the letter I'd begun."

Ide followed her gesture, and then turned his eyes back to her face. "You didn't mean to see me, then, or even to let me know that you were going till you'd left?"

"I felt it would be easier to explain to you in a letter – "

"What in God's name is there to explain?" She made no reply, and he pressed on: "It can't be that you're worried about Leila, for Charlotte Wynn told me she'd been there last week, and there was a big party arriving when she left: Fresbies and Gileses, and Mrs. Lorin Boulger – all the board of examiners! If Leila has passed that, she's got her degree."

Mrs. Lidcote had dropped down into a corner of the sofa where she had sat during their talk of the week before. "I was stupid," she began abruptly. "I ought to have gone to Ridgefield with Susy. I didn't see till afterward that I was expected to."

"You were expected to?"

"Yes. Oh, it wasn't Leila's fault. She suffered – poor darling; she was distracted. But she'd asked her party before she knew I was arriving."

"Oh, as to that – " Ide drew a deep breath of relief. "I can understand that it must have been a disappointment not to have you to herself just at first. But, after all, you were among old friends or their children: the Gileses and Fresbies – and little Charlotte Wynn." He paused a moment before the last name, and scrutinised her hesitatingly. "Even if they came at the wrong time, you must have been glad to see them all at Leila's."

She gave him back his look with a faint smile. "I didn't see them."

"You didn't see them?"

"No. That is, excepting little Charlotte Wynn. That child is exquisite. We had a talk before luncheon the day I arrived. But when her mother found out that I was staying in the house she telephoned her to leave immediately, and so I didn't see her again."

The colour rushed to Ide's sallow face. "I don't know where you get such ideas!"

She pursued, as if she had not heard him: "Oh, and I saw Mary Giles for a minute too. Susy Suffern brought her up to my room the last evening, after dinner, when all the others were at bridge. She meant it kindly – but it wasn't much use."

"But what were you doing in your room in the evening after dinner?"

"Why, you see, when I found out my mistake in coming – how embarrassing it was for Leila, I mean – I simply told her I was very tired, and preferred to stay upstairs till the party was over."

Ide, with a groan, struck his hand against the arm of his chair. "I wonder how much of all this you simply imagined!"

"I didn't imagine the fact of Harriet Fresbie's not even asking if she might see me when she knew I was in the house. Nor of Mary Giles's getting Susy, at the eleventh hour, to smuggle her up to my room when the others wouldn't know where she'd gone; nor poor Leila's ghastly fear lest Mrs. Lorin Boulger, for whom the party was given, should guess I was in the house, and prevent her husband's giving Wilbour the second secretaryship because she'd been obliged to spend a night under the same roof with his mother-in-law!"

Ide continued to drum on his chair-arm with exasperated fingers. "You don't know that any of the acts you describe are due to the causes you suppose."

Mrs. Lidcote paused before replying, as if honestly trying to measure the weight of this argument. Then she said in a low tone: "I know that Leila was in an agony lest I should come down to dinner the first night. And it was for me she was afraid, not for herself. Leila is never afraid for herself."

"But the conclusions you draw are simply preposterous. There are narrow-minded women everywhere, but the women who were at Leila's knew perfectly well that their going there would give her a sort of social sanction, and if they were willing that she should have it, why on earth should they want to withhold it from you?"

"That's what I told myself a week ago, in this very room, after my first talk with Susy Suffern." She lifted a misty smile to his anxious eyes. "That's why I listened to what you said to me the same evening, and why your arguments half convinced me, and made me think that what had been possible for Leila might not be impossible for me. If the new dispensation had come, why not for me as well as for the others? I can't tell you the flight my imagination took!"

Franklin Ide rose from his seat and crossed the room to a chair near her sofa-corner. "All I cared about was that it seemed – for the moment – to be carrying you toward me," he said.

"I cared about that, too. That's why I meant to go away without seeing you." They gave each other grave look for look. "Because, you see, I was mistaken," she went on. "We were both mistaken. You say it's preposterous that the women who didn't object to accepting Leila's hospitality should have objected to meeting me under her roof. And so it is; but I begin to understand why. It's simply that society is much too busy to revise its own judgments. Probably no-one in the house with me stopped to consider that my case and Leila's were identical. They only remembered that I'd done something which, at the time I did it, was condemned by society. My case has been passed on and classified: I'm the woman who has been cut for nearly twenty years. The older people have half-forgotten why, and the younger ones have never really known: it's simply become a tradition to cut me. And traditions that have lost their meaning are the hardest of all to destroy."

Ide sat motionless while she spoke. As she ended, he stood up with a short laugh and walked across the room to the window. Outside, the immense black prospect of New York, strung with its myriad lines of light, stretched away into the smoky edges of the night. He showed it to her with a gesture.

"What do you suppose such words as you've been using – 'society,' 'tradition,' and the rest – mean to all the life out there?"

She came and stood by him in the window. "Less than nothing, of course. But you and I are not out there. We're shut up in a little, tight, round of habit and association, just as we're shut up in this room. Remember, I thought I'd got out of it once; but what really happened was that the other people went out, and left me in the same little room. The only difference was that I was there alone. Oh, I've made it habitable now, I'm used to it; but I've lost any illusions I may have had as to an angel's opening the door."

Ide again laughed impatiently. "Well, if the door won't open, why not let another prisoner in? At least it would be less of a solitude – "

She turned from the dark window back into the vividly lighted room.

"It would be more of a prison. You forget that I know all about that. We're all imprisoned, of course – all of us middling people, who don't carry our freedom in our brains. But we've accommodated ourselves to our different cells, and if we're moved suddenly into new ones we're likely to find a stone wall where we thought there was thin air, and to knock ourselves senseless against it. I saw a man do that once."

Ide, leaning with folded arms against the window frame, watched her in silence as she moved restlessly about the room, gathering together some scattered books and tossing a handful of torn letters into the paper basket. When she ceased, he rejoined: "All you say is based on preconceived theories. Why didn't you put them to the test by coming down to meet your old friends? Don't you see the inference they would naturally draw from your hiding yourself when they arrived? It looked as though you were afraid of them – or as though you hadn't forgiven them. Either way, you put them in the wrong instead of waiting to let them put you in the right. If Leila had buried herself in a desert, do you suppose society would have gone to fetch her out? You say you were afraid for Leila and that she was afraid for you. Don't you see what all these complications of feeling mean? Simply that you were too nervous at the moment to let things happen naturally, just as you're too nervous now to judge them rationally."

He paused and turned his eyes to her face. "Don't try to just yet. Give yourself a little more time. Give me a little more time. I've always known it would take time."

He moved nearer, and she let him have her hand.

With the grave kindness of his face so close above her she felt like a child roused out of frightened dreams and finding a light in the room.

"Perhaps you're right – " she heard herself begin, then something within her clutched her back, and her hand fell away from him.

"I know I'm right. Trust me," he urged. "We'll talk of this in Florence soon."

She stood before him, feeling with despair his kindness, his patience and his unreality. Everything he said seemed like a painted gauze let down between herself and the real facts of life; and a sudden desire seized her to tear the gauze into shreds.

She drew back and looked at him with a smile of superficial reassurance. "You are right – about not talking any longer now. I'm nervous and tired, and it would do no good. I brood over things too much. As you say, I must try not to shrink from people." She turned away and glanced at the clock. "Why, it's only ten! If I send you off I shall begin to brood again; and if you stay we shall go on talking about the same thing. Why shouldn't we go down and see Margaret Wynn for half an hour?"

She spoke lightly and rapidly, her brilliant eyes on his face. As she watched him, she saw it change, as if her smile had thrown a too vivid light upon it.

"Oh, no – not tonight!" he exclaimed.

"Not tonight? Why, what other night have I, when I'm off at dawn? Besides, I want to show you at once that I mean to be more sensible – that I'm not going to be afraid of people anymore. And I should really like another glimpse of little Charlotte." He stood before her, his hand in his beard, with the gesture he had in moments of perplexity. "Come!" she ordered him gaily, turning to the door.

He followed her and laid his hand on her arm. "Don't you think – hadn't you better let me go first and see? They told me they'd had a tiring day at the dressmaker's, I daresay they have gone to bed."

"But you said they'd a young man of Charlotte's dining with them. Surely he wouldn't have left by ten? At any rate, I'll go down with you and see. It takes so long if one sends a servant first." She put him gently aside, and then paused as a new thought struck her. "Or wait; my maid's in the next room. I'll tell her to go and ask if Margaret will receive me. Yes, that's much the best way."

She turned back and went toward the door that led to her bedroom, but before she could open it she felt Ide's quick touch again.

"I believe – I remember now – Charlotte's young man was suggesting that they should all go out – to a music hall or something of the sort. I'm sure – I'm positively sure that you won't find them."

Her hand dropped from the door, his dropped from her arm, and as they drew back and faced each other, she saw the blood rise slowly through his sallow skin, redden his neck and ears, encroach upon the edges of his beard, and settle in dull patches under his kind, troubled eyes. She had seen the same blush on another face, and the same impulse of compassion she had then felt made her turn her gaze away again.

A knock on the door broke the silence, and a porter put his head into the room.

"It's only just to know how many pieces there'll be to go down to the steamer in the morning."

With the words she felt that the veil of painted gauze was torn in tatters, and that she was moving again among the grim edges of reality.

"Oh, dear," she exclaimed, "I never can remember! Wait a minute; I shall have to ask my maid."

She opened her bedroom door and called out:

"Annette!"

"*No-one can make you feel inferior*
without your consent."

– Eleanor Roosevelt

Unheard[1]

by Yenta Serdatsky

translated by Dalia Wolfson

Dr. Anna Shenkin, dentist, sees off her last patient and feels her breathing relax. She looks around the room.

Silence. Shadows quiver on the walls; night is coming.

She goes to the window and looks out at the street. It's grey out, the rain keeps falling; people rush through the mud, umbrellas up. Miserable! she thinks to herself.

The elderly maid brings in a lamp, and its weak light shines on the room. Anna turns away from the window and as her gaze falls on the old woman, she shivers involuntarily, as though seeing her for the first time. How hunched she is, how wrinkled! Such dead eyes... such gray hair...

The maid retreats. Anna stands in front of a mirror, and her tall figure stares back at her with large dark eyes. Her mood lifts a bit, then shifts. New lines catch her eye in the reflection; her soft skin will soon crease there into wrinkles. A sadness washes over her. Only yesterday she plucked two gray hairs from her head. The beginning of the end... what a horror! One day she'll look just as lonely as her maid – the only difference is that her maid will remain a maid, and Anna, the dentist, will go on pulling teeth... What a life! What for? Why?

Anna begins to pace around the room.

If only someone would come! Something gnaws at her from

---

1 published in 1913

inside. She wants someone to confide in, to talk everything out...What is this life? What does one live for?

A knock at the door. Oh, only let it not be another toothache!

No, thank God – it's an acquaintance. And Anna brightens: this one, surely he'll hear her out.

His name is Avrom, but they call him "The Pessimist". He's short, around thirty years old, with a pale face, a trim dark beard and sad black eyes. He greets her half-heartedly and takes a seat in the nearest chair, still in his dripping wet coat. Rain pools around his chair. A puddle forms on the clean floor. Lost in thought, Anna doesn't notice.

Avrom crosses his legs, puts his face in his hands, sighs deeply. She feels awkward. She looks at him and doesn't know what to do.

Suddenly, he pulls his chair closer and looks her straight in the face: "You, Anna. Are you also sad today?"

She feels her breath come easier, she opens her mouth to speak: "I've been feeling so troubled..."

But he won't let her get a word in.

"What good is our sadness?" he blurts out, then starts picking up speed, " – Or, for that matter, what's the point of our happiness? Why do we drag ourselves across this earth? What good does it do for us?" And away he goes, one long monologue, his voice bitter and cynical. He's saying what she would say, too, but that doesn't make it any better; on the contrary, her chest feels tight. She wants to express something but the words get stuck in her throat... if only she could speak about her feelings, get some relief from the weight on her heart...

"Avrom, listen to me! I've been feeling so troubled today..." she tries to interrupt. He waves her away, nervously, and picks up again, talking even faster, more insistently, as though to prevent her from interrupting again.

Unheard

Ten minutes later he's gone. And she hasn't uttered a word.

Her burden feels even heavier, more painful. She's seized from inside by a darkness – bitterness, doubt, envy, pain.

"How utterly selfish!" She fumes. "Comes over, speaks his mind, gets what he needs... then he's off!"

The clock strikes, jolting her out of her thoughts. Another guest arrives. She steels herself.

Can she talk to him? She glances at his face, his cheery smile. Will he even listen? Will he understand? Maybe... Oh...

The guest takes a notebook out of his pocket, opens it and asks excitedly: "Mademoiselle Shenkin! I have three new poems, would you like me to read them to you?"

And before she can respond, he begins to read them aloud, in a coy voice:

"Inside a garden grows a rose –

See how she bathes in sunny rays!"

She hears him warbling on and doesn't understand a word. Why is his head cocked to one side? It's annoying.

"A flaming fire, burning bright

But my heart blazes, so blood-red..."

A few more rhymes reach her ears.

What's brought on this despair? She asks herself. She listens to her heart thudding. What is it telling me? Why won't it stop?

"Whaddaya say, Anyut? What do you think of my poems?" His voice reaches her.

"Your poems?" She stares at him, a little lost. "The poems... Oh... I don't know..."

"There are some really excellent ideas here ... pure gold... pearls!" She barely hears his eager voice, almost doesn't notice him leaving.

Sang his little song and left... The visitor gone, she feels angry again. And then startled, all of a sudden – the clock's bell chimes so loudly, the whole flat seems to shake. Dancing, whirling, her friend Manya bursts in – a short girl, blonde, wild hair, her face flushed. Giggling, she throws herself on Anna.

"Ha, ha, ha, Anyuta! Oh, Anyusha, Anyusha, if only you knew what I did to them this time! Hahaha!"

Manya's a brat, a clown, she's always playing pranks. Anna has always loved her for her silliness, but right now the laughs grate on her nerves.

"Manitshka, please, leave me alone... I'm not in the mood, I have a headache..."

Manya doesn't wait around. Still laughing, she flutters out of the room like a breeze.

Alone again. She just flew in, Anna thinks, didn't even ask how I am... Her face darkens with one thought after another. Not a single friend... no-one to talk things through with... They come to use me, they take and they take... And her heart trembles and rages on.

The clock chimes six. She jumps – it's almost time, one of her friends must be on their way, surely? She goes through them in her head – who might actually listen?

Vera, Maria, Berta, Sonia, Etsha, Big Boris, Little Boris, Pavel, Isidore, Samuel, Misha... and yet... and yet she doesn't feel sure about a single one.

They're so free and haven't a care, here's a samovar, there's a bite to eat – but not one will listen to her. They like to keep things light-hearted. Sadness engulfs her. Not a single friend... And no-one to hear what's in my heart...

All of a sudden she remembers – Kreynin! – and feels instantly cheered. She throws on a coat and a scarf and hurries out of the house.

Kreynin was her father's friend. A loyal friend, she knows that, she grew up around him, used to call him "Uncle". He'd bring her playthings, kiss her and call her "my child!"

How could I have forgotten about him, she thinks to herself. I'll talk it out with him… and my heart will feel so much lighter. Oh, how good that will be!

***

Stepping into Kreynin's home, she regrets her decision immediately. Kreynin is sitting there, his hands on the table, dozing. A lamp with a green shade casts a dim light on the modest room. She scans it all quickly: soot-smudged walls and ceiling, spiderwebs everywhere. The old furniture. A wave of sorrow passes through her. An iron bedframe with filthy sheets, a shabby oilcloth thrown over an old couch, two chairs, a bookshelf and a worn-out writing table. That's all there is. The table is littered with things: books, newspapers, writing utensils, a couple of bread rolls, some sugar in a wrapper. A teapot and a glass of tea, poured not long ago. A thick layer of dust on every surface. Scraps of paper, used collars, cigarette butts and spent matches on the dirty floor. In a corner, an overturned kerosene canister with an awful smell that stinks up the room.

Anna sighs heavily. How depressing! She begins backing away when suddenly Kreynin stirs.

"Khaneleh!" He exclaims. "What a nice surprise! How are you, my child? Come here, sit down! How's it going? Tell me!"

He's the only person I can really speak to, she thinks. Anna tries to settle down in the mess around her. Yet her despair only grows at the sight of Kreynin's gaunt face, pale and wrinkled…

"But it will feel better to speak from my heart," she reassures herself. She wants to start talking.

"I hope you're well?" She asks politely, sitting down on a

chair facing him. And Kreynin seems to have been waiting for just that question.

"How should I be, my child!" he pounces. And, clinging to the chance to speak lest it escape, he begins talking rapidly in his broken voice. He tells her everything – about his lonely, solitary days (he's a childless widower), his complaints about insomnia, and about old age that has crept up on him unannounced. The longer he speaks, the more heated his words.

Anna gets up, her body heavy, and watches him. She can tell that he can't even see her any more. His pale lips tremble, mouthing something, as though he wants to make a long confession, a plea, a request...

"What use is my life? What good am I? What happens next? What comes at the end?"

Fragments of his talk reach her ears, burning like hot lead dripping onto her heart. "Soon I'll look like that... talk like that..." She shudders. And suddenly she gets annoyed.

Why is he still talking? She glares at his toothless mouth. If only he'd pause, just for a moment! Her whole being resonates with one demand: To speak to somebody, to unburden my heart!

"Listen, Khanaleh..." Now Kreynin's wrapping up, he's taking her by the hand, "Listen, my child, you've come to me and I feel like a new-born. I feel young again! Talking things out with you, it's as though a heavy stone was lifted from my heart... I feel so light, so wonderfully light again... I swear, it's true, Khanaleh, on my friendship with your father. Come again, please come more often to visit!"

And then he looks at the old clock on the wall.

"It is late," he says, "You should really be heading home."

*"If you are silent about your pain,
they'll kill you and say you enjoyed it."*

— Zora Neale Hurston

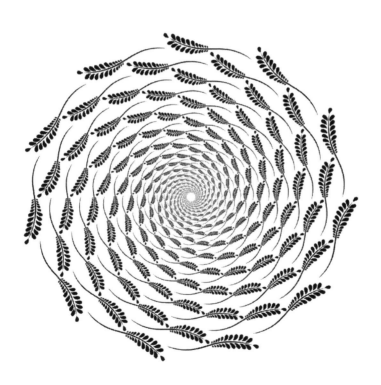

Fog

by Gabriela Mistral

translated by Stuart Cooke

The fog has been thickening
into an ashen-blue blanket;
blinding the sea, she steals
our clutch of archipelagos:
crooked, cunning woman
who walks with clumsy steps.

She blurs Chiloé,
reaches as far as Tierra del Fuego
and juggles forms, the shapes
of boy and deer,
whisks away my bulk
just so they'll cry.

I already know her tricks
of cutting corners
and playing blind man's bluff
with the shepherd or the muleteer.
Now she's playing her ever-lasting
game with us,
forging whales and octopi
from an idle, enchanting sea.
She treats us like we've drowned,
are lost, captive,

Fog

even though we're underneath her,
just as God made us: whole.

I whisper to my kids
that it's not solid, that it's breath,
that its arm won't choke,
that it's a dead yawn, nothing more,
that we're not fighting with a hero
but with white nonsense.
And we crack the blue egg
with lancets of dialect,
and we smash it up
with our two warm bodies.

In the aquarium of fog
swarming with monsters,
the man who rowed three oceans
has settled down to tell stories;
he speaks the slow channels,
conjures the straights,
like someone weaving worlds
with hands and gestures.

Now the old man's telling
the long, worn tale
of the coasts eaten
by the hard-mouthed ocean,
and he is talking to the Antarctica
that we have and we haven't.

From his mouth, Antarctica
rises like a halcyon in flight,
the divine white animal,
arrogant and sleepy.

Virginia's Sisters

And so with her we sleep,
fraternal and meek,
the little deer of symbol
and the feverish Indian.

We end up just where
they end up in the stories,
the loving Mother who is earth
and ends in sacred silence;
but the three of us find
the tightly-sealed secret,
the unknown whiteness,
the untouched Mystery.

Natalia[1]

by Fausta Cialente

translated by Laura Shanahan

Natalia said she had to go out, to send a telegram home. Obtaining this modicum of freedom, which ran counter to provincial customs, involved such fuss that when she found herself outside, alone, it seemed to her that the grey but gentle face of her liberty was sketched lightly on the walls of the town.

By this time Malaspina would already be waiting for her. At the end of the street she saw a carriage pull up; she climbed in and it crossed her mind that she could take a roundabout route and keep her young man waiting. Instead, tapping on the glass, she called out to the coachman: "The Albergo del Papa."

***

Leaning against one of the portico's columns, his feet at the edge of a puddle, Malaspina felt weary – almost feverish. His journey had been strenuous and riddled with anxiety, and now every time a woman passed by, skirting around him, his heart missed a beat and left him breathless. The entrance to the hotel was beneath the portico – it was a fairly modest hotel, but he would take a room there for the night if Natalia wanted to

---

1 Excerpted from the 1930 novel: Natalia is visiting her childhood friend Silvia. During the First World War Natalia wrote letters to a young soldier called Malaspina, who has asked to meet her in the town where Silvia lives.

meet him the next day too. His anguish arose from uncertainty as well as from excitement: it was like being vaguely seasick, and he felt almost nostalgic for those bare yet faithful acacia trees he had left behind, betrayed for the sake of standing by this wall, tormented by the winter wind. He didn't dare think *she might not come*, but felt his heart inflate with rebellious outrage in response to some appalling injustice which at that precise moment was falling like a boulder upon an obscure innocent creature somewhere in the world, crushing it to the ground, leaving it flat and wretched.

And yet a carriage had pulled up, black and dripping; above it he saw the glistening-wet back of a coachman, who was holding the reins and lowering his whip. Malaspina felt faint with emotion. In the window, through the rain, Natalia's eyes were bright and tranquil; her appearance was like an astonishing, unexpected springtime, fresh as an almond within the plush darkness of the mothball-scented carriage; and as he gazed at her, motionless and overcome, the carriage door opened, a hand reached out and a clear, calm voice said: "Come on, get in!"

The carriage juddered off again. Her voice seemed to him not only calm but sweet, and her gloved hand remained in his, held tight. He found, with a spasm of his heart, that she was less beautiful than her pictures had led him to believe, and could not understand why she seemed nonetheless better in person. Perhaps because it was truly her, and no longer just a picture. Desperately, he asked himself: *What do I do now? Kiss her? But how can I?*

Her eyelashes were lowered now, and while feigning modest shyness she was in fact thinking: *He's a nice enough looking boy... Yet I don't like him. No, I really don't think I can... And how am I going to tell him? I just don't know.*

He was the first to speak, his voice breaking with emotion: "Forgive me... I've had to come a long way... and at this time of year…" But his breath was heavy, a little sour. She looked away and thought again: *Why did I come? Why don't I just tell him, right now, to get out and go on his way?*

The town passed by slowly – the pot-bellied grilles on the ground-floor windows, and behind them a few bored faces that were just then forgetting their troubles, and the weather, and yawning at the beginnings of an overcast sunset beyond the rain-pearled panes of glass. The silence in the carriage had gone on too long for Malaspina who, painfully intimidated, began to say in a warm, choked voice: "Natalia…" but she did not let him go on and her voice, cold as a blade, swiftly pierced his heart and dug mercilessly into it: "We made a mistake, you must see that – I knew this would be too difficult; I saw before you did… that perhaps you didn't feel as you should have. But I hope that now you understand. You must see, it would have been better if none of this had happened."

Indeed, Malaspina now knew – the boulder had rolled silently down an invisible slope – who the flat, wretched man was, face-down in a dirty stream. But his shyness and his pride were like outsized roots twisting around him, tugging him underground, suffocating him; perhaps all she now saw was a fragile shrub with small, pitiful, anaemic leaves. He would say nothing in defence of the love he had come to feel for her – with every right, as he well knew. Love, tenderness and now despair were shameful wounds to which he must not confess, and he broke out in a cold sweat at the idea that he might fail to hide them. His head was spinning like a windmill; the world was empty and frigid as a tomb. What could he do but look on as this scene of betrayal played out?

Natalia was fresh as springtime – that was exactly how she had looked to him – and her cruel will would keep her that way even as she grew old, amid that mothball smell. At fifty years old, in her black carriage, she would drive through ever-new streets and dig her blade into other young hearts, ones that had not yet even been born. Malaspina could not avenge himself; and yet he did not know that Natalia had turned her head away not so much from indifference but because his dense breath was bothering her. His misery got the better of his pride for a moment, and in a treble voice he said to her: "Your letters were the most beautiful book I have read in my life. What should I do with them?"

"I don't want them back… Perhaps for a while yet they may still be the most beautiful thing in your life."

It was a dismal and conceited wish. She had forced a mountain to collapse, and now seemed to be trying to impose order on its continued crumbling.

"Goodbye," he replied in the most contemptuous tone he could muster through the little sea of tears threatening to drown him, and he got out while the horse was still trotting onward. The carriage jolted and swayed to one side. Little more than a quarter of an hour had gone by.

***

'… All this was nothing yet, believe me, Jacopo: when the dizzy daze of those first kisses, which I could not decently avoid, had subsided, up from somewhere that was certainly not my heart rose something that had no place in that scene – something you know all too well – my sense of irony. I was almost shaking from the fear that I would start laughing. All the while he was telling me of a room that awaited us who knew where, since we couldn't very well carry on in that rickety old carriage – my lower back still aches from how it shook us about. As he got out, he said to me: "Tomorrow, if you like…" Well, would you have consented to some vague 'tomorrow'?

Instead I replied: "Today, right now – I don't want to hear another word about tomorrow," because at least if he agreed, he would clearly be in the wrong. He agreed, the fool! He didn't see it was a trap. I could have asked anything at all of him, but we spoke no more – I had backed myself into a corner and I must have looked very anxious, because every now and then he squeezed my hand as if to encourage me, not knowing that I had plenty of courage and that the worst was yet to come.

At the entrance to the hotel, before getting out of the carriage, I let down a veil from my hat – farcical, I know, but it had to be done. The place was rather modest: there wasn't even a lift; we had to climb the stairs on foot. The room, too, was modest (he informed me that he had chosen this hotel so as not to run the risk of anybody seeing me there) and I went straight to the window to look out. Through the gap between the plain but well-starched curtains I saw it was still raining; there was a carriage parked by the stables outside and all the straw was soaking wet. In the room, there wasn't so much as a chair – doubtless they had forgotten to put it back after cleaning the room, for clean it was. In short: a bed, a table, a washstand. But nothing to sit down on except for the bed, which I found most annoying, believe me. Malaspina had begun again to apologise for all these shortcomings, and indeed for the seediness of the whole situation, but really it was my fault, he said, because I had wanted to meet him in a town that was neither my home nor his. "But you live in the countryside!" I said to him, a little irritated, and he looked surprised.

What could we do but sit down on that bed? Standing there looking at each other was just too ridiculous. I must repeat, the room had only three things: a bed, a washstand, a table. And some soap in a little dish. These humble surroundings hardly offered scope for a vista, and yet a vista has remained in my mind. It is the one he described to me: his home, his fields, his horses… and he talked also of marriage, of a wedding that must take place as soon as possible, he having suffered so much during the war, just as he wrote in his letters. But when he said 'get married', I wanted to reply: "Are you mad?" – and I also felt the urge to laugh, as if that meagre single bed were already garlanded with orange blossoms for the wedding night. My sole desire was to get out of there as quickly as I could, but I didn't know how to get past the locked door – he had the key. Among the dark stains on the mirror I could see my pale face, and this too irritated me. The bed had warmed up a little, but he didn't dare touch me. We could have been stuck in this stalemate for heaven knows how long, since neither he nor I was brave enough to admit defeat. Meanwhile the light was fading; the gaps between the curtains were filling with darkness; the scent of the soap floated through the air (it seemed to me like the sweet soul of a little death); and in that penumbra I saw his sad face, his eyes glistening as if on the brink of tears, and I felt I had to make something happen, something that couldn't happen through us just sitting there. So I said: "I hope you understand..."

It didn't mean much, this remark of mine, but a reply or a question from him could perhaps have got us a long way. He settled for drawing me a little closer to him; his lips lingered at the base of my neck (I must remind you that I was fully-dressed – I had taken off only my hat); I felt those lips get hotter, burning me like a fiery seal – and all the while I watched a little vein on his forehead swell and throb. I thought that, if it were cut open, I would see thick, dark blood flow out; perhaps I trembled a little, and perhaps that was why his hands suddenly gripped my hips firmly, found themselves, somehow, on a dangerous path, and would soon have got the better of my stupid irony. I didn't want to shout out, but I defended myself with hostility. My salvation came in the form of two hotel porters who, just at that moment, were dragging something very heavy – most likely a trunk – along the corridor. They were labouring in silence so as not to disturb the guests, and I heard the wood creaking and the men wheezing as they pushed. I, too, struggled, and just then they crashed against the door. The blow made the whole room shake; the windows jangled and the men outside cursed. I threw myself off the bed without a sound, and Malaspina jumped up to block the doorway. But the door hadn't opened at the blow, and the men now were moving on, grumbling – I heard them go down the stairs. When Malaspina turned around I already had my hat on and the veil down.

In acid tones, I told him: "I'm going down to find a carriage; you, meanwhile, will pay the bill." I don't even know what his response was; I don't know if he spent the night at that hotel; as I emerged into the cool rain, my first thought was that he didn't know where I was staying and he wouldn't be able to trace me. The flooded, mud-covered streets came to meet me, holding out their lamplit arms, and behind my fleeing steps they wove a maze in which Malaspina would surely be lost.'

Natalia

***

That evening, the fires in the bedrooms had been lit. Crouching down on the rug, Natalia kicked off her slippers and warmed her feet in front of the hearth. Her stockings, which had been not just damp but soaked through after her wanderings in the rain, had dried out now, so she took them off and left them in a pile by the fire. She had written a long letter to her brother and was satisfied with the day now concluded: her adventures and inventions were so closely and potently entangled in her memory that she could barely distinguish between them.

Silvia came and went between the two rooms, the connecting door remaining open. She tidied up the garments strewn about the room, and in response to her asking why on earth Natalia had written such a long letter to Jacopo when she had only just sent the telegram home that had kept her out for so long, Natalia responded that the telegram was only to confirm she had arrived, and her brother and Nina would undoubtedly be expecting something more.

"So did you write about me, then? About Mamma?" asked Silvia, stopping and looking down at her with curiosity and a hint of severity.

Smiling slyly, Natalia said: "Yes, I told him you've grown ugly as sin – and I don't know how I'm going to bear it!"

"What a stupid little liar you are! I'd really better read it, that letter of yours, since you're obviously hiding something from me – I'm going to have to keep an eye on you…"

Enveloped in a soft white dressing-gown, she sat down next to Natalia after tossing a cushion onto the rug. Natalia, too, was in a dressing-gown: a kimono of smooth yellow silk, which she pushed back a little on her chest to show that, underneath it, she was naked.

"Look, I've got nothing else on," she murmured. "But I'm perfectly fine in front of this lovely fire… Today's been

pretty awful – there were so many people at the post office…"
Quickly, she thrust her hand under Silvia's nose, cutting off
any further questions. "The scent of that orange I peeled
earlier is still on me, can you smell it? I like it."

For a few moments they listened to the deep silence of the
house. "Your mother's asleep," she added, under her breath.

"Asleep, yes." Silvia let out a faint sigh. They thought of
the old woman, who in reality, as they both knew, was not
asleep, but got up every so often to straighten the wicks of the
candles burning before the portraits of the dead boys, to water
the potted plants, to adjust the curtains and make sure they
were properly closed, before dropping off at dawn and then
dozing through almost the entire day.

Silvia was now violently illuminated by the flames from a
newly added log, and every now and then Natalia stole a glance
at her before turning back to the fire, not wanting to look as
if she was spying on her or – as in fact she was – entranced
by her quiet beauty. It seemed to her that the curve of Silvia's
mouth took its shape from the lingering silence, a silence that
did not necessarily signify either foolishness or coldness. In
spite of the bereavements that had brought sorrow into her
home, she had not lost that old habit of lapsing into silence
with a faint smile on her face; yet the possible reasons for what
appeared to be a mysterious, peaceful happiness unsettled
Natalia – because really she knew nothing about Silvia's life.

No, not quite nothing, came the unexpected thought: and this
fiancé of Silvia's, who perhaps had hardly even seen her and
barely touched her at all, began to expand in her imagination
until he had taken on the improbable dimensions of a hulking,
vulgar, violent being – though from Silvia's brief account of
the episode he had emerged as an almost non-existent figure.
Had he held her in his arms, perhaps? Had he pressed those
breasts concealed beneath the white dressing-gown? Had he
written to her from the trenches during the war – ambiguously

worded letters like poor Malaspina had written to her? (She was dreaming, now, in a kind of daze.) She could see him before her, with the wide, blood-red nose of a heavy drinker, the low and menacing brow of a delinquent, hands covered in hair...

The log in the fireplace burst, sending a shower of sparks into the air. Silvia remained silent, beautiful and serene, certainly unaware of how Natalia had saved her from that loathsome creature: the image that had emerged from the flames had already vanished, leaving only a pile of hot ashes. The fire was languishing now, and there was no other light in the room; shadows slid down the walls, slipped out of the paintings, felt their way blindly about the room. She could no longer even see the portrait of her father. (*And how would I be able to see that, fool that I am – the fire is here in Silvia's room; the one in mine has gone out.*) But a heat that did not come from the flames was now scorching her feet, climbing slowly upwards towards her mind.

Of the affair now concluded and condemned to the past – the abandonment of Malaspina – she had said nothing to Silvia, despite her earlier intentions; in fact, she now felt that doing so would be enormously embarrassing. She would be incapable of inventing an outrageous yet convincing ending to the tale, as she had in her letter to Jacopo, and the truth would be painful to recount – a little ridiculous, too. This house, darkened by so many bereavements, the old adulteress, the blind walls, could have made the perfect setting for the story of her and Malaspina. But the quiet, faded nobility of Silvia's existence – her beauty – had compelled her to renounce what now seemed only a mediocre adventure. Silvia's voice and her smiles delicately pricked Natalia's skin, like the tender thorns of a wild rose. The secret of her birth seemed to wrap her entire being in mystery: she sparkled with luminosity within its hold, and perhaps this attraction had played a part in Natalia's rejection of the unfortunate Malaspina. But if now he was wandering the streets with the memory of her, bitter and scornful, coursing through his mind, she felt neither culpability nor remorse. Hadn't she been disappointed, too? Yet this did not prevent her from moving on – tomorrow was a new day, and she realised that already she was setting the scene for the next act. That little white flower at the hem of a skirt trailing on the grass by a well, back in her childhood – could it truly have led her to believe that nothing and no-one had, since then, breached the hem of that skirt? Now, the vision mingled with a desire to somehow bless the mourning that had kept Silvia apart from it all and preserved her in the state in which she now saw her: healthy, chaste and silent.

The log, now almost entirely embers and covered with a fine layer of grey ash, crumbled to pieces with a faint crackle. But although Natalia was fascinated by the silence and stillness, she could not help remembering the hidden depths she had sensed in Silvia when they were both reading the words Jacopo had written so many years ago on the back of a sheet of music. And now the fire languishing in the hearth ignited fiercely within her, calling to her like the edge of a precipice: she was not so astonished, then, to find her hands, quicker than her conscious will, slipping under the lapels of the white dressing-gown – and her hands must have been really quite cold, since the warmth of those soft breasts felt so gratifying to her touch. She found them simultaneously firm and yielding. Briefly, she thought: *If I had to tell someone about this, where would I find the words?* But she could not see that Silvia's eyes were veiled, because the glow from the flames scarcely illuminated the hem of the dressing-gown, and she could not have explained how it was that, kissing her, she managed to push her down slowly onto the rug.

So she was mature, now, the silent virgin: like a ripe fruit she had fallen, coming to rest in Natalia's arms.

I didn't mean for this to happen at all, she thought in confusion, and nonetheless she used Silvia's body as confusedly she had dreamed of doing; but it was the other woman alone who experienced unanticipated pleasure, and from that body, irrigated by bliss, gratitude rose up like a wave. Natalia was conscious of being the cause of this, and maybe she hadn't intended to go so far. Silvia no longer shuddered in response to her caresses, but perhaps they had touched the secret of that enduring stillness; meanwhile Natalia's unexpectedly skilful hands had lost the aroma of the innocent fruit, and her warm feet could feel the andirons cooling in the fireplace.

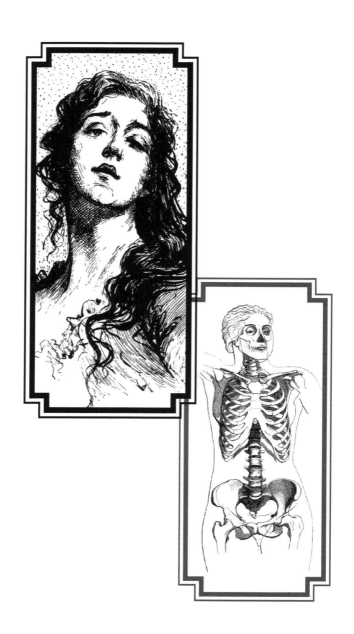

What makes this century worse?

Anna Akhmatova

translated by Olga Livshin

What makes this century worse than any before it?
Maybe that, for once, it noticed the world's sorrows,
black smoke rising from them. And it touched the heart
of this most painful ulcer. Still, it could not heal this.

The earthly sun's still shining in the west;
our cities' roofs, still blazing in its rays…
Here a white creature chalks the houses of the dead
with crosses, calls the ravens, and the ravens fly.

Broken[1]

by Nataliya Kobrynska

translated by Hanna Leliv

1.

No young man in the village was more handsome than Maksymykha's son, Lukyn. He was as tall and slender as the elm tree that stood by the river next to his widowed mother's house.

The girls would feast their eyes on him every Sunday: he would usually be dressed in a white shirt with an embroidered collar cinched with a wide leather belt. He'd drape a new jacket over his shoulder, and put on a hat with peacock feathers. At dances, in the church, or at work – he was the best-looking of all the young men, unrivaled among his peers. A face bright like the sun, sky-blue eyes, lush black curls, and a neat moustache.

Even his mother would glance at him and smile. "Who does he take after?" she wondered. Her daughters were pretty, too, but they looked more like her and her husband. However, they were no match for Lukyn! He did seem to take after one person in the family, though, specifically, her elder sister Frasyna – she was so beautiful back in her day, there were none who could rival her. Maksymykha might've thought it odd, if she hadn't given birth to him herself. Her sister had the same blue eyes, the same hair, and was almost as tall.

Her daughters were older than Lukyn, and she had married them off to rich farmers – but she could only pray for an

---

1 published in 1918 under the title 'The Cripple'.

equally good match for her son.

He might easily find himself an even better catch, marry the richest girl in the village – it was just that she thought none of them were good enough. "I should ask around, find him a wife from another village," Maksymykha often thought to herself.

Her household was not very affluent, though. She was nowhere near as well-off as her sister, Frasyna, who had married a prosperous man and was rolling in money. Frasyna had never wanted to marry the man and complained about her parents forcing her, but she became one of the richest women in the village, and now she had many things to boast about. Maksymykha may not have been as wealthy as her sister, but she had a good enough income to welcome a daughter-in-law into her home.

Her house couldn't have been better – with a shingled roof! And she had her own field, some horses, and some cattle. If Lukyn were to marry a girl with a good dowry – then Frasyna's wealth would pale in comparison to hers. Lukyn was exempt from the draft, so his mother started looking for a wife for him as soon as he finished school.

She'd often talk with the other women in the street or outside the church and complain about her asthma, and all the hard work around the house that made it impossible to take care of herself properly.

"Don't you get any help? Well, at least you have a young man in the house," the women would tell her. "Don't provoke the Lord! Everyone dreams of such a son."

"But he doesn't do women's work."

"Of course not. Men know their place, and women know theirs. A daughter-in-law would do you good."

That was exactly what Maksymykha had been hoping they'd say.

"I pray to God for a decent and hard-working one," she

would reply slowly.

"Don't worry. I'm sure he'll find himself a fine young lady. He's such a nice boy. He'll know it when he sees it. They'll be queuing up to marry him, don't you worry."

Maksymykha would come home and recount these conversations to her son. He'd only smile, pleased with himself and what people said about him. But then again, why would they say otherwise? He knew all too well that there was no girl who wouldn't want him. Any of them would marry him should he care to propose. He'd consider them in his mind, one by one, as if counting ducks filing along a riverbed.

Many of the local girls were pretty; many were rich and hailed from good families too. Marunia had intense black eyes. Sofiya was tall and blonde. Iryna's face was pretty as an apple. Erstyna had a fine long braid. But none could compete with Malanka, a girl who served in his aunt Frasyna's household.

Lukyn didn't know why Malanka seemed like the prettiest girl he'd ever seen. It all started one day when he took his horses to the river, and she was doing laundry at the rock. He tiptoed up to her quietly and put his hands around her waist to scare her.

And she did get scared. She jumped to her feet, angrily, nostrils flaring. They stood like that for a while facing one another.

"Are you insane?" Malanka said, breaking the silence.

"I just wanted to scare you."

"Go to hell!" she snapped and, turning away, went home.

Lukyn felt like he'd only just met her – for the first time he saw how tall and pretty she was and what kind of passion she had in her eyes. He couldn't stop thinking about her ever since that day. To see her more often, he began visiting his aunt, finding new excuses each time: he'd say he needed a piece of rope; or his sharpener got lost somewhere, and he had to borrow a new one; it was high time to cut the grass for the cow. He didn't really need an excuse to visit his aunt, of course, but he looked for one, anyway, pretending that he wasn't going there just to see Malanka.

His aunt loved him. Whenever he dropped by, they'd chat, and if he said he needed to hurry back home, she'd say, laughing, that work was not like a hare, it wasn't going anywhere. But no matter how happy his aunt was to see him, Lukyn often became a little irritable when they had their chats. He was much happier to find Malanka home alone, although that rarely happened.

His uncle, a strict man, cared for his wife and rarely sent her out to work in the field. It was Malanka who was supposed to do all the hard work on the property. Lukyn also valued hard work and admired Malanka for her readiness to get stuck into the worst chores, but it annoyed him that his uncle burdened her with so much.

"Whoever marries her won't regret it," he thought, watching her pitch the hay onto the stack with her pitchfork. Her slender body leaned so nicely, and her face had turned red with the exertion. "Perhaps it could be me?" This thought suddenly dropped out of the clear blue sky, then disappeared. Yet, he couldn't forget the idea.

At first, Malanka treated his advances as a young man's trickery and kept her distance. But when he promised he'd marry her, she gave herself to him, body and soul.

Maksymykha was furious and cried. This was not the daughter-in-law she'd hoped for. She felt ashamed that her son was about to marry her sister's servant. But Frasyna took the side of the young couple. She had no children of her own and Malanka was like a daughter to her.

"She's a decent, hard-working girl," she said, trying to console her sister. "Let him marry her if he loves her."

Frasyna breathed a sigh of relief. She thought of her own

youth and her first love. Maksymykha was well aware that her sister had been fond of their neighbours' son, but their parents would not hear of their union. He'd owned only half of the house and a small part of the vegetable patch. And he'd also had to save for a dowry for his sister.

After that, their parents didn't have to wait too long for another suitor: Frasyna soon met an eligible bachelor who owned a house and a good deal of land. Frasyna had taken on the running of the household by herself because their parents had died a short while later. Although the couple were very well-off, one day Frasyna burst into tears in front of her sister and said she'd give up her entire fortune for just one kiss from the neighbours' son.

Maksymykha glanced at her sister out of the corner of an eye, remembering this. Frasyna noticed and smiled ruefully.

"I may not be young anymore, it's true, but my heart tells me: Don't separate them, sister, or they'll cry their hearts out and curl up and die because of you."

Maksymykha wasn't happy about the union, but she knew there was nothing she could do to make Lukyn turn his back on Malanka. He barely listened to his mother, and was glad that Frasyna had taken their side.

***

The wedding could not be delayed, so after Saint Peter's Day, Lukyn brought his young wife home. Maksymykha didn't take much to her daughter-in-law.

"A daughter-in-law full of pride, and with 'dowry' in her belly — that's who he's brought me," she said to herself angrily. She said nothing in front of other people though — why make them laugh? But the atmosphere at home was tense.

Malanka could not please her mother-in-law, no matter how hard she tried. It eventually came to the point of them arguing and cursing each other – seldom at first, but then more and more often. The mother complained to her son, and the wife to her husband, and sometimes, all hell broke loose, and Lukyn would just leave the house.

But Maksymykha wasn't destined to live with her daughter-in-law for long. She had trouble with asthma. One day she caught a bad cold and was gone in less than two weeks. She went to her final resting place so quietly that no-one even noticed. It just so happened that when she died everyone was outside.

Lukyn grieved for his mother but most of all, he regretted that she passed away so quietly, as if she'd never lived in the first place. She hadn't said a single word before her death. It would have been easier for him if she had reproached him instead of just passing away in silence.

He stared at her a long while as she lay in her coffin on the bench, and he would have given almost anything to hear just one word from her. But she kept silent; her lips were pressed tight, as if sealed by a curse. Or maybe it was all those times he'd shouted at her, "Be quiet!" in anger. This was his punishment now, and he'd have to answer to God for it.

But no matter how much he blamed himself, the house was as silent as if touched by angels. It was transformed into a house of peace and quiet, which only saw discord when they scolded their children for misbehaving. And they had quite a few of them. God blessed them every year with another.

***

It was already getting dark but Malanka was still bent over the potato patch. The baby was crying in its crib, and it was time to cook dinner, as Lukyn was due back from town soon. But she wanted to finish digging over the potato patch. She'd just gone inside and barely had enough time to start a fire in the stove when Lukyn returned.

"Aren't you making dinner yet?" he asked gently, sitting down on the bench.

"I'm running late because I had to finish turning over the potato patch. It was all overgrown with weeds. Imagine if I hadn't done it on time?"

"It's alright. But try to hurry, will you? I'm hungry."

"It'll just be a few minutes. There's some borscht left over from lunch. Let me just put the *kulesha*[2] on the stove. You were in town for a long time. I thought you'd have been home earlier. If you'd have been here to help, we could have gotten it all done faster."

"I met some people, and we started talking about things."

"Oh. What kind of things?"

"The newspapers say war is coming."

"Oh, come on. I'm more interested in growing potatoes. People have been talking about war since I was a child."

"Well, there you go. They must have brought it here with all that talking."

"It took them a while."

"It's not a joke. They say the war is really coming now. But either way, I'm exempt from the draft, so they won't be able to take me."

A short while later, they did start drafting young men into the army, conscripting almost half of the village. The rest were eventually called up, too. Hearts were heavy with pity for all the young men who were drafted, especially now that everyone was talking seriously about the war.

Mothers cried for their sons, sisters for their brothers, girls for their lovers. Fathers grieved, unaware that soon they'd have to follow their sons themselves.

War had finally broken out, after all.

---

2   Kulesha is a Hutsul corn porridge, cooked in water and served with cheese, butter, and sour cream.

Many people grew anxious, but some tried not to think about it at all. There was simply no time for much reflection. In the village, there had never been enough time for all the work, let alone dwelling on things like war.

All is as God wills. One must eat to live. And if one wants to eat, one must work.

Work engenders more work. Some people took the easy route, but Lukyn and Malanka never shied away from a bit of hard work, and it paid off. Their household income grew. They built the new cattle pens and the hay sheds that his mother hadn't been able to build before she died. They started building a barn, and the frame was already up. All that was left was to cover the roof with straw – and to thresh some wheat for that purpose.

Unfortunately, Lukyn did not realise that he would never get a chance to harvest the wheat. The war that he had barely thought about was creeping closer and closer. Out in the fields, people often felt the earth shake from the explosions in the distance. But they still went on believing that the war would never reach them. They were only anxious about the increasing number of men being called up. Rumours began to spread that even those exempt from military service would be drafted. Malanka was horrified to hear this, but Lukyn still refused to believe it. "People say all kinds of things," he said. "But that doesn't always mean things will happen as they say."

One day when he had just harnessed his horses to the cart and was about to leave for the field, the local magistrate came to their house.

"What does he want?" Malanka asked as she stood outside and saw him coming.

"I'm being called up."

Malanka covered her face with her hands and burst into tears."Don't worry. I'm exempt. I'll just have to go and put in an appearance."

But Lukyn was drafted after all, and was told to get ready to leave in two weeks. At first, he felt as if nothing had really happened, but then things seemed to have turned upside down. Everything felt strange, like nothing belonged to him any more. He looked at his house but it seemed like a different house, and his wife was no longer his wife, and his children – no longer his. One of them would run out of the house and grab the hem of his coat, but he felt like it was someone else's child. And his wife began crying all the time, ripping his heart apart.

He had another week at home. Every day, every night, brought him closer to the terrible date, and he could not delay it, could not put it off. Days alternated with nights. Only two days were left, but he no longer cared – he might as well leave now, he felt so sickened by the prospect. What difference did a couple of days make?

The last two days soon passed, too.

On the day he was supposed to leave, he felt numb. He sat on the tree stump next to the shed and stared at the vegetable patch. Large red poppies were coming into bloom, smaller ones poking up their blond heads among them. He became fixated on the flowers. The large, red ones with their black centres and the other, small blond-headed ones, all blooming there regardless –

Suddenly, everything changed. "Oh please God, no!" a voice deep inside him cried out, and he clenched his fists tightly. "What right do they have to tear me away from my own land, my home, my loved ones?!"

His chest heaved in violent revolt. His arms dropped, his head hung low, and he wept like a baby.

He heard someone weeping at his side. It was Malanka. She was sitting down on a pile of logs in the backyard, but he did not notice that she was there. He turned around.

"Why are you crying like that?" he said angrily and stood up. He went to the shed and took the cattle out to the water.

Broken

It was too early to leave but he could not bear to stay home any longer and see his wife, his children, and the red poppies that now made him nauseous.

When it was time to leave, he glanced at the religious icons on the wall, looked around the house, and stared at the unfinished barn. Malanka followed him with their children in tow, crying so hard, it was as if she was mourning a dead man. But a dead man's soul would be standing before God in judgment, and such a man would no longer care about his body – whereas Lukyn could almost picture his death, his funeral. The children were wailing in unison when he pulled his sobbing wife towards him for one last hug.

Not long afterwards, the men were herded onto a train like cattle. Some men were crammed inside the traincar, others were told to climb onto the roof. The confusion, the screaming, the crying – it all merged together in one terrible commotion. Lukyn wanted to see his wife and children one last time but could not push through the men to get to the door. And then the train whistled and jerked, dragging them, as if tethered on a leash, into the unknown...

Malanka returned home, feeling like a widow. She sat on the bench and wrung her hands. Only her children, who were growing hungry, shook her from her desolation.

Three weeks later, she received a letter from Lukyn. He asked about her health and how she was doing, said that he was doing drills, and mentioned the names of their fellow villagers who were also there beside him. A second letter arrived shortly afterwards in which Lukyn asked her to send him a kreutzer because his money was running out.

There were rumours that the wives would get compensated if their husbands were drafted into the army, but then something completely unexpected occurred.

The terrifying sound of shooting that had been echoing around the village came to an abrupt end. Some villagers thought the war was over, when all of a sudden, yells were heard: "Soldiers! Soldiers are coming!"

The soldiers arrived on horses lugging enormous cannons. They were exhausted and filthy, black with soot – and starving, may God have mercy on them all.

They asked for bread. People brought them everything they had but there wasn't much. Some hoped to see their relatives among the troops but no-one from their village was in that motley crowd. Our troops had been sent to fight with the French, they said.

For three days and three nights the troops traipsed like ghosts about the village. Malanka went around staring at each of them till her eyes hurt, trying to see if Lukyn was among them. She didn't sleep. She didn't eat. She gave some leftovers to her children and took the rest of the food out to the soldiers. Word spread that the enemy would be arriving soon.

"Tomorrow! The Russians are coming tomorrow!"

People went numb with fear.

***

A day passed, then a second and a third, but all was quiet. People almost forgot about the war when they suddenly heard the screams: "The enemy! The enemy's here!" Some villagers ran in whatever direction the road would take them. Others were sorry to leave their work behind, but fled just the same.

A few were at a complete loss, frozen in fear. The enemy troops streamed in like water – and this continued for the whole year. The villagers heard no more news about their own troops or the army.

***

Broken

The Russians were everywhere. The villagers felt as if they'd fallen into a bottomless pit. No news, no rumours, no-one coming to the rescue. No-one knew what might happen. Their crops were destroyed, and the enemy seized their harvests.

Malanka lived all alone with her small children. No sooner would she lie down to get some rest than she'd hear soldiers pounding on the front door. A dozen men would barge in – and she could do little to stop them.

If only they didn't rob her. Some of them spoke a language she could more or less understand and even shared their food with her, but others just came and scraped the pots clean.

On one occasion, they came and took all the hay from the shed. She cried and begged them to leave it but they just laughed at her. People were frightened that they would take the cows, too. They might leave you be if you had only one, but if you had two, they'd seize one, to be sure. Malanka had two cows, one of them a heifer. People told her to sell them – even selling them cheap was better than having them taken by the enemy.

One day – she'd gone over to her neighbour's – her children started screaming. She hurried back only to see enemy soldiers pulling the heifer out of the pen. Neither her crying, nor her screams or curses were any use, they took the cow as if it was rightfully theirs. She sobbed over that heifer day and night. The neighbours tried to bring her to her senses. Aunt Frasyna berated her, saying, "Did you want to lay down your life for a cow and make your children orphans?" But there was no consoling her. "If Lukyn had been here, he wouldn't have let this happen! He would've protected the cow!" she kept saying.

"Oh, Lukyn, my darling, why don't you send us a word about yourself? Are you no longer alive? Is a raven picking over your bones?" she lamented, weeping.

People hoped that their soldiers would return and drive the enemy out but as the months passed and no news arrived, they lost any such hope. Some women forgot that their husbands were away fighting, shedding their blood, and shamefully, they went with the soldiers – heaven forbid.

"May the Lord punish them!" Malanka often cursed.

"Look at her. She'd better keep her nose out of it! Acting like she's a saint!" one woman who took it personally snapped.

And then something surprising happened. The enemy troops seemed to be thinning out. People couldn't believe their eyes. But then they saw the enemy soldiers pile their belongings onto their carts, lead their horses away, and run around the houses taking everything, even the bleach to do their laundry. Someone said: "Your troops are coming back. They'll be here in a week."

More and more enemy soldiers came down from their positions atop the hills. They pulled up their cannons and dug a trench across the entire length of the village. People would stop working in the fields, and watch them dig, while the enemy troops mocked, "What are you afraid of?" they asked. "Our cannons will be firing out there beyond the village. If anyone is going to be shooting at you, it will be your own troops!"

"They may be shooting at you, but we might get hit too. Bullets don't choose who they hit. Soldier or civilian, they don't care," people said.

Late one afternoon, there came a loud roar and whistling noises, a hellish whizzing, then a hail of iron. Black smoke arose in dense plumes.

Everyone ran for their lives. People grabbed whatever they could and left – some on foot, others on horse carts. They ran to the woods or neighbouring villages as fast as they could.

Malanka barely had time to collect her children. Her aunt was riding on a horse cart just ahead of her. Malanka threw the things she grabbed on her way out of the house onto the cart and walked behind it with her children. When the firing was heavy, people dropped to the ground and lay still until it quietened down. Then they stood up and hurried away.

There was a long whistling sound in the air, followed by a crackling and a roar so massive it shook the earth. A column of smoke swirled up. Malanka hugged her children and hunkered down. One child slipped and fell. She wanted to grab hold of her but she fell into a ditch. She groped around to gather her children in the darkness. Three of them were still close to her, while the other two were crying a short distance away. There were no horse carts and no people nearby. Finally, she found the two children, and they all sat huddled together for warmth. It began raining, and water streamed into the ditch. The children cried for food. She remembered a sack of bread she'd put onto Aunt Frasyna's cart – perhaps it was still there. What should she do in her misery? The older children were easier to handle, but the younger ones? Oh God. What did a child know? Eating and sleeping, that was it. It was pitch dark outside.

Suddenly, she saw a flash of light that looked like a lamp in a house. She peered into the darkness and saw that it was really a house with the light on.

"This way," she said to her children. She took the youngest one in her arms, and the others followed behind. They started walking toward the house – across the water, the rocks, and the logs. The door was open, and a fire was burning in the stove. Several soldiers were drying their wet uniforms. A few pots and bowls sat on the shelf, upside down, and on the floor, there was a pillow and someone's tattered dress. The family that lived in that house had clearly had no time to pack before leaving.

Malanka stood in the doorway, petrified.

"What do you want?" one of the soldiers asked.

"Have you got any bread? A crust maybe? My children are hungry, but I don't have anything to feed them."

"We don't have any food, either. All this family left was

empty pots," another soldier said with a bitter smile.

She was about to leave when the first one picked up a bag and, rummaging through it, took out a piece of dried bread.

"You are one lucky woman," he said as he handed it to her.

The children reached out for the bread but it was so hard she couldn't break it. She looked around the house to see if there was water but she didn't see any.

"That's alright," she thought. "I'll find some water somewhere else to soak it in." She said thank you and left. She sat on the ground under a large withered tree not far from the house and hugged her children. This was how they spent the rest of the night.

When dawn broke, Malanka looked around, searching for a path toward the nearest village. Going back was out of the question – she had to catch up with the group she'd been with. But which way did they go? There was no point in guessing; she just had to go wherever the path took her.

So she walked on. They reached another village. People had abandoned this one, too. The houses stood empty, their doors and gates agape. An old woman was sitting by her wicker fence, clutching at her chest in a coughing fit. She said everyone had fled, and they were probably gathered outside the next village down the road. At least, that was what another woman who'd returned to look for her missing child had told her.

Malanka looked at her own children, counting to make sure everyone was there. She asked the old woman which way the villagers had fled and headed in that direction.

Past the third village, she saw a large pasture. It was so crowded with people you could barely move. Asking around, she learned where her fellow villagers were gathered. Malanka's legs were aching by the time she finally found Aunt Frasyna huddled in an open field next to her cart with her husband and servant, as if a thunderstorm was about to hit. Fortunately,

Frasyna still had some food left from the bundle she managed to take upon leaving her house, so Malanka fed her children.

They survived three days in these conditions. Some people left to find out what was happening with the army. One person even ventured as far as their village. The braver ones claimed it was safe to return home – the troops had marched in the opposite direction. The only things scattered along the roads now were dead bodies, and the houses on one side of the village had been destroyed or burned out.

On their way back, people raked over the remains of dead bodies with pitchforks, as they'd already decomposed. The stench was so heavy one could barely breathe. The houses on the hill where Malanka once lived stood more or less intact. There were a few horse carts by her house, left by soldiers who had been there rummaging around. Inside, she found only a broken bed and the bench. The table was missing, and pottery shards were scattered on the floor along with some loose straw. A wooden bucket lay on the vegetable patch, broken.

Malanka went to the patch but as she bent over to pick up the bucket, something banged above her head, and that bang was the last thing she heard.

People saw what looked like a burning letter drop down out of an airplane. Then came a loud roar, and everything was engulfed in smoke. Many people were wounded. A few soldiers were killed, and Malanka was hit directly and blown to pieces. People struggled to gather her remains. There was hardly anything left to put in the coffin. They hammered together a wooden box, small as a child's, and buried her without a service or the tolling of bells. There was no priest to put the final nail in the coffin.

2.

Poor Lukyn struggled to come to terms with his fate after he'd left his house, his wife, and children, and set off down the road to war. He was not the only one. They pushed them on like a flock of sheep – first, they joined one group, then another one. They trudged ahead blindly, like a herd of cattle.

Lukyn shuffled along like a dead man. He did what the others did – woke up, walked, ate, went to sleep – but he felt as if someone else was doing it. He found it strange to hear people talking, laughing, joking.

Days passed by. Others complained about the food or bad sleep but he didn't care about these things. His thoughts were elsewhere – with everything he'd left behind, his house and the farm, his wife and children.

They did not keep the troops in the same place for long – they took them farther away from the village for the drills. Lukyn was obedient and did whatever they told him to do. Still, he did not escape the occasional reprimand and punishment. At first, he thought they picked on him for no reason. But later, he realised he didn't always hear what they were saying to him.

***

Still, these things were nothing compared to the horror they were to face on the front line. No-one knew when it was supposed to happen but everyone was bracing for it, terrified. The drills would have been tolerable but for the anticipation. Everything was easier to tolerate if you weren't alone. Lukyn did not like his fellow soldiers at first but got used to them slowly. They all had the same destiny – and the same grief and sorrow.

One morning, they sat about waiting, but then in the afternoon, they were ordered to pack up and leave. In the evening, they arrived at the railway station. It was drizzling, so the men sitting on top of the train cars fared the worst. Inside, it was so crowded that one could hardly turn around. Lukyn, his back pressed to the wall, was staring out through the drizzle and thinking about his family.

A few of his fellows sang folk songs, *kolomyikas.*[3] Were they truly happy? Or were they only trying to cheer themselves up? He didn't care. They sang on and on without stopping. Someone broke into a song about an eagle and a gray falcon. "Oh, eagle, have you been to my homeland?" The words burst out of Lukyn's chest, and he found himself joining in. But even after everyone else had fallen silent, he kept on singing, asking the eagle again and again if it had been to his homeland.

He had no clue, either, how long they had been traveling for. He'd lost track of time a while ago – sometimes, he did not know what day it was. It did not matter if it was a Friday or a Sunday when you served in the army, since you followed the same routines every day.

Day gave way to night a few times, and then it was day again and night again, and they finally stopped in an open field. It was noon when they were ordered to get off the train. "Is this it?" they wondered. The question sent a chill down their spines despite the fact that it was scorching hot, and their foreheads were dripping with sweat.

***

They had barely finished digging their trenches when the enemy cannons roared. They returned fire – the rumble, the banging, the commotion was so loud, it was as if the whole world was coming to an end.

Bullets went flying, and the cannons roared back as they dug their wheels into the muddy ground. The soil was sent up

---

3 A fast-paced folk song that originated in Kolomyia, in the Hutsul region of eastern Halychyna.

into the air as bushes and trees were uprooted. The sky grew darker with smoke, lit up with fiery flashes. People were falling like sheaves of straw. Terrifying screams could be heard along with the roar of the cannons and the swoosh of bullets. One thought kept flashing through Lukyn's mind: "Death! Death! Death is here, now!"

Suddenly, a thought took him away from it all, and he saw Malanka standing before him. How was she? Did she know that...? But he did not get to finish this question. He felt something plunge into his shoulder, and he dropped, limp, to the ground.

He lay still for a long time. Was he no longer alive? Death's sickle had come to reap him, too! It had sent him a bullet – or maybe a whole handful of bullets – and he would have to part with his life, just like everyone else.

After a while, he felt an arm next to him, the fingers spread out. Whose arm was it? Why did it clench and unclench its fingers? Perhaps it was his arm? Right. Yes. It *was* his arm. He unclenched his fingers one more time and clenched them again. Then he sat, propping himself up on an elbow. Was he alive? Nothing badly hurt. Only his cap was missing, and his knapsack had blown away.

He heaved a deep sigh of relief, feeling a bit stronger. Hope gave him the energy to look around. The battle was over. But his troubles were not. The army had to spend the winter in the trenches among snowdrifts. When the snow melted, they often had to trudge knee-deep in water, and if there was frost, they'd freeze to the ground overnight and would have to tear their coats off in the morning. And there was so much work, heaven forbid. Digging trenches, lugging firewood from the forest – there was never a moment's rest.

Only letters from home, which hadn't arrived for a while now, helped him cope with the misery. The letters were full of gloom, but at least he knew what was happening. Malanka didn't just write about herself and the children but also about things going on in the village. He no longer cared about that stuff, though – all he wanted to hear about was Malanka. He would've given up half of his life just to see her again.

***

With the arrival of Spring, rumours spread among the soldiers that the enemy was advancing again. Everyone was hoping the war would end soon, but now it seemed to be flaring up anew. They were ready, but the enemy struck just when they least expected. The shooting began in the morning and went on for several days, almost without stopping. The destructive fire left the trenches and barricades on the frontline in ruins.

There was hardly anything left of the trenches. Everything and everyone was in total chaos. Devilish roars, screaming, exploding grenades, the commotion of people, horses, cannons, and military machinery – it all swirled in a hellish dance. Soldiers were falling in droves, the horses too, kicking their legs up in the air. Lukyn saw a man next to him sway and drop to the ground, hit by a deadly bullet. A few steps away, a soldier was finishing off another man with the barrel of his rifle. It was the last thing he saw, as the world darkened suddenly, and he felt himself stifled by a red fog.

***

When he came to his senses, he found himself on a bed surrounded by strangers. His eyes fell on a woman wearing a bonnet. "Malanka!" A voice inside him called out. However, excruciating pain cut off his thoughts. He had no idea how long he had been lying there, slipping in and out of consciousness, but whenever he came round, he'd see that woman in the white bonnet. When he finally was able to focus his eyes more clearly, he knew it was not Malanka.

The nurse lifted his head carefully and wrapped it with white rags. She did the same thing with his leg. Once he got to the point of being able to stay awake longer, he would move his wounded leg and feel not only pain but some other, bitter sensation.

One day, he realised where that feeling had come from, and a terrifying pain gripped his heart: his leg had been amputated below the knee. His heart bled without stopping. What would he do without a leg? How would he live? How would he earn his daily bread?

He grabbed his bandaged head, tore the rags away, and threw them on the ground. Blood began gushing forth, but he did not care. He'd rather have been dead than live as a cripple! And again, he had no idea what happened next. When he came to, his mind felt as if he'd plunged into a dark abyss that he could not and would not leave.

But that was not the end of his misery. He could hardly get used to the thought that he'd have to live without one leg when another revelation came to him, wounding his pride even more.

The nurse had left a box next to his bed, its lid shining like a mirror. He looked into that shining lid and went numb. One eye was smaller than the other, his lip was cut, and his whole face was distorted. His reflection terrified him even more than the fact of losing a leg.

He remembered himself as a young, sprightly lad. All the girls in his village had fancied him. Malanka had once been enchanted by his handsome looks. What if it terrified her to see him like this, now? Wouldn't she be disgusted by him? He was so ugly – and without a leg, as well. Wouldn't it have been better if he'd died, if a bullet had pierced his heart, putting an end to it all?

Broken

Part of him wished he was dead but another part still yearned for life. What did one's looks matter if one lost one's life? Whatever he looked like, at least he was still alive. He was only worried about what she, Malanka, would think. People would probably shudder at the sight of him but he did not care about them. He cared only for her, for Malanka!

***

After a while, he was transferred to another hospital. They fixed him an artificial limb and gave him a document exempting him from further military service. He was free. He could return home. But why wasn't his heart rejoicing, as he was so eager to get back to his nest that he wished he could fly there?

When the time came to go home on the train, he felt an odd thrill. Oh God! Once he had almost lost hope that he would ever return, that he would even survive. But as he approached his village, he began to despair again. How would he face Malanka? What would she say? Would he be able to work around the house like he used to?

***

There was his village. There stood his house. For the first time in his life, he was nervous about going home. As he came closer, a fear enveloped him, his heart was pounding. But then he was devastated as he saw the state of his home. The windows had been knocked out, the door was propped up and padlocked, the roof stripped bare, the wicker fences torn down, the shed was damaged.

He went up to the window. The house was empty – not a living soul inside. He sank down on the bench and wept bitterly. What had happened? Where were his wife and children?

He lost track of time, sitting there – all he felt was a terrible aching inside his chest.

"Lukyn? Is that you?" a woman asked him.

Lukyn stared at her with a vacant look.

"Don't you recognise me?"

"Ivanykha?" he said quietly, as if to himself.

"I'm your neighbour. Oh God, what happened to you? I was just trying to see if it was really you…"

"Where's my wife? My children?" he blurted, the words tasted like ash in his mouth.

"Don't you know?"

"Where's my wife? My children?" he yelled.

"Don't you know…? Malanka was killed."

"Malanka! Where? When? How?"

"There was a big battle here. At first, she ran away with the children, but no-one can outrun fate. It'll find you no matter where you are. And it found her in front of your house, right where I'm standing now. A ball from the flying ship fell on her and crashed her. Aunt Frasyna took the children in – what would they do here all alone?"

Lukyn gasped, "Oh God!" and he wept again like a child. Someone must have seen him, because he was still sitting on the bench, devastated, when Aunt Frasyna came with his children.

She clasped her hands when she saw him. The children did not recognise him, at first. The youngest one did not even know he was their father. Aunt Frasyna wanted to give the children back to him but she realised that he was not in any fit state to care for them.

Lukyn was half-dead.

***

Broken

"You have no idea how hard it's been to try and bring him back to his senses," Aunt Frasyna told the other women outside the church. "He misses her, and he's still grieving so much I don't know what to do. Oh Lord! I even lied to him and said she slept around with some Russians and that she didn't really care about him – I just wanted to make it easier for him, so he wouldn't grieve as much. But he wailed so loud the whole valley could hear his cries …"

On hearing those words, Lukyn had felt as if a horse had knocked him to the ground; his chest had tightened, his heart had been pierced anew. A cripple! A cripple! So ugly. Without a leg.

But now, what was even worse – was his broken, bloody heart…

Sunset

Antonia Pozzi

translated by Sonia di Placido

Black threads of poplars
black threads of clouds
over the red sky —
this is the first grass
freed from snow
transparent
one thinks of Spring
and watches
if at a turn
arise primroses —

But the ice greys the pathways
the fog induces sleep in the troughs
the slow pallor devastates
the colours of the sky.
Night falls
not one flower is born
it's Winter — O Soul —
it's Winter.

Once upon a Time[1]

by Ling Shuhua

Translated by Leilei Chen 莫譯

After school, the sunset obligingly tinged the windows of C University's East Building with orange gold. Up in the mezzanine, three or four girls dressed in light blue and lilac checks or stripes were passing by, chatting and laughing. Yunluo was tidying up in her bedroom when someone suddenly shouted from the yard: "Juliet, Juliet, Romeo is here!" A chain of giggles followed.

The University was putting up *Romeo and Juliet* to celebrate its tenth anniversary. Yunluo was selected to play Juliet. Yingman, who played Romeo, was a grade above and always joked around. A happy, tall northerner in her twenties. Yunluo didn't talk to Yingman much, even hated her since she made fun of Yunluo in front of the class during rehearsals, which was so embarrassing. Yet strangely, every time she heard Yingman call her Juliet, Yunluo felt her heart skip, and not out of anger.

"Shoot," Yunluo said to herself, pretending not to hear the call. "Rehearsal again."

The three or four girls upstairs in the mezzanine burst out laughing again. Yingman shouted at the top of her lungs: "Juliet, hurry up! Aren't you worried about driving Romeo crazy?"

Yunluo felt annoyed and could ignore her no more. She threw the washed handkerchief aside, stuck her head out

---

1 1926 short story

from behind the door and said, "Rehearsing that damn play again? I'm coming. I haven't finished revising for tomorrow's exam yet..."

Yunluo couldn't resist the urge and went downstairs reluctantly, pouting.

After they finished the last rehearsal that night, Yingman accompanied Yunluo back to her dorm. Sitting under the light, she watched Yunluo let down her hair, making it into a loose braid, and putting on a western style nightgown with laces across the bosom and around the sleeves. Perhaps out of fatigue from the show, Yunluo's cheeks were a pale shade of red, running all the way to her drooping eyelids. She was too tired to open her pretty eyes any wider even if she had wanted to; she looked gentler somehow and lovelier.

"Huff, I'm exhausted!" Yunluo patted her back gently as she lay down on the bed.

"Mind me doing that for you, Juliet?" said Yingman, smiling and moving closer, looking at Yunluo's pale skin and delicate chest under her unbuttoned collar, and down below the soft, rising curve of her breasts. Her little bow-shaped mouth was more charming, opening slightly, curving at the corners and adding slight dimples to her cheeks. This made her even more adorable than before when she was about to kiss Romeo in the rehearsal. Fragrant smells from either her body, hair, or makeup wafted from behind the bed curtain, sweet and intoxicating.

Yingman suddenly lay down on the bed and put her arm around Yunluo's neck and said, "I can't hold off. What's so sweet? Let me smell it!"

"Don't annoy me again! Let go!" Yunluo smiled, pushed her away gently.

"I can't let go. Or, I'll die!" Yingman hugged her tightly regardless.

Meiling, a roommate, pushed the door open and laughed when seeing them right there: "Don't die yet, Romeo. I give you permission to take our Juliet. Big Sister Zhu, do you agree?"

Big Sister Zhu, reading in bed under a blanket, also laughed: "I have to, don't I? Go to bed, Meiling. Don't make a nuisance of yourself being the third wheel!"

As they were laughing, Yingman buried her face in Yunluo's chest, inhaling her scent. No-one knew if Yunluo was too tired to resist, or if she liked her chest being covered by something warm and soft; she stopped shouting and murmured, smiling: "You're choking me to death!"

It wasn't until later when Madam Zhou, the dorm supervisor, came in to check the room that Yingman got up reluctantly and left for her dorm at the back campus.

***

It was raining hard the following night after they finished the show. Yunluo asked that Yingman come back to her room for a while because of the rain. Holding a small umbrella and each other's waist, they hopped into Yunluo's room. Meiling greeted them, laughing: "Aha, here come Romeo and Juliet as a couple! I've just made some tea. Come and have some, you love birds." She looked at Yunluo's face for a minute, then suddenly threw herself onto the bed, giggling.

"What's so funny, little monkey?" Yingman couldn't help laughing, too.

"You chuckled a lot backstage earlier. Did we do anything wrong?" asked Yunluo.

"That was so funny, this evening – " Meiling burst out laughing again.

"You should change your nickname to Laughing Monkey

starting tomorrow! Why were you laughing all the time?" Yingman said, feeling puzzled.

"Oh Lord, I was in stitches!" Meiling sat up, rubbing her eyes. "You'll be doubled up if I tell you. You two were really into your roles today. When it came to the kissing scene, I was hiding behind the curtain and noticed two students, guys sitting in the front row – it's said they are Yang Yuqing's two elder cousins – they were glued to it, watching with their mouths wide open as if they were expecting some candy. Another kid in the front row chanced to pick up his dad's cane from the ground, the curved head happened to hook one of them in the mouth. The other one hurried to take the cane out, leaving his mouth wide open and laughing like an idiot at the same time. It was hilarious! Didn't you see them?"

Yunluo and Yingman couldn't help giggling. Big Sister Zhu tossed her book aside and said, "Meiling is a real storyteller! How could that guy not feel the cane inside his month?"

"Ask someone else if you don't believe me. I'm not the only one who saw it." Meiling ran out, laughing.

Yingman smiled at Yunluo who blushed even more. They sat on the bed, talking and giggling.

After a while Meiling dashed back in: "It's raining so hard, I almost slipped over just now. Good news, Romeo, no need to leave tonight. Mrs. Wu told the people downstairs a moment ago that Madam Zhou is not feeling well and won't be able to come to check the dorm tonight."

"Let's close the door and go to bed." Big Sister Zhu winked at Meiling, who went and locked the door obligingly.

After a while the lights went off. Yingman stood up and said, "I should leave now, shouldn't I?"

"Don't – " Yunluo pulled her down. "It's raining so hard, you…"

"This bed is too small to fit me."

"Don't you know how to accept a favour, Romeo? Juliet wants you to stay, and you're saying, no?" said Meiling, sticking her head out of her blanket.

"I'm not saying no, but it might be too cramped and she'll be uncomfortable." said Yingman while taking off her top and skirt, and lying down by Yunluo's side.

The air in the room was humid and had an earthy smell. The rain still pitter-pattered in the courtyard. Meiling burst out laughing again, breaking the dead silence of the night: "Can you tell me what comes after 'may all lovers', Big Sister Zhu?"

"Isn't it 'unite in marriage'?" Big Sister Zhu answered. "Go back to sleep. No more nonsense."

Yingman put her face against Yunluo's, murmuring with a smile: "Did you hear – united in marriage?"

"Shut up, or I won't sleep with you." Yunluo poked her and then laid her head on Yingman's chest.

Waking up at midnight, Yunluo found herself warm under the blanket, her head on a soft arm, her waist under a hand. She suddenly felt an indescribable sense of comfort that she had never experienced before. This feeling of warmth seemed to have dispelled all the emptiness, fear, and loss she was used to feeling when waking up in the middle of the night. She tucked the blanket under Yingman's shoulders to keep the draught out.

Yingman woke up suddenly, realizing that Yunluo was right next to her, watching her, face to face. The rain had stopped. The moonlight gently shone through the curtain. Yunluo felt embarrassed when she noticed that Yingman had woken up. She covered her eyes and hid her face in Yingman's shoulder, whispering: "How come you're also awake?"

Yingman tried to lift Yunluo's face up for a look, but the other kept on snuggling into Yingman's shoulder, which tickled. Yingman's lips happened to touch Yunluo's forehead, then she couldn't help kissing her again and again.

Yunluo murmured, "Did you sleep well?"

"Very well!" Yingman touched Yunluo's smooth cheeks and said, "What if I wasn't a woman...?"

"Shh! Go back to sleep." Yunluo pinched her lightly and put her face against Yingman's, and together they fell asleep.

After that night, Yingman and Yunluo took a walk together on campus almost every evening. Their classmates began to recognise them from afar and made way for them with a smile.

One night – perhaps half a month later – when the moon was casting its silvery light on the ground, they entered the university campus shoulder to shoulder, hands around each other's waists. They started talking about how much they had missed each other over the past two days, then sat on the pavilion railing, gazing at the moon. Yingman murmured: "How lovely the moon is! Tonight the moonlight feels unusually bright, she's smiling down on us. Look how pretty her smile is!"

Yunluo frowned at Yingman and said, "You're always happy. How come I can't see her smile? Her face looks cold and pale to me, and if she smiled, it would be a snigger. She makes me feel uneasy. I usually feel sad when I look at the moon, as it reminds me of my late father and sister, and I miss my mother and brother." While she was speaking, tears appeared at the corners of her eyes, glittering under the moonlight. Yingman wiped them away.

"You're such a softie! Even the moonlight and a light breeze make you cry!" She smiled and kissed Yunluo's face, pushing back the strands of her hair that were being tangled by the wind. Yunluo's tears ran freely as Yingman wiped them away, so much that she ended up sobbing on Yingman's shoulder. This startled her friend.

"What's happened, my darling?" Yingman whispered. She

held Yunluo tightly, her face close to hers.

But Yunluo only cried even more. Yingman gently encouraged her to speak, and she finally said, "It's all so pointless!"

Yingman stared at her at a loss for words. She wiped her tears away and said, "Why do you think that life is pointless? What's the matter? Tell me. I really don't want you to feel sad."

Yunluo sighed, she looked paler and even more pitiful. She stared at Yingman for a while, then suddenly gripped her hands, and said bitterly, looking down: "How I wish you were a man!"

"Must I be a man to know what's on your mind?" Yingman smiled.

"Of course not. I mean it's no use telling you!" She lowered her head even more.

"You shouldn't hide your worries from me. Aren't we like one and the same? Your worries are mine. Why can't you tell me?"

"I don't want you to feel sad for me, that's why." She looked at the moon silently for a while and said. "I got another letter from my elder brother saying that his Section Chief keeps asking him to act as a matchmaker for me and him. My brother said he was a decent man and revered his mother… he feels bad declining him again."

Yunluo lowered her head again. "Think about it – I haven't even met him. Yesterday I heard Yuying talking about this man, he's been running around looking for another wife, even though his wife died not even two months ago. She seemed to be one of his targets. Then, he starts chasing me too without waiting to hear Yuying's reply…" Yunluo said angrily. "My brother has written me seven or eight letters, though, saying that his boss favours him a lot because of me, asking me to trust him and decide as soon as possible."

Yingman listened in silence at first, but her eyes seemed to well up with tears as Yunluo stopped talking and looked at her. She asked with concern, "What are you going to say to him?"

"I haven't written back yet. I mean, I just want to spend my whole life with you, and that man... my fear is that my mother and brother won't..."

Yunluo looked up at Yingman and was about to cry again. Yingman couldn't say a word but was weeping quietly with her.

"Don't be so sad. Don't be so sad, my heart is breaking." Yingman wiped her tears away with a handkerchief.

"Where there's a will, there's a way. Why can't we stay together forever? Haven't the schoolteachers Chen Wanzhen and Miss Chu lived together for five or six years already? Why can't we be like them? Don't believe there's only one way. I think I love you more than I could love any man. Don't you know that? Why can't you marry me?"

The cloud in Yunluo's face seemed to have faded a little. Upon hearing the question, she frowned slightly, not believing it was possible, but she was afraid to say no. As she remained silent, Yingman put her hands on her friend's shoulders and looked right into her eyes, urging: "Won't you marry me? Write back to your brother telling him to turn that man away!" Yunluo cast her eyes down slowly the way a girl does, feeling shy with strangers. Yingman looked away, her mouth gasping as if she couldn't breathe in the foul air. Yunluo suddenly hugged her and said in English, "My God, how can I live without you! I love you. Say you love me too."

They looked up at the moon. It shone down from the sky in its silvery, sparkling dance costume as if smiling and congratulating them. The mild night breeze of early May sent the fragrance of the white roses beside the west wall to waft over them, as if a bottle of fine wine had been opened and poured into their cup of joy, waiting for them to take a sip.

"You are the moon, I'm the star beside it..." Yingman

looked up with a smile and stepped down from the pavilion, holding Yunluo's hand.

"You'll never leave me alone, and I'll stay with you forever..." said Yunluo, lowering her head as she kept walking.

Their love bloomed like the blossom on the peach and plum trees and the rose bushes on campus. When their schoolmates gossiped about Yunluo and Yingman, no-one used their real names any more; they were known simply as Romeo and Juliet instead. Even Mrs. Wu, who sold dim sum in the dining hall and only stopped by briefly for an hour, knew them by their nicknames.

The summer holidays started. Yingman accompanied Yunluo to Tianjin and saw her off on the train to Jinling before getting a ride back home. When it was time to depart, Yunluo had held on to Yingman's hand, weeping so much she couldn't utter a word.

The first day Yingman arrived home, she wrote a letter in her room and had it mailed straight away. Her parents, brother and his wife teased her for having fallen in love and for not being as silly and playful as before.

Yingman waited for a week after she sent her first letter, but didn't hear anything back. Then she sent two express mails in a row. One day, while she was looking at the photos of herself with Yunluo, a letter arrived; the words inside touched her deeply:

"... How could you doubt that I would forget you? It's I who fear that you may one day forget me! I know I don't deserve your love. First of all, I'm not as clever as you are, I don't work hard and always want to have fun, so it's impossible to catch up with you. Working hard at home is totally out of the question. We have guests visiting every day since I came back, asking my mother for my hand in marriage. It's so annoying. Before their visits, my mother keeps on nagging me to dress up nicely and put on makeup. Yesterday, I felt upset and didn't do as she asked. She kept going on during supper time that her daughter had grown older and bolder, that her words were no longer any use. I couldn't do anything but hold back my tears with a smile and listen to her complaints. Sigh. Since my father died, she has been through a lot raising me and my brother.

"Forgive me for the late reply. This is the first letter I've ever written after coming back home. I was gazing at the moon for quite a while last night, thinking of you. You must be having lots of fun at home and may not have time to look at the moon. Right? My star, my shining star, do you see the sparkle of my tears?"

Yingman took the letter to her lips and kissed it again and again with tears in her eyes. After going to bed that night, she lit the candle and read it a few more times, the black words blurring as she fell asleep, the letter still in hand.

She dreamed often of Yunluo walking towards her, wearing pretty clothes, with tears staining her pale, flushed, face, then suddenly she'd panic that Yunluo had died, and she'd wake up weeping. This became a laughing matter in her family.

Yingman had not heard from Yunluo for two weeks since she received her first letter. She was worried and restless, and was longing to return to school every day.

Later on, the war broke out in Jiangsu and Zhejiang provinces, train transport between Tianjin and Shanghai was cancelled, and it took more than twenty days for letters from Shanghai to arrive in Tianjin. There was nothing she could do other than worry. In the beginning she woke up from her nightmares sobbing at night. Later, the nightmares subsided, and she couldn't even see Yunluo in her dreams, as she was wracked with anxiety. Sometimes, she heard people telling her in her dream that Yunluo was seriously ill and couldn't write her a letter, that she should go visit her, then she wanted to go but her parents forbade her. She became so upset that her crying would wake her mother in the next room; then she could only close her eyes and pretend to be asleep.

Yingman had been waiting week after week but had heard nothing from Yunluo. The war wasn't over yet, but the summer holidays were near the end. Yingman bid farewell to her parents and went back to school in Beijing a week before the new semester started. She was disappointed to learn that the dorm supervisor hadn't yet received Yunluo's registration date.

Yingman had mailed countless express letters and even thought about sending a telegraph, but she had never done that before and would need to ask someone to do it for her, and besides she had heard that telegraphs often couldn't get through between Beijing and Nanjing during times of military conflict. She was so worried that she'd just lay in bed gazing at the ceiling and the top of the mosquito net.

Close to dusk, Yingman went out for a walk on campus. The Jiangnan chrysanthemums blooming beside the pavilion brought back memories and she walked out of the garden with tearful eyes. She wanted to go back to the dorm and wash the dirty handkerchiefs accumulated over the past few days and that too reminded her of Yunluo again: Yunluo used to take all the handkerchiefs and wash them voluntarily. She came across other couples while walking across the sports fields, strolling and chatting, hand in hand, shoulder to shoulder, appearing more intimate than she had noticed before. After a while one or two couples noticed her and called to her with a smile, "Hey Romeo, why not come and have a walk with us?" Then they smiled at her contentedly, which saddened her even more.

As the golden twilight shone on the dorm windows, cheers and laughter burst forth from inside – she found herself hating – for no reason – people that laughed out loud, thinking they looked stupid, and she especially hated them looking at her as they laughed. She moped about in the corridors, silently cursing those who were having fun, and felt infuriated when they did. Hmph, laugh… to death…

She suddenly overheard someone mention "Yunluo," so she paused to listen. A student from Room No. 3 said, "Are you guys talking about Yunluo? She and my sister are married to two brothers now."

"Is she married?"

"Yes. My sister told me in her letter. She said, the family name of her brother-in-law's new wife was Xie, said she was really pretty and had been in my school for two years. Who can that be if not Yunluo?"

Yingman felt a pain in her heart when she heard those words; later she recalled hearing "so pretty, the bridegroom's happy... the bride was smiling," etc., but she couldn't take it in. Everything seemed to go dark in front of her eyes, then Yunluo's crying face appeared, then Yunluo in her bridal dress, her head covered with a pink chiffon veil, her dress with sparkling beads, standing there with a smile...

She fainted and fell flat on the floor. The people talking inside the room came out and were so scared that their lips turned blue. They cried out, anxiously, "Oh, Lord! What's happened to her? What's happened to her?"

Later, the students carried her to bed. Lying there, she opened her eyes and saw people crowded around her, gabbling, but she was too tired to listen to them, she had to close her eyes again. In her dream, Yunluo seemed to be weeping... or smiling, or weeping again.

Yingman didn't want to see anyone, anymore. "Huff!" She let out a long sigh. The people gathered around her all said, "Finally... finally, she's back!"

Their Religions and Our Marriages[1]

by Charlotte Perkins Gilman

It took me a long time, as a man, a foreigner, and a species of Christian – I was that as much as anything – to get any clear understanding of the religion of Herland.

Its deification of motherhood was obvious enough; but there was far more to it than that; or, at least, than my first interpretation of that.

I think it was only as I grew to love Ellador more than I believed anyone could love anybody, as I grew faintly to appreciate her inner attitude and state of mind, that I began to get some glimpses of this faith of theirs.

When I asked her about it, she tried at first to tell me, and then, seeing me flounder, asked for more information about ours. She soon found that we had many, that they varied widely, but had some points in common. A clear methodical luminous mind had my Ellador, not only reasonable, but swiftly perceptive.

She made a sort of chart, superimposing the different religions as I described them, with a pin run through them all, as it were; their common basis being a Dominant Power or Powers, and some Special Behaviour, mostly taboos, to please or placate. There were some common features in certain groups of religions, but the one always present was this Power, and the things which must be done or not done because of it. It

1 Excerpted from the novel *Herland*, 1915

was not hard to trace our human imagery of the Divine Force up through successive stages of bloodthirsty, sensual, proud, and cruel gods of early times to the conception of a Common Father with its corollary of a Common Brotherhood.

This pleased her very much, and when I expatiated on the Omniscience, Omnipotence, Omnipresence, and so on, of our God, and of the loving kindness taught by his Son, she was much impressed.

The story of the Virgin birth naturally did not astonish her, but she was greatly puzzled by the Sacrifice, and still more by the Devil, and the theory of Damnation.

When in an inadvertent moment I said that certain sects had believed in infant damnation – and explained it – she sat very still indeed.

"They believed that God was Love – and Wisdom – and Power?"

"Yes – all of that."

Her eyes grew large, her face ghastly pale.

"And yet that such a God could put little new babies to burn – for eternity?" She fell into a sudden shuddering and left me, running swiftly to the nearest temple.

Every smallest village had its temple, and in those gracious retreats sat wise and noble women, quietly busy at some work of their own until they were wanted, always ready to give comfort, light, or help, to any applicant.

Ellador told me afterward how easily this grief of hers was assuaged, and seemed ashamed of not having helped herself out of it.

"You see, we are not accustomed to horrible ideas," she said, coming back to me rather apologetically. "We haven't any. And when we get a thing like that into our minds it's like – oh, like red pepper in your eyes. So I just ran to her, blinded and almost screaming, and she took it out so quickly – so easily!"

"How?" I asked, very curious.

"'Why, you blessed child,' she said, 'you've got the wrong idea altogether. You do not have to think that there ever was such a God – for there wasn't. Or such a happening – for there wasn't. Nor even that this hideous false idea was believed by anybody. But only this – that people who are utterly ignorant will believe anything – which you certainly knew before.'"

"Anyhow," pursued Ellador, "she turned pale for a minute when I first said it."

This was a lesson to me. No wonder this whole nation of women was peaceful and sweet in expression – they had no horrible ideas.

"Surely you had some when you began," I suggested.

"Oh, yes, no doubt. But as soon as our religion grew to any height at all we left them out, of course."

From this, as from many other things, I grew to see what I finally put in words.

"Have you no respect for the past? For what was thought and believed by your foremothers?"

"Why, no," she said. "Why should we? They are all gone. They knew less than we do. If we are not beyond them, we are unworthy of them – and unworthy of the children who must go beyond us."

This set me thinking in good earnest. I had always imagined – simply from hearing it said, I suppose – that women were by nature conservative. Yet these women, quite unassisted by any masculine spirit of enterprise, had ignored their past and built daringly for the future.

Ellador watched me think. She seemed to know pretty much what was going on in my mind.

"It's because we began in a new way, I suppose. All our folks were swept away at once, and then, after that time of despair, came those wonder children – the first. And then the whole breathless hope of us was for *their* children – if they should have them. And they did! Then there was the period of pride and triumph till we grew too numerous; and after that, when it all came down to one child apiece, we began to really work – to make better ones."

"But how does this account for such a radical difference in your religion?" I persisted.

She said she couldn't talk about the difference very intelligently, not being familiar with other religions, but that theirs seemed simple enough. Their great Mother Spirit was to them what their own motherhood was – only magnified beyond human limits. That meant that they felt beneath and behind them an upholding, unfailing, serviceable love – perhaps it was really the accumulated mother-love of the race they felt – but it was a Power.

"Just what is your theory of worship?" I asked her.

"Worship? What is that?"

I found it singularly difficult to explain. This Divine Love which they felt so strongly, did not seem to ask anything of them – "any more than our mothers do," she said.

"But surely your mothers expect honour, reverence, obedience, from you. You have to do things for your mothers, surely?"

"Oh, no," she insisted, smiling, shaking her soft brown hair. "We do things *from* our mothers – not *for* them. We don't have to do things *for* them – they don't need it, you know. But we have to live on – splendidly – because of them; and that's the way we feel about God."

I meditated again. I thought of that God of Battles of ours, that Jealous God, that Vengeance-is-mine God. I thought of our world-nightmare – Hell.

"You have no theory of eternal punishment then, I take it?"

Ellador laughed. Her eyes were as bright as stars, and there were tears in them, too. She was so sorry for me.

"How could we?" she asked, fairly enough. "We have no punishments in life, you see, so we don't imagine them after death."

"Have you *no* punishments? Neither for children nor criminals – such mild criminals as you have?" I urged.

"Do you punish a person for a broken leg or a fever? We have preventive measures, and cures; sometimes we have to 'send the patient to bed,' as it were; but that's not a punishment – it's only part of the treatment," she explained.

Then, studying my point of view more closely, she added: "You see, we recognise, in our human motherhood, a great tender limitless uplifting force – patience and wisdom and all subtlety of delicate method. We credit God – our idea of God – with all that and more. Our mothers are not angry with us – why should God be?"

"Does God mean a person to you?"

This she thought over a little. "Why – in trying to get close to it in our minds we personify the idea, naturally; but we certainly do not assume a Big Woman somewhere, who is God. What we call God is a Pervading Power, you know, an Indwelling Spirit, something inside of us that we want more of. Is your God a Big Man?" she asked innocently.

"Why – yes, to most of us, I think. Of course we call it an Indwelling Spirit just as you do, but we insist that it is Him, a Person, and a Man – with whiskers."

"Whiskers? Oh yes – because you have them! Or do you wear them because He does?"

"On the contrary, we shave them off – because it seems cleaner and more comfortable."

"Does He wear clothes – in your idea, I mean?"

I was thinking over the pictures of God I had seen – rash advances of the devout mind of man, representing his

Omnipotent Deity as an old man in a flowing robe, flowing hair, flowing beard, and in the light of her perfectly frank and innocent questions this concept seemed rather unsatisfying.

I explained that the God of the Christian world was really the ancient Hebrew God, and that we had simply taken over the patriarchal idea – that ancient one which quite inevitably clothed its thought of God with the attributes of the patriarchal ruler, the grandfather.

"I see," she said eagerly, after I had explained the genesis and development of our religious ideals. "They lived in separate groups, with a male head, and he was probably a little – domineering?"

"No doubt of that," I agreed.

"And we live together without any 'head,' in that sense – just our chosen leaders – that *does* make a difference."

"Your difference is deeper than that," I assured her. "It is in your common motherhood. Your children grow up in a world where everybody loves them. They find life made rich and happy for them by the diffused love and wisdom of all mothers. So it is easy for you to think of God in the terms of a similar diffused and competent love. I think you are far nearer right than we are."

"What I cannot understand," she pursued carefully, "is your preservation of such a very ancient state of mind. This patriarchal idea you tell me is thousands of years old?"

"Oh yes – four, five, six thousand – ever so many."

"And you have made wonderful progress in those years – in other things?"

"We certainly have. But religion is different. You see, our religions come from behind us, and are initiated by some great teacher who is dead. He is supposed to have known the whole thing and taught it, finally. All we have to do is believe – and obey."

"Who was the great Hebrew teacher?"

"Oh – there it was different. The Hebrew religion is an accumulation of extremely ancient traditions, some far older than their people, and grew by accretion down the ages. We consider it inspired – 'the Word of God.'"

"How do you know it is?"

"Because it says so."

"Does it say so in as many words? Who wrote that in?"

I began to try to recall some text that did say so, and could not bring it to mind.

"Apart from that," she pursued, "what I cannot understand is why you keep these early religious ideas so long. You have changed all your others, haven't you?"

"Pretty generally," I agreed. "But this we call 'revealed religion,' and think it is final. But tell me more about these little temples of yours," I urged. "And these Temple Mothers you run to."

Then she gave me an extended lesson in applied religion, which I will endeavour to concentrate.

They developed their central theory of a Loving Power, and assumed that its relation to them was motherly – that it desired their welfare and, especially, their development. Their relation to it, similarly, was filial, a loving appreciation and a glad fulfillment of its high purposes. Then, being nothing if not practical, they set their keen and active minds to discover the kind of conduct expected of them. This worked out in a most admirable system of ethics. The principle of Love was universally recognised – and used.

Patience, gentleness, courtesy, all that we call "good breeding," was part of their code of conduct. But where they went far beyond us was in the special application of religious feeling to every field of life. They had no ritual, no little set of performances called "divine service," save those religious pageants I have spoken of, and those were as much educational as religious, and as much social as either. But they had a clear established connection between everything they did – and God. Their cleanliness, their health, their exquisite order, the rich peaceful beauty of the whole land, the happiness of the children, and above all the constant progress they made – all this was their religion.

They applied their minds to the thought of God, and worked out the theory that such an inner power demanded outward expression. They lived as if God was real and at work within them.

As for those little temples everywhere – some of the women were more skilled, more temperamentally inclined, in this direction, than others. These, whatever their work might be, gave certain hours to the Temple Service, which meant being there with all their love and wisdom and trained thought, to smooth out rough places for anyone who needed it. Sometimes it was a real grief, very rarely a quarrel, most often a perplexity; even in Herland the human soul had its hours of darkness. But all through the country their best and wisest were ready to give help.

If the difficulty was unusually profound, the applicant was directed to someone more specially experienced in that line of thought.

Here was a religion which gave to the searching mind a rational basis in life, the concept of an immense Loving Power working steadily out through them, toward good. It gave to the "soul" that sense of contact with the inmost force, of perception of the uttermost purpose, which we always crave. It gave to the "heart" the blessed feeling of being loved, loved and *understood*. It gave clear, simple, rational directions as to how we should live – and why. And for ritual it gave first those triumphant group demonstrations, when with a union of all the arts, the revivifying combination of great multitudes moved rhythmically with march and dance, song and music, among their own noblest products and the open beauty of their groves and hills. Second, it gave these numerous little centres of wisdom where the least wise could go to the most wise and be helped.

"It is beautiful!" I cried enthusiastically. "It is the most practical, comforting, progressive religion I ever heard of. You *do* love one another – you *do* bear one another's burdens – you *do* realise that a little child is a type of the kingdom of heaven. You are more Christian than any people I ever saw. But – how about death? And the life everlasting? What does your religion teach about eternity?"

"Nothing," said Ellador. "What is eternity?"

What indeed? I tried, for the first time in my life, to get a real hold on the idea.

"It is – never stopping."

"Never stopping?" She looked puzzled.

"Yes, life, going on forever."

"Oh – we see that, of course. Life does go on forever, all about us."

"But eternal life goes on *without dying.*"

"The same person?"

"Yes, the same person, unending, immortal." I was pleased to think that I had something to teach from our religion, which theirs had never promulgated.

"Here?" asked Ellador. "Never to die – here?" I could see her practical mind heaping up the people, and hurriedly reassured her.

"Oh no, indeed, not here – hereafter. We must die here, of course, but then we 'enter into eternal life.' The soul lives forever."

"How do you know?" she inquired.

"I won't attempt to prove it to you," I hastily continued. "Let us assume it to be so. How does this idea strike you?"

Again she smiled at me, that adorable, dimpling, tender, mischievous, motherly smile of hers. "Shall I be quite, quite honest?"

"You couldn't be anything else," I said, half gladly and half a little sorry. The transparent honesty of these women was a never-ending astonishment to me.

"It seems to me a singularly foolish idea," she said calmly. "And if true, most disagreeable."

Now I had always accepted the doctrine of personal immortality as a thing established. The efforts of inquiring spiritualists, always seeking to woo their beloved ghosts back again, never seemed to me necessary. I don't say I had ever seriously and courageously discussed the subject with myself even; I had simply assumed it to be a fact. And here was the girl I loved, this creature whose character constantly revealed new heights and ranges far beyond my own, this superwoman of a superland, saying she thought immortality foolish! She meant it, too.

"What do you *want* it for?" she asked.

"How can you *not* want it!" I protested. "Do you want to go out like a candle? Don't you want to go on and on – growing and – and – being happy, forever?"

"Why, no," she said. "I don't in the least. I want my child – and my child's child – to go on – and they will. Why should I want to?"

"But it means Heaven!" I insisted. "Peace and Beauty and Comfort and Love – with God." I had never been so eloquent on the subject of religion. She could be horrified at Damnation, and question the justice of Salvation, but Immortality – that was surely a noble faith.

Their Religions and Our Marriages

"Why, Van," she said, holding out her hands to me. "Why
Van – darling! How splendid of you to feel it so keenly. That's
what we all want, of course – Peace and Beauty, and Comfort
and Love – with God! And Progress too, remember; Growth,
always and always. That is what our religion teaches us to want
and to work for, and we do!"

"But that is *here*," I said, "only for this life on earth."

"Well? And do not you in your country, with your beautiful
religion of love and service have it here, too – for this life – on
earth?"

None of us were willing to tell the women of Herland about
the evils of our own beloved land. It was all very well for us to
assume them to be necessary and essential, and to criticise –
strictly among ourselves – their all-too-perfect civilization, but
when it came to telling them about the failures and wastes of
our own, we never could bring ourselves to do it.

Moreover, we sought to avoid too much discussion, and to
press the subject of our approaching marriages.

Jeff was the determined one on this score.

"Of course they haven't any marriage ceremony or service,
but we can make it a sort of Quaker wedding, and have it in
the temple – it is the least we can do for them."

It was. There was so little, after all, that we could do for
them. Here we were, penniless guests and strangers, with no
chance even to use our strength and courage – nothing to
defend them from or protect them against.

"We can at least give them our names," Jeff insisted.

They were very sweet about it, quite willing to do whatever
we asked, to please us. As to the names, Alima, frank soul that
she was, asked what good it would do.

Terry, always irritating her, said it was a sign of possession.
"You are going to be Mrs. Nicholson," he said. "Mrs. T. O.
Nicholson. That shows everyone that you are my wife."

"What is a 'wife' exactly?" she demanded, a dangerous gleam in her eye.

"A wife is the woman who belongs to a man," he began.

But Jeff took it up eagerly: "And a husband is the man who belongs to a woman. It is because we are monogamous, you know. And marriage is the ceremony, civil and religious, that joins the two together – 'until death do us part,'" he finished, looking at Celis with unutterable devotion.

"What makes us all feel foolish," I told the girls, "is that here we have nothing to give you – except, of course, our names."

"Do your women have no names before they are married?" Celis suddenly demanded.

"Why, yes," Jeff explained. "They have their maiden names – their father's names, that is."

"And what becomes of them?" asked Alima.

"They change them for their husbands', my dear," Terry answered her.

"Change them? Do the husbands then take the wives' 'maiden names'?"

"Oh, no," he laughed. "The man keeps his own and gives it to her, too."

"Then she just loses hers and takes a new one – how unpleasant! We won't do that!" Alima said decidedly.

Terry was good-humoured about it. "I don't care what you do or don't do so long as we have that wedding pretty soon," he said, reaching a strong brown hand after Alima's, quite as brown and nearly as strong.

"As to giving us things – of course we can see that you'd like to, but we are glad you can't," Celis continued. "You see, we love you just for yourselves – we wouldn't want you to – to pay anything. Isn't it enough to know that you are loved personally – and just as men?"

Enough or not, that was the way we were married. We had a great triple wedding in the biggest temple of all, and it looked as if most of the nation was present. It was very solemn and very beautiful. Someone had written a new song for the occasion, nobly beautiful, about the New Hope for their people – the New Tie with other lands – Brotherhood as well as Sisterhood, and, with evident awe, Fatherhood.

Terry was always restive under their talk of fatherhood. "Anybody'd think we were High Priests of – of Philo-progenitiveness!" he protested. "These women think of *nothing* but children, seems to me! We'll teach 'em!"

He was so certain of what he was going to teach, and Alima so uncertain in her moods of reception, that Jeff and I feared the worst. We tried to caution him – much good that did. The big handsome fellow drew himself up to his full height, lifted that great chest of his, and laughed.

"There are three separate marriages," he said. "I won't interfere with yours – nor you with mine."

So the great day came, and the countless crowds of women, and we three bridegrooms without any supporting "best men," or any other men to back us up, felt strangely small as we came forward.

Somel and Zava and Moadine were on hand; we were thankful to have them, too – they seemed almost like relatives.

There was a splendid procession, wreathing dances, the new anthem I spoke of, and the whole great place pulsed with feeling – the deep awe, the sweet hope, the wondering expectation of a new miracle.

"There has been nothing like this in the country since our Motherhood began!" Somel said softly to me, while we watched the symbolic marches. "You see, it is the dawn of a new era. You don't know how much you mean to us. It is not only Fatherhood – that marvelous dual parentage to which we are strangers – the miracle of union in life-giving – but it is Brotherhood. You are the rest of the world. You join us to our kind – to all the strange lands and peoples we have never seen. We hope to know them – to love and help them – and to learn of them. Ah! You cannot know!"

Thousands of voices rose in the soaring climax of that great Hymn of The Coming Life. By the great Altar of Motherhood, with its crown of fruit and flowers, stood a new one, crowned as well. Before the Great Over Mother of the Land and her ring of High Temple Counsellors, before that vast multitude of calm-faced mothers and holy-eyed maidens, came forward our own three chosen ones, and we, three men alone in all that land, joined hands with them and made our marriage vows.

"*True emancipation ... will have to do away with the absurd notion of the dualism of the sexes, or that man and woman represent two antagonistic worlds.*"

– Emma Goldman

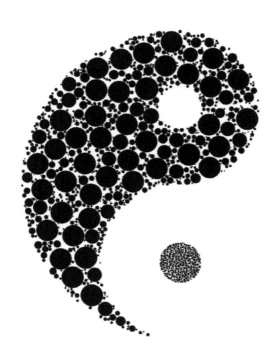

Goodbye, Lebanon

by May Ziadeh

translated by Rose DeMaris

Goodbye, Lebanese mountains.

I'm going far
from your pink rose garlands,
your bright red satin strawberries.

Egypt called in a serious voice,
and already my boat's rocking
bears new fruit –

But sea, whisper your lullabies
please, because I hurt so much.
Soft waves of home, sob for me.

Don't go away so quickly, my love.
Leaving you, my chest is all wound,
wholly tender.

Lebanon,

you made me. Your moody nights
put the darkness in my eyes
and laid a vein of lightning in my soul.

Goodbye, Lebanon

Your white lace waterfalls
wove jasmine vine and lute serenades
all through me,

and my speech is the Spirit
murmuring in your woods.
My capricious seasons are yours:

my soul is sometimes wild,
an egret flying far
beyond the ocean's edge,

and sometimes I curl up
when touched, a tidepool flower
damp with delicate seafoam tears.

Fading from sight, you're a dream
that ends. But grief goes on.
Goodbye, my nest.

I love you, Lebanon. I adore you.
Lebanon, goodbye.

My heart –
pink roses,
red strawberries
– turns to vapour with the word:

Goodbye.

Goodbye.

"You look ridiculous if you dance.
You look ridiculous if you don't dance.
So you might as well dance."

– Gertrude Stein

About the Authors

Anna Akhmatova (1889-1966) was born in Odessa, Ukraine, at the time part of the Russian Empire. Her father was a Ukrainian cossack and her mother was part of the Russian nobility. After her former husband was executed for his alleged role in an anti-Bolshevik conspiracy, Akhmatova fell under the suspicion of the authorities and her poetry was disparaged for its apparent 'bourgeois aesthetic' and 'trivial feminine preoccupations'. Despite this persecution, she chose not to emigrate and carried on writing poetry, eventually gaining recognition both in her homeland and abroad.

Fausta Cialente (1898-1994) was born in Cagliari, Sardinia. Her debut novel *Natalia* was first published in 1930, when it won the Premio dei Dieci. However, Fascist censorship prevented the book from reaching a wide readership; officials in Mussolini's government ordered the author to edit out sections of the book – including what Cialente referred to as a 'small lesbian episode' – but she refused. After her marriage, Cialente moved to Alexandria, Egypt, but kept in contact with the Italian Resistance and spoke out against the fascists on Radio Cairo.

Carmen de Burgos (1867-1932) was an important journalist, activist and author of fiction whose work was banned and largely forgotten during the Franco dictatorship years. As well as being the first woman to have her own column in a major newspaper in Spain, she was also the first female war correspondent, travelling to Morocco to cover the war there. She was an advocate for numerous causes, including the right to divorce, education for women, suffrage, and the anti-war and anti-death-penalty movements.

Alice Dunbar-Nelson (1875-1935) was an American poet, teacher, journalist and political activist. She is one of the key figures of the Harlem Renaissance movement. She contributed to *The Woman's Era*, the first newspaper aimed specifically at African-American women and supported America's involvement in the First World War, believing that it would bring an end to racial divisions. Her poem 'I Sit and Sew' reflects the frustration of a woman who feels unable to contribute directly to the war effort. As well as poetry, Dunbar-Nelson published collections of short stories.

Zelda Fitzgerald (1900-1948) was an American novelist, playwright and painter. Her marriage to F. Scott Fitzgerald drew public attention and she was described by the press as the first American 'flapper'. However, Fitzgerald was disappointed by the critical reception of her work and suffered from mental illness, being initially diagnosed with schizophrenia and then with bipolar disorder. She was hospitalised and endured ten years of electroshock therapy, eventually dying in a fire at the hospital, at the age of 47.

Charlotte Perkins Gilman (1860-1935) was a leading figure in the feminist movement in the U.S. Perkins is best-known for her short story 'The Yellow Wallpaper', an analysis of suffocating domesticity and postpartum depression, as well as an indictment of the 'rest cure' that was often enforced on women experiencing mental health problems. She also became a notable lecturer on social issues such as labour rights and women's emancipation. Perkins published *Women and Economics*, which was translated into seven languages, and which presented radical arguments for the economic independence of women and a criticism of the romanticisation of domesticity.

Sorana Gurian (1913-1956) was a Jewish-Romanian intellectual who was part of the underground opposition in fascist Romania during the Second World War. She contracted tuberculosis in her twenties and spent time at Berck sanatorium, in France, and later studied at the Sorbonne. After returning to Romania, Gurian's anti-fascist activism put her life in danger and she escaped to Italy by entering a marriage of convenience. After her divorce, she lived in Israel and eventually returned to Paris, where she died of cancer at the age of 43.

Radclyffe Hall (1880-1943) was an English writer best known for her novel *The Well of Loneliness*, a novel with lesbian themes. The result of an obscenity trial in 1928 meant that all the printed copies of *The Well of Loneliness* were destroyed and the book was not republished in the UK until 1959 In the author's note to the earlier short story collection 'Miss Ogilvy Finds Herself', Hall writes: 'Although Miss Ogilvy is a very different person to Stephen Gordon, yet those who have read *The Well of Loneliness* will find in the earlier part of this story the nucleus of those sections of the novel which deal with Stephen Gordon's childhood and girlhood and with the noble and selfless work done by hundreds of sexually inverted women in The Great War'. Hall was listed at No. 16 in the top 500 lesbian and gay heroes in *The Pink Paper*.

Magda Isanos (1916-1944) is one of Romania's most important early twentieth century poets. Isanos also worked as a journalist and lawyer and was involved in left-wing activism. When Isanos was six months old, she contracted polio, which had an impact on her health and mobility for the rest of her life. In 1935, Isanos married, but her marriage broke down a year later, after which she began living with her sister and focused her attention on her poetry and her career in law. A second marriage brought her happiness as well as a daughter, but she suffered great losses in the war when a bomb destroyed her home and most of her manuscripts.

Nataliya Kobrynska (1851– 1920) was a Ukrainian writer, socialist feminist, and activist. Due to the fact that women were not allowed to pursue education beyond the elementary level, she was mainly educated at home and studied several languages: German, French, Polish and Russian and read literature from various counties. In 1884, Kobrynska organised the Tovarystvo Rus'kykh Zhinok (Association of Ukrainian Women) to educate women by exposing them to literature and by promoting discussions on women's rights. She wrote her first short story 'Shuminska' (later known as *The Spirit of the Times*, in 1883.

Katherine Mansfield (1888-1923) was born in New Zealand and is considered one of the most important modernist short story writers of the twentieth century. At the age of 19, she left New Zealand and began a new life in England, where she befriended

Virginia Woolf, Lady Ottoline Morrel, D.H. Lawrence and other intellectuals connected to the Bloomsbury Group. Mansfield was diagnosed with pulmonary tuberculosis in 1917, and she died in France aged 34.

Maria Messina (1887-1944) was hailed by Leonardo Sciascia as the 'Italian Katherine Mansfield'. Born in Palermo, she later moved between Umbria, Tuscany, the Marches, and Naples. After teaching herself to read and write, she wrote stories focused on the lives of rural women in Sicily. According to various sources, she was a shy woman who barely ventured outside her home, then later her isolation was exacerbated when she began suffering from multiple sclerosis. In 1910, she received the Medal of Gold for her first book of stories, *Pettini-fini* [Fine Combs].

Gabriela Mistral (1889-1957) from Chile, was the first Latin American author and fifth woman to receive a Nobel Prize for literature. Her poetry was praised by the jury for the way it 'inspired [...] powerful emotions, [and] made her name a symbol of the idealistic aspirations of the entire Latin American world'. Her work as a teacher and journalist also led her to become involved in educational reform. She was a passionate advocate of women's education, a topic she explored in *Lecturas para Mujeres* (Readings for Women).

Fani Popova–Mutafova (1902–1977) was one of the most important Bulgarian historical fiction writers of all time. She was sentenced to seven years of imprisonment by the Bulgarian communist regime during the war because of her alleged "pro-German allegiance". After eleven months, she was released for health reasons, but was forbidden to publish anything between 1943 and 1972. During this period, she translated Italian literature.

Antonia Pozzi (1912-1938) was an Italian poet, photographer and keen mountaineer who enjoyed exploring the terrain of the Dolomites. She was the only child of wealthy, but restrictive parents. Pozzi took her own life at the age of 26 and left behind diaries, notebooks, letters, and over three hundred poems. None of her poetry was published in her lifetime. After her death, Pozzi's father published revised versions of ninety-one of her poems, censoring anything that hinted at her struggles with her faith or her romantic life. Her poems were not restored to their original form until 1989.

Yenta Serdatsky (1877-1962) pursued her radical ideals and literary ambitions in turn-of-the-century Warsaw, and fled from persecution to New York City in 1906. Factory girls, tired peddlers, refugee intelligentsia and community activists populate her tales. Despite her talent, the reviews of her only book, *Geklibene Shriftn* [Collected Stories, 1913], were critical and misogynistic. Serdatsky stopped writing for several decades, but in the late 1940s she began to publish with the *Nyu Yorker Vokhnblat* and continued until her death in 1962.

Ling Shuhua (1900-1990) was a Chinese modernist writer and painter. She also translated English literature and self-translated her own stories into English. The daughter of a concubine and a high-ranking official, Ling studied at Wuhan university, where she began an affair with Julian Bell, Vanessa Bell's son, who was teaching English there at the time. Through her connection with Bell, Ling began a correspondence with Virginia Woolf. Ling dedicated her memoir *Ancient Melodies* to Virginia Woolf and Vita Sackville-West, whom she met in England in the 1940s, and it was later published by the Hogarth Press in 1953.

Dorka Talmon (1906-1957) was born in Poland and became one of the founding members of Kibbutz Ein Hachoresh. The Kibbutz was set up in 1931-2 in Palestine (since 1948 – Israel). Talmon was a very active member of the socialist movement in Poland and was sent on its behalf to assist those who wanted to 'make immigration' (הילע) to Palestine in the 1930s. Talmon died in 1957 after a long illness. 'First Steps' was taken from a collection of writings compiled in a booklet and distributed to Kibbutz members to celebrate its 30th anniversary (1961). It was never formally published and remains in the Kibbutz's archive.

Marina Ivanovna Tsvetaeva (1892–1941) is considered to be one of Russia's greatest poets. She lived through and wrote of the Russian Revolution of 1917 and the Moscow famine that followed it. In an attempt to save her daughter Irina from starvation, she placed her in a state orphanage in 1919, where she died of hunger. Tsvetaeva left Russia in 1922 and lived with her family in increasing poverty in Paris, Berlin and Prague before returning to Moscow in 1939. Her husband Sergei Efron and their daughter Ariadna were arrested on espionage charges in 1941; her husband was executed. Tsvetaeva committed suicide in 1941.

Edith Wharton (1862-1937) is one of America's most celebrated writers. She is best known for novels such as *The Age of Innocence*, *The House of Mirth* and *Ethan Frome*, but also published numerous short stories as well as articles on a variety of subjects such as architecture, design, gardens and travel. She was the first woman writer to receive the Pulitzer Prize for fiction.

Myra Viola Wilds, born in Kentucky (dates unknown), was an African-American writer who began writing poetry in 1911, after she lost her eyesight from years of eyestrain working as a dressmaker. Her collection of poetry *Thoughts of Idle Hours* was published in 1915, anticipating the cultural revival of African-American music, art and literature known as the 'Harlem Renaissance'.

Virginia Woolf (1882-1941) is considered one of the most important modernist writers and was a founding member of the artistic and literary 'Bloomsbury Group'. She pioneered the 'stream of consciousness' narrative device in novels such as *Mrs. Dalloway* and *To the Lighthouse* and is also well-known for her collection of essays *A Room of One's Own*. Based on the lectures she gave to the women's colleges at the University of Cambridge, these essays focus on the history of women's writing and the relationship between creativity and financial independence.

May Ziadeh (1886-1941) was a Lebanese-Palestinian poet, essayist, translator, intellectual, and feminist who passionately advocated for the emancipation and education of Arab women who helped to break ground for female Arab writers. Published in 1911 under the pen name Isis Copia, Ziadeh's collection of poems, *Fleurs De Rêve* [Dream Flowers], was her literary debut. She is considered to be a pioneer of Oriental feminism.

About the Translators

Leilei Chen 莫譯 published the traditional and simplified Chinese versions of Steven Grosby's *Nationalism: A Very Short Introduction* in 2017 and 2019. She translated Margaret Laurence and published the Mandarin versions of "The Loons" and "The Half-Husky" in 2022. Her poetry translation of 马辉 *I Have Forsaken Heaven and Earth, but Never Forsaken You,* is forthcoming in 2023. Her English translation of "Women's Nonfiction Writing in China" by 张莉 is forthcoming in *TranscUlturAl* in 2023. Her translation of contemporary Chinese ecological literature is forthcoming in 2024. She authors *Re-orienting China: Travel Writing and Cross-cultural Understanding.*

Stuart Cooke lives in Brisbane, Australia, where he is an Associate Professor of Creative Writing and Literary Studies at Griffith University. His books include *Speaking the Earth's Languages: a theory for Australian-Chilean postcolonial poetics* (2013) and a translation of Gianni Siccardi's *The Blackbird* (2018), and he is the co-editor of *Transcultural Ecocriticism* (2021).

Rose DeMaris is working on a creative English translation of *Fleurs de Rêve*, the debut poetry collection of Lebanese-Palestinian author May Ziadeh, which was originally published in French in 1911. Some of her translations of Ziadeh's poems have appeared in *Asymptote* and *The Los Angeles Review.* Rose's original poetry appears in *New England Review, The Los Angeles Review of Books Quarterly, Narrative, Image*, and elsewhere. She holds an MFA in Poetry from Columbia University, teaches creative writing, and lives in New York City.

Sonia di Placido is a graduate of University of British Columbia's Creative Writing MFA Program, member of the Editorial Board, *Prism International* Magazine, she has published 3 chapbooks and two books of poetry, *Exaltation in Cadmium Red,* 2012 and *Flesh,* 2018 by Guernica Editions. Sonia has works in various genres and journals: poetry, plays, fiction, CNF, essays, translation, and reviews. Sonia was a Juror for the League of Canadian Poets' Pat Lowther Award awarded to Canadian Women Poets of distinction National Poetry Month 2022. She is currently writing her first novel.

Slava Faybysh translates from Spanish and Russian. In 2022, his co-translation of Ainur Karim's play *Chins Up! Shoulders Back!* won first place in the ALTA Plays in Translation Contest. In 2024, the Modern Languages Association will publish his translation of Carmen de Burgos's *Divorce in Spain*, and also forthcoming from Corylus Books, is a thriller by Argentine author Elsa Drucaroff. Short translations have been published in the *New England Review, Asymptote Journal,* and *Another Chicago Magazine.*

Mira Glover has been translating academic material from Hebrew into English researching her parents' roots from their birthplace in Poland through their pioneering years when setting up a Kibbutz in Palestine (now Israel) from 1932 to 2000. She worked with the Kibbutz archive, researching the history, ideology and complex relationships within a unique social, economic and psychological construct and then she translated this into English to produce an historical record of her family's roots.

Nina Kossman is a bilingual poet, memoirist, playwright, short story writer, translator of Russian poetry, novelist, and artist. She has authored, edited, and translated 9 books of poetry and prose. Her work has appeared in over 90 magazines and anthologies and has been translated into many languages. She is a recipient of several awards, including an NEA fellowship, and grants from the Foundation for Hellenic Culture, the Onassis Public Benefit Foundation, and Fundación Valparaíso. Her plays have been produced in several countries.

Hanna Leliv is a translator originally from Lviv, Ukraine. She was a Fulbright fellow at the University of Iowa's Literary Translation Workshop and mentee of the National Centre for Writing's Emerging Translators Mentorship Programme. Her translations of contemporary Ukrainian literature into English have appeared in *Asymptote, BOMB, Washington Square Review, Circumference,* and elsewhere. In 2022, her translation of *Cappy and the Whale,* by Kateryna Babkina, was published by PRH UK. Currently a fellow at the Leslie Center for the Humanities at Dartmouth College.

Olga Livshin's poetry and translations appear in the *New York Times, Ploughshares,* the *Kenyon Review,* and other journals. She is the author of *A Life Replaced: Poems with Translations from Anna Akhmatova and Vladimir Gandelsman* (Poets & Traitors

Press, 2019). Livshin co-translated *A Man Only Needs a Room,* a volume of Vladimir Gandelsman's poetry (New Meridian Arts Books, 2022), and *Today is a Different War* by Lyudmyla Khersonska (Arrowsmith Press, 2023).

Juliette Neil is a translator and writer. She has lived in both the U.S. and Italy and continues to try to exist in both places at once. She likes to think about language, transition, narratives of womanhood, and movement.

Petya Pavlova is a freelance translator born in Sofia who has made London her home. She is a Chartered Linguist, member of the CIOL and the ITI. Some of her translations have been published in *Trafika Europe* and the 95th anniversary anthology edition of PEN Bulgaria. She is always on the lookout for titles by Bulgarian women writers to introduce to an English-speaking audience.

Gabi Reigh moved to the U.K. from Romania at the age of 12. In She won the Stephen Spender Prize (2017). Her work has been published in *Modern Poetry in Translation, World Literature Today, Another Chicago Magazine, Open Democracy, TES Supplement, The L.A. Review of Books,* amongst others. She was shortlisted for the Society of Authors' Tom Gallon short story prize in 2018.

Laura Shanahan lives in Bath and translates Italian and French, while also working as an editor. She holds a BA in Modern Languages and an MA in Literary Translation Studies. Her translations of short fiction by Elsa Morante, Anna Maria Ortese and Viola di Grado have been published in the *Journal of Italian Translation* and *World Literature Today.* She was runner-up in the 2018 *World Literature Today* Translation Prize, and has been both shortlisted and longlisted in the John Dryden Translation Competition.

Dalia Wolfson is a scholar and translator living in Boston, MA. She received her BA in Comparative Literature from the University of Penn-sylvania, and she is currently a graduate student of Comparative Literature at Harvard University. She was the recipient of a 2021-2022 Yiddish Book Center Translation Fellowship and a 2023 MusART Residency. Her translations from Hebrew, Russian and Yiddish into English have appeared or are forthcoming in *Asymptote, Scrawl Place* and *Consequence Forum,* among others. She is editor of Texts and Translations for the Yiddish Studies journal *In geveb.*

Diverse Writers to read:

Volta by Nikki Dudley
ISBN 978-1-912430-55-0 Price £9.99

Bone Rites by Natalie Bayley
ISBN 978-1-912430-87-1 Price £9.99

Pomegranate Sky by Louise Soraya Black
ISBN 978-1-906582-10-4 Price £8.99

Shambala Junction by Dipika Mukherjee
ISBN 978-1-910798-39-3 Price £9.99

The River's Song by Suchen Christine Lim
ISBN 978-1-9006582-98-2 Price £9.99

Sacred by Eliette Abecassis
ISBN 978-0-9536757-8-4 Price£9.95

Intelligent Non-Fiction to read:

Virginia Woolf in Richmond by Peter Fullagar
ISBN 978-1-913641-28-3 Price £16.99

Unravelling Women's Art by PL Henderson
ISBN 978-1-913641-15-3 Price £19.99

50 Women Sculptors ed Cheryl Robson
ISBN 978-0-993220-77-7 Price £24.99

Art, Theatre & Women's Suffrage by Irene Cockroft
& Susan Croft ISBN 978-1-906582-08-1 Price £9.99

The Original Suffrage Cookbook ed LO Kleber
ISBN 978-1-912430-13-0 Price £12.99

The Women Writers Handbook ed Ann Sandham
ISBN 978-1-912430-33-8 Price £14.99

Women Make Noise: Girl Bands from Motown to the Modern
ed. Julia Downes ISBN 978-0-956632-91-3 Price£15.99